THE BOOK OF MAYHEM

THE LAST ORACLE BOOK THREE

MELISSA MCSHANE

Night Harbor Publishing

For my mom,
who finally loved one of my books

I hurried along the sidewalk toward Abernathy's front door, bags in hand. It was about ninety degrees outside, and at nearly eighty percent humidity the air felt like a hot, wet washcloth wrapped around me. Stepping into the comfort of the store was like walking into a refrigerator, cool and dry. Whatever Abernathy's had for a cooling system was more than a match for the mugginess of a Friday afternoon. It would have to be, to keep all those books in ideal condition.

I breathed out in relief as the smell of roses surrounded me, faint but unmistakable. Even fainter was the smell of unfinished wood from the yellow 2x8s the many bookcases were made of, and the scent of old paper and ink from thousands of books. The bookcases stood at irregular angles to each other, making crooked corridors narrow enough in places that only one person could pass. Abernathy's looked strange even for a used book store, and casual customers usually went away in disgust when they discovered how unorganized it was. But for those who knew the secret, it was a place of wonder.

"Satisfied?" Judy said. My co-worker was perched on the stool behind the cash register and sounded more than a little smug.

"Are you always this pleased with yourself when you're right?" I dumped the bags containing a couple of boxed salads and some bottles of Diet Coke, beaded with sweat, on the counter with its cracked glass top.

"Yes. Always."

"Well, you were right. I should have let you go to the market. But it's just next door, and I get so tired of being inside all day. I just wanted to see the sun for five minutes."

"It's overcast."

"*Now* I know that. Anyone come in?"

"I think everyone's waiting for the storm to pass. It should rain in an hour or so, the forecast says." Judy picked up a salad and hopped down from the stool. She was tiny, at least three inches shorter than average-sized me, but she carried herself like a six-foot-tall Amazon warrior. "But let's eat anyway. The afternoon shift might be busier."

I took my own salad and drink and made a face. "I wish you'd stop calling it that. It's pure stupidity on the part of the factions."

"I make allowances for how new you still are to this world. Conflict between the factions is inevitable. It's why my father and Parish worked out this arrangement."

"I hate it." Two months earlier, when animosities between the Nicollien and Ambrosite factions had been high, their respective leaders William Rasmussen and Ryan Parish had worked out a system in which Nicolliens used Abernathy's in the morning and Ambrosites came in the afternoon. I'd refused to go along with it, but they'd imposed it on their people anyway. And now it had become the de facto rule. Why couldn't they just behave like grownups?

"It's worked, hasn't it? No more tension between customers, no more loud arguments."

I scowled again, but followed her to the break room, where I pulled out my chair with more than usual force. "If I can stay impartial, why can't they?"

"You've got more incentive. The Accords impose sanctions if a custodian of a Neutrality isn't impartial. Take it up with the Board if you're so annoyed."

"They'd just say 'suck it up, cupcake.' Not in so many words."

"I could hear Lucia saying it that way, though."

"In exactly that way." Lucia Pontarelli, custodian of the Gunther Node of magic and local law enforcement in the magical community of the Pacific Northwest, had an acerbic turn of phrase when she was irritated. When she wasn't irritated, too, come to think on it. "I've been afraid to ask her what she thinks of the Board of Neutralities after being acquitted of the charge of partiality."

"She hasn't behaved as if anything is different. I have to say, I don't like her much, but I respect her."

"Me too. Though I like her more than you do."

Judy paused with a forkful of mixed greens halfway to her mouth. "Did you hear the door?"

I'd heard the bells chime, but was hoping to pretend otherwise. It was a rare day when I actually got five minutes to eat my lunch in peace. I dropped my fork and sighed. "I'll be back."

The man by the door was unfamiliar to me, but then I didn't know more than a fraction of the magi in the Portland community, let alone those who drove from farther afield to visit the oracle. "Welcome to Abernathy's," I said. "Can I help you?"

"Just an augury," he said. As if there was anything 'just' about paying for a prophecy from the world's only living oracle. Though 'living' wasn't really the right word. Maybe.

"Do you have it written down?"

He startled, as if I'd goosed him. He was a crane of a man, his hands held close before him as if clutching a lady's purse. "Um...yes," he said, dipping into his back pocket and pulling out a wallet. "It's in the form of a question."

"Good. Thank you." I accepted the creased slip of paper from him and smiled, but it didn't put him at ease. "I'll just be a minute." I turned and walked between the bookcases and into the timeless peace of the oracle.

The color of the light went slightly blue, and brightened, as if the sun was shining unimpeded by the overcast that covered the sky. Dust motes flickered through the sunbeams, drifting along on a breeze I couldn't feel. I walked at a normal pace, trying not to let my hunger make me impatient. Not that it would disturb the oracle, who never seemed affected by my physical or emotional condition. I was its hands, carrying out the answers to requests made by those who knew how to ask. They brought their questions, and the oracle chose a book they had to study and analyze for the answer. The oracle wouldn't answer every question—for example, nothing beginning with the word "who"—but most people went away from Abernathy's satisfied.

I took a look at the augury question. *Can I trust my new business partner?* I'd have probably used Abernathy's catalogue for that question; it provided simple answers, particularly yes/no answers, for a fraction of the cost of an augury. But it wasn't my business to tell other people theirs.

Ahead, I saw a glow brighter than the blue-tinged air and walked a little faster. My stomach was reminding me I hadn't finished my lunch. I turned a couple of corners, sidled between two bookcases, and found the glowing volume: *The Partner*, by John Grisham. I'd never read it and had no idea what it might tell my customer.

I pulled it off the shelf, and the blue glow vanished, replaced by an almost electric tingle. It had been two months since the oracle had come under attack by someone who'd tried to destroy it by making it give false auguries, but I still felt relief every time an augury came off successfully.

I opened the cover. *Mitch Hallstrom, $725*. Funny how the oracle always priced its auguries in numbers divisible by 25.

When I returned to the front, Hallstrom was standing where I'd left him, eyeing our antique cash register. But he wasn't what left me feeling breathless. Another man stood near the door, looking elegant and handsome in a pearl-gray three-piece suit with an emerald green tie and pocket square. I swallowed against the sudden lump in my throat and turned my attention to Hallstrom, feeling pinned by the gaze of the newcomer.

"$725, Mr. Hallstrom," I said.

He startled again, looking just like the crane I'd imagined him as. "I...that's too much. I can't afford it."

He wasn't the first to have this problem. "I'm sorry, but Abernathy's price is final. I can hold the book for you while you gather the payment—and you can pay in *sanguinis sapiens*, or trade in kind—"

"What does that mean?"

"It means we'll accept other books in exchange for this one. It has to be a lot of books, though, and they have to be in good condition."

Hallstrom nodded. "I can do that. I'll come back before closing, just...don't lose the book, okay?" He was out the door before I could say anything else.

Willing my cheeks to stay their normal pink, I said, "Hi, Malcolm."

"Good afternoon," Malcolm Campbell said. "You don't mind that I'm here before two?"

I laughed, and didn't think it sounded forced. "You're practically the only person other than me who doesn't care about the restrictions. And you know I'm not enforcing them."

"I don't want to cause trouble for you."

Other than emotional trouble, but that's not your fault. "You won't. Mr. Rasmussen already dislikes me, and you being here won't make it worse. You need an augury?"

"Safe deposit box."

I was keenly aware of his tall, powerful presence behind me as I led the way through the store to the basement steps. I'd had a huge crush on him, and he'd told me he had feelings for me, but with him being an Ambrosite, we couldn't be together without violating the Accords, which said I had to be impartial in my treatment of both factions. And "impartial," according to everyone I'd asked, meant a custodian couldn't date a member of either faction.

So I'd moved on. Sort of. My boyfriend Jason was cute, and nice, and I liked him, and...those were all wishy-washy words, weren't they? But there was no sense my pining after what I couldn't have, even if my heart still leaped every time Malcolm came through the door.

"I haven't seen you in a while," I said, then felt like an idiot. What if he thought I'd been looking for him? What if he thought it meant I still cared? Which I didn't. Which was a lie. But I didn't want him feeling sorry for me and my hopeless feelings.

"I've been in Phoenix, training some new teams."

"Phoenix in July? What is it, 120 degrees in the shade? That's crazy!"

"Well, you know 'insanity runs in my family. It practically gallops.'"

"It would have to. Training couldn't wait until winter?"

I caught him looking at me with a funny expression. "You missed it."

"Missed what?"

"'Insanity runs in my family'? *Arsenic and Old Lace?*"

"Oh." Now I did blush. "You're right. I completely missed it."

An awkward silence fell. We both loved old movies and had a running game trying to stump each other with quotes. "I don't think either of us has ever missed before," I said, gamely trying to make a joke of it even though I felt as though I'd somehow let him down. "What should my penalty be?"

"Watching it again, of course." Malcolm put his key in the lock. I quickly inserted mine and removed the box from the cabinet. "You could watch it with your family."

"That would be nice." I took a deep breath. "Or I could see it with Jason. He's not into old movies, but he might like that one." Maybe someday I'd stop feeling uncomfortable about mentioning Jason in front of Malcolm if I did it often enough.

"Everyone likes that one." Malcolm turned away, dismissing me.

I hurried upstairs and into the break room, where Judy was just throwing away her trash. I flung myself into my seat and shoveled salad into my mouth, praying Judy wouldn't notice anything was wrong.

"Campbell's here, isn't he?" Judy leaned against the counter next to the microwave, which was new and looked out of place next to the thirty-year-old refrigerator, and folded her arms across her chest. Judy was too damned observant.

"Safe deposit box," I mumbled, and swigged my Diet Coke.

"You have got to let go of him."

"I know that, Judy!" I said, spraying bits of lettuce into the box. "I have Jason. He's more than enough for me. This isn't a big deal."

"Are you sleeping with him?"

"With Jason? Not that it's any of your business, but yes."

"Then it had better not be a big deal. It's not fair to him." Judy left the room, closing the door behind her.

I flung my fork at the trash can and shoved my plastic salad box away. My crush *wasn't* a big deal. This was just me being stupid. It would pass, especially if Malcolm kept going away on these training missions.

I pulled out my phone and started to call Jason, but remembered he was at work and his boss didn't like him taking personal calls. We'd do something tonight, probably with Viv and her latest boyfriend whose name I'd forgotten, and I wouldn't think about Malcolm Campbell at all.

I got up and threw away my trash, then went back to the front counter. Judy wasn't there. She was probably doing something in the office, working on that new customer database she was so proud of. It was going to make our lives a lot easier, so I was happy to let her do it.

I put Hallstrom's book away under the counter, then leaned on the cracked glass top with both elbows and hoped Malcolm had finished and left while I was eating. I didn't need my calm disturbed any more today.

Footsteps echoed from deeper within the store, and Malcolm emerged, dusting his hands on a white handkerchief he then tucked away inside his coat. He gave a good impression of a wealthy, cultured man, owner of a private security company, but I'd seen him fight, and knew that impression concealed the true man—a powerful, skilled ex-military operative who put his life on the line defending humanity against monsters from another reality. No wonder I had trouble not being attracted to him.

"Thank you," he said. "I'll see you later."

"Are you off for more training?" I tried to sound blasé. His absence could only help me feel calmer.

"No, I'm home for the next little while." He lowered his voice, though there was no one to hear us. "Invader presence in the city has gone up in the last week or so, which means my team is on alert. A lot of teams are, frankly. You may see an upsurge in augury requests."

"Thanks for the warning. Say hello to the team for me, would you?" I was good friends with his teammates Hector, Olivia, and Derrick, and the new awkwardness between me and Malcolm meant I saw less of them.

"I will. Good afternoon, Helena."

When he was gone, I hopped down and went into the stacks. The oracle wasn't active, so they were just ordinary bookcases, but I felt comforted being surrounded by them. "I still don't know what I'm doing half the time," I whispered, "but I feel as if I'm being guided, and that's thanks to you. I hope I'm living up to your expectations." I never felt stupid, talking to the oracle even if it wasn't present, but I certainly didn't want anyone else hearing—

"Who are you talking to?"

I turned around fast, catching myself on one of the bookcases. I knew that voice. A blond woman, tall and buxom, stood looking at me with her hands on her hips, her mouth quirked in a familiar smile. I saw it in the mirror every morning.

My hands gripped the bookcase so hard my fingers tingled. I drew in a breath and said, "*Cynthia?*"

2

"Surprised?" my sister said. Her smile broadened, and she took a step toward me. I let go of the bookcase to hug her. Surprise wasn't the word for it. Dread would be more like it.

"Of course! When did you get in?"

"This morning. I talked to Mom and she gave me this address. I have to say, Hellie, this isn't what I expected. Don't you even alphabetize?" She wore an expensive-looking tan suit with a skirt that came to above her knees and a pale blue silk shell that showed off her excellent figure. She drew one finger across one of the upper shelves and showed me the dust clinging to it.

Familiar irritation rose up in me, and I tried to ignore it. Telling her I hated being called Hellie would only remind her to do it more often. I walked away, wanting her out of the stacks. "There's a special organizational system. What are you doing in Portland?"

She sauntered along behind me. "Business conference, plus I wanted to see my loving family, starting with my favorite baby sister."

"I'm your only sister." *And I'm not a baby.*

"Therefore my favorite." She smirked at me and patted my cheek. "You coming to dinner? Mom said to ask. She also said to invite your boyfriend. Hellie, haven't you dumped that waste of space Chet already?"

"I did, thanks for asking. She meant Jason. We—"

"I can't wait to meet him." She lounged against the countertop and picked at a flaw in the glass. There were a lot of them. I ought to get the top replaced. "I wish I could introduce you to Ethan, but he had to work. Busy life, trading stocks on Wall Street."

"I'm sure it is." Tension built behind my eyes the way it always did when Cynthia showed up. She was worse now than when we'd been kids, but maybe that was because she had more with which to lord it over me—hot model turned stockbroker boyfriend, successful career, expensive apartment somewhere fancy in New York City...the list went on. I reminded myself that I was the custodian of a powerful magical entity and smiled pleasantly.

The door opened, sending bells jingling. "Helena, I—oh, excuse me," Malcolm said. He had a slip of paper in one hand and held the door with the other. "I realized I wanted you to find me that book, after all," he continued, his eyes focused on Cynthia. She, for her part, was at full alert and smiling like a cat in a purring competition.

"No problem," I said, taking the augury slip from him. "This is *my sister*, Cynthia. Cynthia, this is a friend of mine, Malcolm Campbell. He's a regular customer."

"*Very* pleased to meet you," Cynthia said, extending a well-manicured hand toward Malcolm.

"It's always good to meet a relative of Helena's," Malcolm said, inclining his dark head toward her with a smile. I wanted to tear Cynthia's hair out by the roots.

"I'll just...go find this book," I said, and practically ran for the oracle.

Once inside, I stopped to calm myself. Cynthia loved pushing my buttons. Therefore, I wouldn't give her the satisfaction. I would perform this augury, and have a pleasant conversation with her, and then she would leave...and I'd have to see her at dinner, and listen to her snide comments, and watch her flirt with my boyfriend the way she always did. *How long is this business trip, anyway?*

Malcolm's augury was relatively inexpensive, something to help him track invaders tonight. I wished I could go along. It would be better than dinner with Cynthia.

"Here you are," I said, handing it to him. "That will be $450."

Cynthia gasped dramatically. "Expensive book!"

"Old books frequently are," Malcolm said, reaching for his suit pocket. He paused, his dark eyes fixed on me in a realization that he couldn't hand over tubes of *sanguinis sapiens* in front of Cynthia. "Will you put it on my account, Helena?"

"That doesn't look like an old book to me," Cynthia said, eyeing the brightly colored cover of *A Child's Encyclopedia of Animals*, vol. 15, POS to RIK.

"Condition is, of course, essential," Malcolm said smoothly. "It was a pleasure meeting you, Cynthia. Thank you again, Helena."

When he was gone, Cynthia fanned herself dramatically. "Why aren't you dating *him*, Hellie? He's positively edible."

Fury swept through me, fury and pain that stunned me, and I managed to say, "He's just a good friend. It's possible to have those, you know."

"I know, but if I were your Jared, I'd be worried."

"His name is Jason, and we're fine, thanks."

"Don't be so snooty, Helena, I'm just taking an interest in your life."

"I think we need a better—oh," Judy said, emerging from the back of the store. She sounded so much like Malcolm had that I suddenly felt like laughing. None of us were used to ordinary customers coming in, it happened so rarely, and watching my friends stumble over their secrets made me feel less miserable. "Who's this?"

"My sister, Cynthia. Cynthia, this is Judy, my co-worker."

"Co-worker? I thought you ran the place." Cynthia eyed Judy narrowly, like a possible rival, though I couldn't think for whom.

"I do. Judy helps. And we have a lot of work to do." I didn't lean too hard on those words, but Cynthia got the message anyway.

"Well, I don't want to keep you from your work," Cynthia said. "I'll see you at dinner, Hellie." She smiled at Judy and swept out of the store.

Judy said, "'Hellie'?"

"I hate it. Never call me that."

"I wouldn't. It sounds like something you'd call a pet. I'd say it's impossible she's your sister, except you look exactly alike."

"We do not."

"All right, she's bustier and taller than you, but aside from that... you even have the same smile."

"Don't remind me." I leaned against the countertop. "What were you going to say?"

"Huh? Oh. I was going to say we need a better system for processing the *sanguinis sapiens*. The safe deposit box you've been using is inadequate, and moving to a larger box just pushes the problem back a few steps."

"Did you have a plan?"

"No, but I thought I'd talk to someone at the Athenaeum access point about how they do it. They handle far more of it than we do and might have a solution."

"Good idea." The Athenaeum, greatest repository of knowledge in the world, accepted only raw magic as payment for accessing its records. If anyone knew what to do with an excess of *sanguinis sapiens*, it was its technicians Guille and Irina. "How's the database coming?"

Judy scowled. "I realize it was my idea and I therefore have no excuse to bitch, but I think we need to hire someone to do the data entry. I'm going blind from reading those records."

"I'll think about it. I can take a turn at typing, too."

"So long as business continues to be slow, that would help. But if we get too many requests—"

The door swung open. "I've got payment," said Hallstrom. He carried a filing box filled with what smelled like the remnants of a forest fire. Blackened leather bindings peeked out at the top. "I know they smell a little smoky, but they're in good condition."

I ran my fingers along the spines. They came away clean. Apparently the blackness was age rather than soot. "Let's see if Abernathy's will take them," I said, and removed the first book and opened to the title page. It was clean, if age-yellowed and spotted near the edges, and nothing was written on it. I glanced over my shoulder at the book-cases. *Are you paying attention?* "Not this one," I added, setting it aside.

On the title page of the second book, in faintly golden script, was the number $75. "Seventy-five dollars," I told Judy, who tapped a note into her phone.

"Is that a lot?" Hallstrom said. He leaned over to look at the book's page, which to him would be blank. "It seems like a lot."

"We'll see," I said, reaching for another book. I had no idea what criteria the oracle used to decide how much a book was worth, though I guessed the value might have something to do with how readily it could turn the thing into an augury. I was mostly just glad I didn't have to figure out values myself.

Hallstrom ended up with about six hundred dollars in credit and gratefully came up with the balance in cash. "You don't know how much this means to me," he said, clutching his augury to his thin chest.

Nope, I really don't. That's how it works. "You're welcome," I said, and let out a deep breath when he was gone.

"I hate the grateful ones," Judy said.

"Judy!"

"I do. They make me feel uncomfortable, like I'm getting credit for something I didn't do. Literally didn't, since I'm not the custodian." She didn't sound bitter about that the way she would have half a year ago.

"I feel that way too, but it's gratitude we're accepting for the oracle, so I think we should be gracious about it."

Judy shrugged. "I'll put these away if you like, and you can take a turn at the keyboard." She gathered up the pile of books, which was quite large, and staggered away into the stacks. I let her do it. It wasn't as if Abernathy's had a shelving system; it operated on principles of indeterminacy, in which not knowing what was in the store meant anything could be in the store, so we just neatly shelved books any old place.

I typed customer information into the database for about forty-five minutes, until two o'clock, when the Ambrosites arrived, making the second rush of the day. Their auguries kept me busy for a couple of hours, but I never minded. Time spent in the oracle energized me, made me feel cheerful, and I had plenty of friends among the Ambrosites I enjoyed chatting with, just as I did among the Nicolliens. I was impartial the way the Accords demanded. Too bad—I cut off that line of thinking before it could ruin my mood. Malcolm was a friend, too.

When things slacked off around five, I called Jason. "Hey, hon," he said. It was how he always answered the phone when I called. I didn't really like it, but it seemed like a stupid thing to make a fuss over.

"You're busy tonight, right?" I hopped onto the tall stool and kept one eye on the front door.

"Um, no, should I be?"

I sighed. "You might wish you were busy. My sister's in town and my mom wants us all to come for family dinner."

"Your mom's cooking? Is it salmon again? I thought I'd died and gone to heaven."

"I don't know what she's cooking, but did I mention my sister is in town?"

"You did. I'd love to meet her."

I leaned my elbows on the glass countertop and closed my eyes, searching for inner peace. "Jason, she's a bitch. She'll flirt with you and insult me and my parents will ignore it."

"She can't be that bad."

"I assure you she can."

There was a tiny pause, almost imperceptible. "Look, hon, if you don't want me to come—" His voice had that little whine in it that got on my nerves.

"It's not about you."

"Then what is it about?"

I sighed again. "Nothing. I just don't like her. Will you come tonight?"

"It sounds like you'd rather I didn't."

I hated when he got his feelings hurt. It made me feel like I had to back down to cheer him up. "If I have to go, I'd really like it if you were there. I'll feel less defensive."

"All right. And I promise not to flirt with your sister. As if I'd want to with you in the room."

"That makes me feel better," I said, though it sort of didn't. "You want to meet at my parents', or should I pick you up?"

"Why don't I pick you up? Then afterward, we can come back to your place and fool around."

It was back to that again. "You know I prefer your place. It's bigger, and more comfortable—"

"We never go to your apartment. I'm starting to think you've got a bunch of ex-boyfriends' bodies stashed there."

"No, but my meth lab takes up all the extra space."

Jason laughed. "All right, pick me up at six-thirty."

When he'd hung up, I stared at my phone for a while. It was true, I'd never invited him to my apartment, and I didn't know why. It would certainly be convenient for me and my work, especially if he spent the night—not that I'd spent the night at his place yet, either. My reluctance was just another reminder that as much as I liked Jason, there was still a distance between us he didn't seem aware of, a gap I didn't know how to bridge. He was cute, and smart, and funny, and the sex was good—so what was the problem? *You know what the problem is*, I told myself, and went back to mindlessly typing names and addresses.

By six o'clock I was sick of the keyboard and mentally prepared for a happy family dinner, not that I was likely to get that. I locked up the store, said goodbye to Judy, and drove off toward Jason's apartment. He lived in a nice, quiet part of town, and I was mostly honest when I said I felt more comfortable at his place. My apartment above the store, which had once belonged to a custodian named Silas Abernathy, was about seventy years old and still decorated in that classic style. It also lacked adequate heating and cooling, Abernathy's system not extending to the second floor, and fronted on a relatively busy street whose noise penetrated the walls day and night. At least at Jason's apartment I wasn't distracted by the sounds of cars driving past all the time.

Jason lived about ten minutes from my parents' house, in an upscale apartment complex with white brick facings on the ground floor and the upper levels painted forest green. Cute little hedges lined the walkway facing the parking lot, making the tiny yards look like a long row of English cottages. Jason came bounding out the door when I drove up. "I was watching for you," he said, unnecessarily, and leaned over to kiss me. His hair, blonder than mine, flopped down over his very blue eyes. "I've been thinking about you all day."

"Really? What have you been thinking about?"

He ran his finger down the line of my neck. "I'll show you later," he said, smiling.

"Mmm, something to look forward to."

"Dinner's not going to be that bad, Hel."

"I hope not." I had no reason to be that optimistic.

My parents lived near Happy Valley, a name that struck me as ominous tonight. *Don't be an idiot. You're setting yourself up to be miserable.* A late-model BMW was pulled up in the driveway of the ranch-style house when we arrived. "Your sister?" Jason said.

"Cynthia always rents one when she comes to visit. I think it's her favorite car. They may keep it reserved just for her." I hoped that sounded like the joke I intended and not as bitter resentment. Jason laughed, so I was probably all right.

We went in through the side door and into my mother's kitchen, redolent with spicy smells. "Helena! Jason! I'm so glad you're here!" my mother said, setting aside a pan covered in asparagus stalks drenched in melted butter and parmesan and embracing us both. "Why don't you set the table, both of you? Your father's on the patio, grilling steaks," she told me, "and Cynthia is in the back, freshening up."

Of course Cynthia wouldn't be doing any work. She was a guest.

Jason and I got stacks of plates and handfuls of silverware and started setting the old walnut dining table. I reflexively straightened the tablecloth. "I didn't think Dad was allowed to grill anymore, after the Mother's Day Incident."

"He has to learn just like anyone. And he's been practicing all summer." My dad was good at just about everything except cooking. Why Mom, nearly a cordon bleu chef, was encouraging him to pursue the art was a mystery to me.

My younger brother Jake came bounding up the stairs from the basement. "Hey, Hel. Hey, Jase." He waved at us but didn't pause on his way to the bathroom to wash up.

"We're the only ones doing any work," I complained.

"You're my responsible child," Mom said with a smile.

Dad opened the sliding glass door, letting in the aroma of perfectly grilled steaks. "Food's ready, if I'm not mistaken."

"It smells wonderful, Dad," Cynthia said, emerging from the rear of the house. She'd changed into shorts and a fitted T-shirt and looked gorgeous as usual. She saw Jason and stopped. "Please tell me you're not Jason," she said, "because I want to steal you from my sister."

My jaw went rigid. Jason laughed. "Helena said you were funny," he said. "I'm Jason, and you must be Cynthia."

Cynthia flicked a glance at me. "Lucky you," she said with a tiny smile. I made myself relax. Jason wasn't going to be swayed by her obvious flirting, and I could endure her little jabs. And the steaks smelled fantastic.

They tasted fantastic, too. "Really good, Dad," I said with my mouth full. Dad beamed.

"I haven't had anything this good in weeks," Cynthia said. "Maybe I should come home more often."

"Maybe you should," Mom said. "How's your meeting going?" She passed me the rice pilaf and I served myself another scoop.

"We start Monday. It should be incredibly boring, lots of talking, lots of posturing."

"You came awfully early for a Monday meeting," I said.

"I wanted some family time. Nothing wrong with that, is there, Hellie?"

"Of course not," Dad said. "We'll have to think of things to do as a family. There's a music festival going on downtown, or a movie. Tomorrow afternoon?"

"I have to work then," I said.

"Oh, right."

"We can still get together. Helena won't mind, will you, Hellie?"

"Not at all. There's plenty of other things we can do together later." I felt a little relieved at the idea of not having to enjoy forced family fun. Then I felt bad. I loved spending time with my family, even if Cynthia had to be along.

My leg buzzed with an incoming text. I reached for it, then put my hand on the table. "Sorry."

"Mom still has the no phones during dinner rule, huh?" Cynthia took a bite of asparagus and licked butter off her lips.

"It's a good rule," I said, picking up my knife and fork. My phone buzzed again. "Sorry."

Cynthia turned her attention on Jason, who sat to my right. "So tell me, Jason, how long have you and Hellie been dating?"

"Almost two months." Jason glanced at me, smiling, and I was cheered by it.

"And you've already met the fam. Brave, Hellie."

I smiled pleasantly at her. "Yes, considering we've never met Ethan. I almost wonder if he exists."

"Be nice, Helena."

"It was a joke, Mom. Of course Ethan exists. I just think, after two and a half years, it's time we met him."

"Ethan's very busy. He hasn't taken a vacation in over three years." Cynthia glared at me. It cheered me further.

"I'm sure we'll meet him eventually. Your father and I have talked about taking a trip to New York sometime later this year."

"You have? Why is this the first I've heard of it?"

"We're not obligated to tell you our every plan, Helena." Mom smiled at me to take away the sting. "It's just something we were thinking about."

"I'd love to show you around town," Cynthia said. "Like I'm sure Helena would do for me, if she had time."

"I...what?" It was so unexpected I fumbled my fork. It hit my plate with a dull chime.

Cynthia smiled. "I know you're tied to that little store of yours, but don't you think it would be fun to take in the sights together?"

Take in the sights? "Cynthia, you used to live here."

"It's been six years. I'm sure everything's changed."

I looked around the table for some kind of rescue. My parents looked thrilled. Jason was smiling. Jake had his head down over his steak and was ignoring the rest of us. "I...well, sure. That would be...fun."

"And you can bring Jason along," Cynthia purred, giving him a long, slow look just to irritate me. "You don't mind, do you?"

"Accompanying two lovely ladies around town? I can't imagine anything I'd rather do."

Cynthia laughed. To everyone else, it no doubt sounded pleasantly cheerful. I was the only one it drove crazy.

My phone buzzed again, and I leaped to my feet, nearly sending my chair crashing into the glass-fronted sideboard behind me. "I'm done eating," I said, and ran for the living room, my napkin falling unheeded at my feet.

In the living room, I dropped into one of the suede-upholstered love seats and pulled out my phone. I'd told Viv I was having a family dinner, so whatever this was had to be important. Or, knowing Viv, she was just having a crisis over her latest boyfriend, whose name, I'd finally remembered, was Rick. Her relationships were frequently dramatic, but this one was more dramatic than most.

It wasn't Viv. It was Malcolm.

TERRIBLE ATTACK. QUINCY SERIOUSLY INJURED BY INVADER. THOUGHT YOU'D WANT TO KNOW.

3

I sucked in a breath. Olivia was a paper magus, not a steel magus like Malcolm whose magical aegis made him immune to an invader's attack. The thought of her dead, drained of her magic, horrified me.

The next message read SHE'LL SURVIVE and the third, somewhat longer, said AUGURY VERY ACCURATE THANK YOU. WILL SEE YOU IN THE MORNING FOR ANOTHER AUGURY.

"Is everything all right? You look awful," Jason said.

"A friend of mine was in an accident. She'll be all right, but it's still scary."

Jason put his arms around me and hugged me. "I'm sorry."

"Sorry for what?" Cynthia came in and flopped onto the couch opposite me. "We're going to play games as soon as the washing is done."

"So why don't you help?" I snapped, disentangling myself from Jason.

"I tried. Mom said I was excused. She said you should come help her. Jason can keep me company." She smirked and patted the couch cushion next to her. I shoved my phone into my pocket and left the room, trying not to stomp.

"You could be a little nicer to your sister," Mom said. She was rinsing dishes and loading them into the dishwasher. I gathered a few more plates from the table and dumped them into the sink.

"I was being nice. She's the one who's constantly sniping at me."

"Helena, I know you and Cynthia have never had a close relationship, but can't you see she's trying to change that? She doesn't actually want to see Portland. She wants to spend time with you."

"I don't have a ton of time to spare. Neither does she, if she's got that big meeting all next week."

Mom stopped with a tumbler in one hand and the long-handled scrubber in the other and looked me in the eye. "Just—make an effort, please?"

I sighed and rinsed a handful of forks. "I'll try. But if she keeps making a play for my boyfriend, I'll scratch her eyes out."

"She's just being friendly."

"In most states, we call that flirting, Mom."

Mom laughed. "She's in love with Ethan and has no interest in anyone else."

I started clearing away the other glasses. "Maybe. I think she just doesn't like seeing me with anyone."

"Don't be so negative, Helena."

I heard Cynthia's pealing laugh coming from the living room, overlain with Jason's deeper chuckle. "It's not negative if it's true."

We played board games in teams, Mom and Dad, Cynthia and Jake, me and Jason. Our team lost constantly, no matter what game we played, mostly because I was worried about Olivia, but also because I couldn't help being conscious of Cynthia's attention to Jason. Her constant comments on his play and his appearance went unnoticed by everyone else, and Jason, despite his promise to me, flirted back.

By ten o'clock I was on edge and miserable and ready for the day to be over. When Mom proposed one more round, I said, "I have to work tomorrow, so I think we should go."

"Oh, of course," Mom said. "It's been a lovely evening, hasn't it?"

"It's been great, Louise," Jason said. "Thanks for inviting us. And it was nice getting to know you, Cynthia."

"Same here," Cynthia said. "How about I call you tomorrow, Hellie, and we'll make a plan?"

"Sounds good," I said. "Good night, everyone."

In the car, Jason said, "You want to come back to my place?"

"Listen, Jason, I'm really tired. Maybe some other time."

"I thought that's what you'd say," Jason said.

I shot him a quick glance. His jaw was set and he was looking away from me, out the passenger window. "I have work tomorrow. What was I supposed to say?"

"Work's always your excuse when you just don't want to spend time with me."

"Oh, it's my fault? Maybe you should have gone home with Cynthia."

He turned on me. "What the hell is that supposed to mean?"

I was too tired to be polite. "You promised me you wouldn't fall for her flirting."

"I wasn't flirting! She's a nice person and we were having fun together."

"Call it what you want." I swerved into the parking lot in front of his apartment and parked across two spaces. "You know how I feel about her. You're supposed to be on my side."

"Why does it have to come down to sides? She's not as bad as you made her sound."

So Jason wasn't immune to her charm, after all. Anger burned hot inside me. "Well, you didn't have to grow up with her constantly putting you down and stealing your boyfriends. So excuse me if I don't think your opinion is valid."

"What's new? You never do." He got out and slammed the door behind him, flung open his front door and stormed through. I swore and backed out of the parking lot. He didn't understand.

By the time I reached home, I'd cooled off enough to regret the argument. It wasn't Jason's fault if all he saw was the front Cynthia put on for the world. I shouldn't have been so awful to him. I'd have to

THE BOOK OF MAYHEM

call in the morning and apologize—no, I could text him when I got in. Viv kept telling me there was always something you could apologize for, even when you were in the right, and in this case I'd let my anger at Cynthia spill over onto Jason.

Safely at home with the doors all locked, I texted Jason: I'M SORRY I HURT YOUR FEELINGS. MY SISTER MAKES ME CRAZY. CALL ME TOMORROW? Then I tapped back through my contacts until I found Malcolm's texts. Derrick, a bone magus who could heal most physical injuries, must have healed Olivia—but I didn't know if a bone magus could heal someone of the loss of their magic. All humans were reservoirs of magic, though without an aegis no human could use theirs, and invaders saw humans' magic as their rightful prey. If someone's magic was drained, I didn't think it regenerated naturally, so there had to be some other way of restoring it. I was pretty sure it wasn't as simple as drinking down a tube of *sanguinis sapiens*.

I plugged my phone in, put on my pajamas—men's extra-small button-up, more comfortable than a nightgown—and pulled out my journal. I'd been keeping it for about two months, after reading the diaries of several of Abernathy's former custodians. I wasn't great about writing every day, but I usually managed three or four times a week. I wrote what Malcolm had said about increased invader presence in the city, wrote about Hallstrom's augury, then set the little book aside. It was bound in tan leather and looked very professional, not at all the kind of diary I'd choose for my own journal, if I were keeping one, which I wasn't. I didn't like the idea of my private journal making its way into the Athenaeum someday on the grounds that a custodian wasn't allowed a personal life, or some other justification.

Maybe that was why I hadn't found Silas Abernathy's journal in the Athenaeum. He'd written a book about his travels after abdicating the custodianship, and I couldn't believe he hadn't written about his years as a custodian, but maybe he'd felt it was too personal to make public. I could certainly understand that.

I opened my journal again and wrote: *My sister Cynthia is in town and wants me to show her around. I can't imagine she won't pry into my work life, which means I'll have to work at keeping Abernathy's nature secret. I wonder if other custodians, or magi, ever have to keep the magical world secret from family or close friends? It's already hard enough keeping this from my family, and they aren't inclined to pry.* It probably wouldn't be an issue. Cynthia would be in meetings all day, and Abernathy's looked dull if you didn't know its secret. No trouble at all.

I turned out the light and snuggled into bed. The rosebuds carved into the headboard looked blobby and ugly in the dim light from the window. No, that was my irritation talking. Hopefully tomorrow Malcolm would come with more information, and it would be a better day. It would be hard for it to be worse.

I WOKE to the sound of someone pounding on my apartment door. I blearily stumbled to it, remembering to peer through the newly-installed peephole before unlocking it. "Finally," Judy said, pushing past me. "I should be grateful you've learned to lock your door, but mostly it's just annoying." She had a box of donuts and the air of someone with something on her mind.

I sat at the kitchen table opposite her and nibbled a maple-glazed donut. "What's up?"

"Some interesting news, that's what's up."

I dropped the donut. "Is Olivia okay?"

"Yes—wait, what about Olivia?"

"Malcolm told me last night she'd been badly hurt, but that she'd survive. You hadn't heard?"

"No, but they're Ambrosites, so I wouldn't have." Judy was as impartial as I was, but her being the daughter of the Nicollien leader meant she was privy to certain facts I wasn't. "I'm sure she'll be fine. Campbell wouldn't have told you unless that was the case."

"So if it's not about Olivia, what is it?"

Judy poured us both coffee, then took a bite out of a donut.

"Someone died last night. Not a magus, just an ordinary person. Drained of her magic. But there weren't any invaders in the area when the team showed up."

"I take it that means something."

"Invaders are slow. It's how our magi are able to take them out so easily—well, not *easily*, but you know what I mean."

"So what does it mean?"

Judy shrugged. "No clue. A new kind of invader? Father's had his second in meetings all night, trying to work out what might have happened. And keep it from happening again."

"I though Ms. Guittard was in Seattle." Amber Guittard, a stone magus, was the Nicollien second-in-command in our area and a sweet-voiced woman I liked a lot more than I liked her boss.

"She was. She ward-stepped back last night for this. We had to weaken the wards of our house to allow her to move from Seattle to there."

"Did Mr. Rasmussen tell Ryan Parish?"

Judy made a face and took a fierce bite out of her donut. "I don't know. It all happened in Nicollien territory, so Father may think it only matters to them. He probably should tell him."

"I could tell him."

"You can't. I'm telling you in strict confidence. I shouldn't have said anything, except I wanted you to know Father will probably be in here this morning for an augury about the death. No more traffic than usual, otherwise—Father's trying to keep it quiet. He'd pop a vein if he knew I'd told you privileged information."

"All right." More faction nonsense. I drank more coffee and grimaced. "Malcolm's coming in for another augury this morning."

"In the middle of Nicollien time?"

Her casual way of putting it, as if the Nicolliens had some God-given right to a chunk of my time, irritated me. "I told you I'm not going to hold anyone to that decision. And they respect Malcolm, even if some of them hate his guts."

"Yes, but if he's here when Father is—"

"They can behave like grownups. Mr. Rasmussen knows he has no authority over Abernathy's."

Judy shrugged. "It's you who's going to have to weather the fallout. If I were you, I'd call Campbell and warn him off."

"Malcolm's not afraid of Mr. Rasmussen."

"No, but they hate each other. Like I said, it's your problem, not mine." Judy wiped her mouth and took her coffee cup to the sink to rinse it. "I'm going to work on the database. Shout if there's a fight. I want a front-row seat."

I ate another donut after she left and stared at my phone. Maybe Judy was right. I could at least warn Malcolm—no, that would mean being partial, unless I was equally willing to warn Rasmussen, which I wasn't. Damn them all for being so touchy and stupid.

Judy had been only partly right; there were more Nicolliens at the door than usual when we opened at ten, but all of them were hunters wanting auguries to guide their teams, as Malcolm had suggested. I had to get them to form a line...maybe I needed one of those little wheels that spat out numbered tickets. I took the day's first augury slip and walked into the oracle.

When I emerged, the store was deathly quiet, more quiet than the oracle had been. Everyone waiting for an augury had their attention fixed on Malcolm, who looked as composed as ever in a charcoal-gray suit with a cherry-red waistcoat and tie. The hostility was thick enough to swim through. I bit back a handful of harsh words and handed the book to the plump middle-aged woman waiting near the cash register. "It's $300, Barbara," I said. "Wait here and I'll get Judy to take payment."

I walked at a measured, calm pace toward the back of the store, went into the office, and shut the door behind me. "Malcolm's out there and I think they want to eat him alive."

"I warned you," Judy said without looking up from the computer.

"Well, I need you to come take payments and fill out the receipts. There are a lot of them today."

Judy shoved the chair back and stood, stretching like a cat. "It's never boring here, at least."

"That's not true. It was really boring last Tuesday."

"So I exaggerated. Mostly it's not boring."

The crowd hadn't moved while I was gone. "Next," I said, and escaped into the oracle.

When I returned the second time, the tension wasn't quite as great, though all the Nicolliens eyed Malcolm like they were hoping he'd sprout fangs and attack someone. "Here you are," I said to the augury's recipient.

"This is supposed to be Nicollien time," the man said. "Why don't you—"

"Why don't *you* tell me how to run Abernathy's?" I said brightly. "Oh, wait, that's none of your business. You all know the time restrictions your leader placed you under aren't binding on me. And you're all free to come here any time you like. As is Mr. Campbell. That will be $600. Judy will take your payment."

The man snarled at me, and in the corner of my vision I saw Malcolm tense. I stood my ground, though my heart was beating a little too fast because the man was heavily muscled and taller than me. Slowly I crossed my arms over my chest and glared back. He might be an idiot, probably was an idiot, but he wasn't stupid enough to attack the custodian of Abernathy's, especially on the premises. Finally he took the book from my hands and turned his back on me. I caught Malcolm's eye and could almost feel him quivering with the desire to attack the man. It was nice to know he was still my defender, whatever else might have passed between us.

I did another four auguries before Malcolm handed me his slip. "I should have waited," he murmured, "but once I was here, I couldn't leave without looking as if they'd chased me out. I apologize if this makes trouble for you."

"It's no trouble, and don't you dare let them frighten you."

He smiled, an amused, sardonic expression. "'Frighten' is hardly the word I'd use."

"Well, I thought 'intimidate' would be insulting."

"Indeed." He glanced over his shoulder at a beefy man and a tall, muscular woman who were glaring at us. "I believe they think I'm taking up too much time."

"That just makes me want to spin out this conversation further. So, seen any good movies lately?"

His smile broadened. "Stop tormenting them," he said, but I could tell he wanted to laugh.

It took me a while to find Malcolm's augury, which turned out to be another volume of the child's encyclopedia I'd given him the day before. We'd never had the full set, and it was looking increasingly scanty with all the gaps from the missing volumes. I checked the title page—still $450—and carried it back to the front counter. "It's—" I began, then registered that the room, which had been still and tense before, had gone positively glacial. I put the book on the counter. "Mr. Rasmussen," I said.

The tall, well-dressed man standing by the door inclined his head to me, for all the world like a king acknowledging an obeisance. His round-framed glasses made him look like a professor of some obscure discipline, but his eyes, light blue and cold, reminded you that he had power and was not afraid to use it. "Ms. Davies," he said.

"Are you here for an augury? Because I'm afraid you'll have to wait."

"I don't mind," said the short woman who was next in line after Malcolm. "I'm sure no one minds."

Heads nodded. I wished I could slap them silly for being sheep. "That's up to you. Mr. Campbell, that will be $450."

Malcolm handed a tube of *sanguinis sapiens* to Judy, who was smiling like this was the best entertainment she'd seen all week. "Thank you, Miss Davies."

The unexpected courtesy made me want to laugh. He hadn't called me that in months. "My pleasure."

Malcolm tucked his book under his arm and strolled toward the door, only to come up short as one of the men surrounding Rasmussen stepped into his path. "I beg your pardon," Malcolm said quietly. "Let me pass."

The man didn't move. Without breaking eye contact, Malcolm

said, "I have a right to use the store, Rasmussen. Please ask your monkey to step aside."

The man growled and raised a fist as if to punch Malcolm. Rasmussen said, "McCorkle, enough. Stooping to childish insults, Campbell?"

"Merely offering an opinion. Your man gives the impression of a trained animal off his leash. You should be careful where you take him. Not everywhere is neutral ground."

"You were warned not to come to Abernathy's at this time. You're the one who should be careful."

"When the custodian tells me she's enforcing your self-determined rules, I'll abide by them. Until then—" Malcolm leaned forward until he was within inches of McCorkle's face, which really did look simian. *"Get out of my way."*

McCorkle flinched and stepped aside. "Thank you," Malcolm said, once again the picture of an elegant gentleman who would never dream of starting a fight in a bookstore, and the door jingled shut behind him. I let out my breath slowly. I'd almost hoped to see Malcolm start a fight, but that would only have ended badly. Though probably not for Malcolm.

"An augury, Ms. Davies? If you're finished daydreaming."

I flushed angrily and snatched the augury slip out of Rasmussen's hand. "Just one moment."

Safely within the oracle, I closed my eyes and willed myself calm. Rasmussen tested my impartiality more than anyone else. He'd wanted me to abdicate the custodianship in favor of Judy, and he made no secret of the fact that he still believed I wasn't suited for the job, even though I'd seen the store through two challenges to its existence. It was so tempting to turn back around and tell him the oracle had rejected his augury—but I'd promised myself never to lie about what Abernathy's did, even if I was the only one who would ever know. Besides, whatever augury he wanted would benefit more than just himself, so it would be selfish and cruel of me to punish those other people just to piss Rasmussen off.

I unfolded the piece of paper. *Where is the creature who killed Tiffany Alcock?*

I took a few more steps before the name registered. Then numb horror struck me. The paper fluttered out of my nerveless grip. I turned and ran out of the oracle.

4

"Tiffany Alcock?" I said.

Rasmussen's lips went white. "If you can't keep your mouth shut about an augury," he said, "I will be forced to take it up with the Board of Neutralities."

"Come with me," I said, grabbing his arm and pulling. He stood firm, yanking his arm free of my grasp. I saw Judy's shocked face for half a second as I swiveled around and took hold of him again. "This is *important* and it's about your augury, and I will start shouting if you don't follow me this instant."

I had no idea how I looked. Crazy, probably. Whatever my expression was, it made Rasmussen wave off his attendants—*monkeys, they do look like monkeys, flying ones like in* The Wizard of Oz—and follow me to the office, Judy trailing in our wake.

Inside, I shut the door and sat on the edge of my tan melamine desk. Its top felt as cold as the ache in my chest. "Tiffany Alcock is dead?"

"I believe that's the girl's name, yes."

"She's a friend. Not a close friend. She was at my birthday party. She—" I shoved off the desk and paced the room, passing between Judy and her father like a bumper car between two posts. Silas Abernathy's photo watched me, and I imagined I saw compassion in his eyes. "You're sure it's her?"

"We're always sure about these things, Ms. Davies," Rasmussen said, and to his credit, he didn't sound as severe as he had a few seconds ago. "I'm sorry for your loss."

"That's—" I waved my hand in the air. I couldn't think of a response to that. Tiffany, cheerful Tiffany, dead at the...they didn't have hands, they had tentacles, or pincers, or a million grasping tendrils, but whatever they were, they'd killed her. "Thank you. I'm sorry I ruined your augury, I was just so surprised—you have to write it again, a little differently."

"I know." Rasmussen opened the office door for me. "I'd suggest giving you time to grieve, but I think you'd prefer we destroy her killer."

At that moment, I liked Rasmussen. "I would. Thanks."

Rasmussen accepted paper and pen from one of his flunkies and wrote a line in flowing script. I was beginning to feel everyone around me had better handwriting than I did. I took it eagerly and walked into the oracle—

and into a flying, screaming storm of books. Wind battered me, ruffled pages so hard I expected to see them tear free and whirl away. Shielding my face with one arm, I peered at the augury slip, holding it tightly so it wouldn't blow away: *Where is the invader that killed Tiffany Alcock?*

"No augury?" I shouted, and the storm died away, leaving my ears ringing and my eyes watering from the force of the wind. "You don't have to be so violent when you won't give an answer," I muttered, and combed through my ponytail with my fingers. I never could predict when the oracle would refuse to answer, and it was always a shock. This time, it was a shock and a horrible disappointment. The first augury would have been fine if I hadn't been so stupid, and now...

I returned to Rasmussen and handed him the augury slip. "There's no augury," I said dully. "I'm sorry. The oracle won't answer this question."

There was a sharp sigh as every Nicollien in the room took in a startled breath at once. You'd have thought I'd just told Scarlett O'Hara I didn't give a damn. "Why not?" Rasmussen demanded. "You're going to let your dislike of me get in the way of finding—" His mouth shut sharply.

"I want this augury more than you do, Mr. Rasmussen. I don't have any control over what the oracle chooses to answer."

Rasmussen glared at me. "I won't put up with this treatment. The Board is going to hear about this."

"And you know what they're going to tell you. I have to accept every augury from those who have means to pay. The oracle isn't obliged to give an answer. I'm sorry."

The monkeys made a flying V around Rasmussen as they left the store. I slumped against the counter. "Who's next?"

It was nearly lunchtime before all the Nicolliens' auguries were finished. Judy didn't say anything the whole time, just patiently accepted payments and wrote down names in the ledger and filled out receipts. I drifted in and out of the stacks like I was in a dream, not a nightmare and not a pleasant dream, but the kind where you hover just below waking and real things seem unreal. Finally, I came to myself, realized I was staring at the bells hanging over the door, and scrubbed my eyes with the heels of my palms. "Is that really it?"

"I'm sorry about your friend," Judy said, shutting the ledger and putting it away. "Even if she wasn't very close."

"It's too unreal to believe. I've seen someone killed by an invader, but I barely knew him. This is...Tiffany and I were in school together. We were both on stage crew freshman year. Part of me just refuses to believe it. The other part of me can't stop thinking about her mom. They were really close."

"Let's eat, and we'll worry about that later," Judy said. "You said leftover pasta primavera, right? I'm not sure how good that is reheated."

"Me neither. But it was really good the first time, so it's worth trying."

We ate in silence, each of us preoccupied with our own thoughts. Judy was probably going over the database and calculating how much longer it would take to be finished. I couldn't stop thinking about Tiffany Alcock. I should call someone...but I didn't know her mom well enough...maybe Viv? Viv was closer to Tiffany than I was; she ought to know. I pulled out my phone. Judy arched an eyebrow at me, but said nothing.

I called Viv, but disconnected before she could answer. It was the lunch rush at the diner where she worked, and if Viv hadn't heard the news, I didn't want to distract her. Instead I texted IMPORTANT NEWS CALL ME LATER and put my phone away.

"Was she a friend of Viv's?" Judy asked.

"Yeah. But it can wait." Something else was bothering me, but I couldn't figure out what. Something about Tiffany...but I had no more information about her death than that she'd been killed by an invader. Or—

I pushed back my chair and hurried into the stacks, searching the floor. There hadn't been time to clean up after the oracle's tantrum— it was hard to think of its refusals as anything else, though it wasn't really alive in a conventional sense—and books lay on the floor, some of them open on their faces, which made me wince. I found the place I'd been standing when I read the first augury slip and began hunting through the mess. After a few minutes, I found the little piece of paper. *Where is the creature who killed Tiffany Alcock?*

Creature. Invader. Such a tiny difference. I carried the paper back to the break room, where Judy was finishing off her Diet Dr. Pepper. I hooked my folding chair with my ankle and pulled it away from the battered table. "The first one said 'creature,'" I said. "The second one, the one the oracle refused, said 'invader.'"

"And?"

"I don't know. It's just that the oracle didn't reject the first augury. That was my fault. And changing just one word changed the whole outcome. It's as if it's saying it wasn't an invader that killed her."

"What else could it be?" Judy wiped her mouth and began clearing her trash.

"I don't know. How can they tell if someone's been killed by an invader?"

34

"It's almost impossible for anyone but a bone magus to tell the difference between a stroke victim and an invader death. Stroke, aneurysm, heart failure—I can't remember what else an invader death looks like. Mostly the difference is the body won't have any magic left in it."

"So what happens to our magic if we die naturally—or I guess I mean, if we're not killed by an invader?"

"It drains away over time. Wardens have their magic harvested so it doesn't go to waste, but an average person, someone not involved in the Long War, they just lose it gradually. So a dead person with no magic—that's an invader's victim. But, again, only a bone magus can tell if someone's had their magic drained."

"So Tiffany—" My throat tightened, and I took a drink of Diet Coke. "A bone magus found Tiffany and saw her magic had been drained, because without an invader lurking nearby, there would be no reason to suspect one had killed her."

"Presumably."

"So maybe it really is a new kind of invader."

"They're not all the same, you know. There are some—" Judy lowered her voice, as if this was a big secret—"that are even intelligent. Like, as intelligent as humans. We never see those."

"Then how do you know they exist?"

"There are reports of people encountering them centuries ago. Trying to negotiate with them. But they're as evil and rapacious as their stupider cousins, so that never went anywhere." Judy pushed her chair in. "I'm going to go work on the database until the afternoon shift comes in." She grinned. "Tell me you don't think of them that way."

"I don't think of them that way." *Much.*

I went into the stacks and began picking up books and slotting them into the shelves wherever they'd fit, not paying attention to the titles. If I had a better memory, I wouldn't be able to do this, because I'd know what was in the store and that would force the oracle to work harder—or work not at all, possibly. I straightened up a row of books and my fingers came away gray. Cynthia had been right about that—the shelves could use some dusting. I finished picking up all the books and headed toward the back of the store for the basement and the cleaning supplies.

On my way there, the door jingled. I sighed and turned around. One last straggler before the two o'clock rush—and now I was doing it, taking the Nicollien-Ambrosite split for granted. If Malcolm and I were the only ones not respecting it, what were the odds of me getting anyone else to change their mind?

I emerged into the space between the front door and the bookcases and came to a sudden stop. "Cynthia. What are you doing here?"

"I wanted to see you at work," Cynthia said. She was dressed in shorts and a cut-off T-shirt, showing off the navel piercing I hadn't realized she still had.

"My work is boring."

"Oh, I'm sure that's not true."

My phone rang, rescuing me from this increasingly uncomfortable conversation. "What's so important?" Viv said.

"Viv, it's really bad news. Have you heard about Tiffany Alcock?"

"You mean, that she died? Yeah, Sheridan called me this morning. I still can't believe it."

I eyed Cynthia, who had moved around the counter to perch on the stool behind the cash register. "Um, yeah, that was it. It's awful."

"I told Sheridan to let me know what they're doing, you know, funeral and whatever. I thought we should go."

"I want to." I'd have to tell her the real news later. "Oh, and my sister's in town."

Cynthia made a cheerful face and waved. "She says Hi."

Viv groaned. "Is it possible to mail her back to her mother planet?"

"Not really, no."

"Well, if you need me to manufacture prior commitments to keep you out of her clutches, just let me know. I have to go, okay? Talk to you later."

I put my phone away and put on what I hoped was a cheery smile. "You're seriously just going to hang out here for four hours?"

Cynthia ran her thumbnail along a crack in the glass. "Oh, not that long. Just a little while."

"It's going to be so boring. Honestly. People come in and I find them books. Not even exciting books."

"I was hoping to see that hot guy again. You said he was a regular, right?" Cynthia winked at me. My smile went tight. "Oh, don't look like that, I was kidding. Not that I'd mind. Look, if you don't want me to hang around, I can go."

She sounded genuinely hurt under the flippant pose, and to my utter shock I felt sorry for her. "No, it's not that, I just...never mind. Go ahead and stay. Just don't touch the cash register. It breaks easily." With that, I hurried back to the office.

"My sister's back, and she's not going anywhere," I said.

Judy swore. She did it so rarely we both blushed. "Okay, so we won't be able to accept *sanguinis sapiens*," she said, "but I can pretend to use the cash register to take cash payments, and you can fake looking like an antiquarian if anyone brings in a box of books. Not that that happens often."

"It's the milling around I'm afraid of. They need to know to pretend to browse. It won't affect the oracle at all, but you saw how everyone just stood there waiting in line this morning. It looks weird."

Judy bit her lip in thought. "We could post a sign."

"Saying what? 'Act Normal'? No, I'll go outside just before two and warn everyone who's waiting, and we'll just have to hope the late-comers figure it out."

At five to two I told Cynthia I was going to the market and left the store. There were already a few customers waiting outside Aber-nathy's front door, and inwardly I groaned, thinking of how visible they were through the store windows. Cynthia had to think it was crazy.

I drew in a deep breath of warm, damp air and let it out slowly. It didn't matter what Cynthia thought of it. She had no idea how bookstores worked and would probably believe anything I told her about my weird and wacky customers. I quickly explained the situation to those waiting, who managed not to turn and look at Cynthia as I spoke. Then I walked to the market and bought myself another Diet Coke. It was going to be a long afternoon.

I was standing in line to pay when I got a text:

I UNDERSTAND ABOUT FAMILY. SORRY I WASN'T MORE SUPPORTIVE. SEE YOU TONIGHT?

A twinge of guilt struck me. I hadn't thought about Jason at all that day, not even to worry about whether he was mad at me still. MAY HAVE FAMILY OBLIGATIONS, I texted back. WILL LET YOU KNOW. I smiled at the clerk and left the store, taking a big drink from the bottle right outside. Jason deserved better than the half-assed attention I sometimes gave him. I was going to do better, starting tonight.

When I returned, it was just after two o'clock and the store was full of Ambrosites browsing the shelves. So far, so good. "If anyone needs help, please let me know," I said, trying not to look at Cynthia.

"I need help finding an…this book," an elderly woman said, handing me an augury slip. I grasped it gratefully and found an empty aisle where I could step into the oracle.

They kept me busy for an hour, during which time I didn't stop sweating with fear that someone would slip up. One person nearly did, coming out with a vial of *sanguinis sapiens* that Judy swiftly pocketed before telling the woman she'd put it on her account. Three times I came out of the oracle to find Cynthia chatting with a customer, and I quailed again, hoping these magi, not all of whom were used to dealing with normal people in the confines of Abernathy's itself, would be discreet. But Cynthia laughed, and smiled, and flirted, and showed no indication she knew anything was strange. I gradually realized I wasn't going to have to explain away anything unusual and started to relax.

The door burst open. "I need an augury," Hallstrom shouted. "It's an emergency."

The few magi still loitering in the store froze. Judy, writing up a

receipt, whipped around to stare at Hallstrom. Cynthia sat up, frown-
ing. And I grabbed Hallstrom's hand and towed him into the stacks,
saying, "I'll see what I can do, sir."

Deep within the bookcases, I flung Hallstrom's hand away. "Are
you out of your mind? There's a non-Warden in the store!"

Hallstrom paled. "I didn't notice. Did he hear me?"

"Mr. Hallstrom, people on the *moon* heard you. Give me your
augury request, then go back to the front of the store and don't say
anything else. I'll handle it."

The instant the slip of paper was in my hand, Hallstrom vanished,
and the silence of the oracle surrounded me. Despite my anxiety, I
felt myself begin to relax. I'd just have to think of a way to spin it.
Something Cynthia would find believable.

I found Hallstrom's book and emerged from the oracle to find
Cynthia and Judy laughing. Hallstrom, standing nearby, was red-
faced and sheepish. "See, I told you she could find it," Judy said.

"I've never heard of a book emergency before," Cynthia told Hallstrom. "You're a more dedicated reader than I am."

"I guess so," Hallstrom said. He glanced at me as if he thought he
might be in trouble. Since I'd told him to shut up, that was true. I
handed him the book, glaring at him.

"Oh, don't worry, Hellie, he was just enthusiastic about that
book," Cynthia said. "I'll have to look it up. *An Augury*, right?"

"Sure," I said. "And his copy will cost him $1800."

"I don't—" Hallstrom began.

"Mr. Hallstrom, Abernathy's doesn't like it when customers use its
time and then can't pay." The continued laughing was getting on my
nerves. "Do I need to hold this book for you?"

Hallstrom patted his pockets, glanced nervously at the still-
giggling Cynthia, and shook his head. "I have a box of books in my
car, if you'll just—I'll just be right back."

When he was gone, Judy said, "I know we shouldn't laugh at him
when he's standing right there, but he's just so *dramatic* all the time.
Coming in here shouting like it's a matter of life and death, when it's
just a book."

"An expensive book." Cynthia flipped its cover open. "The title's *Anatomy of a Murder*, though. I thought—"

"Augury is the name of...of the series," I said, deftly removing the book from her reach. "You know, like a Hercule Poirot or a Nancy Drew. Like that."

"Ah," Cynthia said, nodding like that made sense, which I knew it didn't.

Hallstrom bumped the door open with his butt and set a box of books on the counter. It was one of those packing boxes from a moving company and was tearing at the bottom. "I hope it's enough," he said.

So do I. Wearily I pulled out the first book and looked inside the cover, then thought to make a show of looking at the binding and pages as if I was evaluating it for real. "$25." If they were all this cheap, this was going to take a while. I glanced at the other customers, who were watching the performance and not even pretending to browse the shelves. I mentally cursed my sister and Hallstrom, then Hallstrom again.

It took nearly half an hour to calculate the value of the books so Hallstrom could pay his bill, then another fifteen minutes to add up the value of the remaining books and put it on his account. By that time, my nerves had frayed almost to the breaking point. Cynthia had watched the process with a tiny, mocking smile that made me want to shove her off my stool and into the street. But she said nothing, so I ignored her.

An hour after that I showed the last of the afternoon shift the door and collapsed into the wobbly metal chair next to it, not caring that it shifted precariously and nearly sent me to the floor. Too bad she couldn't be the last customer of the day. I was past ready for six o'clock to arrive.

"Wow, Hellie, your job is as stressful as mine," Cynthia said, stretching like a cat.

"Wow, Cynthia, thanks for the sympathy," I said sarcastically.

"Hey, I was serious. I thought you just sat around all day, but all those people...it's like none of them know how to find a book on their own."

She did sound sincere, and it embarrassed me. "Sorry. I get keyed up after..." I let my words trail off.

"Yeah, what was up with that? All those people coming all at once. They were even lining up on the sidewalk like they were waiting for permission."

"There's a community college class that lets out at one thirty," Judy said. "We always get a rush around two because of it."

"Ah. Interesting." Cynthia hopped off the stool. "Well, I'm going to get changed, but then Mom and Dad want us to go to this music festival tonight. Want me to pick you up?"

Stunned, I said, "Um...sure?"

"Great. I'll be here at seven, and you can show me your cute little apartment. Mom says the kitchen is divine." She hugged me before I could protest, and let the door swing shut behind her.

I stared at Judy. "What was that?"

"I thought you said she was evil beyond the comprehension of mortal man."

"I did. She is."

"She seemed normal to me. But then she might just be performing for the audience." Judy swept a hand downward, indicating herself.

"I...don't know. I don't trust her. She ruined my sixteenth birthday party by showing up with beer and making all my friends gush about how cool she was. She's never been able to stand it when I have something she doesn't."

Judy nodded. "Like your boyfriend?"

"Like that. She's never given me a real compliment. Ever." I took a step back as the door opened, admitting a couple who had to be a fighting team. "So I'm keeping a very wary eye on her," I added, and stepped forward to accept the augury slip.

5

I had plenty of opportunities to keep an eye on Cynthia. Music festival Saturday night. Picnic in the park on Sunday. Movies and dinner Sunday afternoon. By Sunday evening I was as frazzled as if I'd worked the whole time instead of (theoretically) enjoying myself. Jason, who'd joined us for the movie, offered to drive me home afterward. It wasn't a short drive, and he was uncharacteristically quiet. Finally, I said, "Why aren't you overanalyzing the plot?"

"I was thinking about Cynthia," he said.

My fingers closed hard on the armrest. "What about Cynthia?"

He glanced my way. "Uh...is it too late to pretend I didn't say that?"

"Yes."

My harsh tone didn't shut him up. He went on, "I meant I was thinking about the two of you. You really don't like her, do you?"

"I've told you that before."

"And I know you've never gotten along, from the time you were kids."

My fingers must be leaving permanent marks in the upholstery. "Are you going somewhere with this?"

"Don't get mad, Hel. She just doesn't seem that evil to me."

His soothing tone of voice made me angrier, like *I* was the unreasonable one. "Well, she wouldn't, would she? She wants you to like her, and you're not competition for her in any way."

"Is that really what you think? That you're in competition with her?"

"No, *she* thinks we're in competition. Anything I have, she wants."

"I don't see it."

I removed my hand from the armrest and crossed my arms across my chest. "Are you telling me I'm wrong?"

He had his eyes on the road, so I couldn't tell whether my body language was getting through to him. "No. Just...I think she wants to be your friend."

Okay, so it wasn't. "It's about twenty-two years too late for that. And I think you should stay out of it."

"Are you mad?"

He sounded genuinely surprised, so I controlled my first impulse, which was to start screaming. "I don't like being told that my feelings are invalid, and yes, that's exactly what you just did."

"I didn't mean to."

"Which is why I haven't told you to stop this car and let me out."

Now he glanced over at me. "Helena—"

"Can we not talk about this anymore? I just want to go home."

"All right."

We were silent the rest of the way to my apartment, and when we reached the door, I kissed him goodnight, but didn't invite him up even though I could tell he wanted me to. I hated myself for it, but I couldn't bring myself to share that space with him. *I'm just tired. Another time. Tomorrow, maybe, or next weekend. Soon enough.* It was barely seven-thirty, but I got undressed and crawled into bed in my underwear, feeling as worn out as if I'd been hiking all day. Why did relationships have to be so difficult? I wished I knew what Cynthia really wanted. Clearly Jason was ready to jump into bed with her.

I rolled onto my face and groaned. That was unfair. Jason hadn't responded at all to her flirting, and his only crime was trying to be fair and impartial. I really hated that word.

Cynthia had extorted a promise from me to go shopping later that week, and now I wondered if I'd gone temporarily insane when I'd agreed to it. The last time we'd gone shopping together, she'd pretended to steal a bracelet and then claimed I'd planted it on her. Only some fast talking and security camera footage kept *me* from a trip to the police station. And even then the store manager (male) had let her sweet-talk him into dismissing it all as a joke. It still made me go red with embarrassment every time I had to shop at that store. Whatever she had in mind this time, it certainly wasn't sisterly bonding.

The room was hot and stifling, its one window letting in light that made a glowing spot on the red curtains, like some baleful eye. Tiffany's funeral was in two days, and I wasn't going to be able to go because, naturally, they weren't going to hold it in the evening. I hoped nobody would be offended by my non-attendance, but then I hadn't been a close friend. Viv could go for both of us.

I got up and opened the window a crack, letting in an evening breeze that smelled of exhaust fumes and popcorn from the theater next door. What if it had been someone I was truly close to? Or, God forbid, a family member? Surely the Board couldn't object to me closing for a few hours under those circumstances? I didn't like to think about it, but it was the kind of situation I really should be prepared for, the way old people always said you should have your funeral plans made so you wouldn't be a burden on your kids. I shuddered and went back to bed. I didn't need to think about death anymore.

It occurred to me that maybe I needed to read the Accords—the actual Accords, not the generic assumptions I'd gathered from Judy and Lucia and a dozen other Wardens I'd obliquely asked about dating Malcolm. I was sure everyone I'd talked to was right, because they'd grown up as Wardens, but the Accords governed my life; I should know what they said. As if I had time for any extra reading. Still, it was something to keep in mind. I curled up in my soft, comfortable bed, with the antique frame and the brand-new mattress, and sank into sleep.

THE NEXT FEW days were the busiest I'd ever seen at Abernathy's. The perfect summer weather was bringing the monsters out in packs. Hunting teams from both factions thronged the store, wanting auguries to guide their efforts. I didn't hear anything about unusual types of invaders like the one that had killed Tiffany, but Judy said her father and Guittard were still working on it. Personally, I thought if there'd been one, there could be others, but there was nothing I could do for Tiffany, or anyone else who might be a victim, except help the hunters eliminate the invaders.

I was busy enough I forgot about Tiffany's funeral until Viv appeared, dressed somberly in drab maroon cotton, her bright blue hair clashing horribly with her outfit. She was sitting behind the counter when I emerged from the oracle, ignoring Judy, who was ignoring her in turn. "How was it?" I asked.

"Sad. Lots of crying. Her mom is a wreck. I'd never been to a graveside service before. It's not at all like in the movies." Viv unbuttoned the top button of her dress, which went all the way to her chin. "I hate this dress. I'm never wearing it again."

"Good call," said Judy. "It doesn't suit you."

"Thanks tons."

"I didn't mean it as an insult."

"I don't know how to tell, with you."

"*Stop*," I said, thrusting the book at Judy. "You, take care of this, and *you*...are you leaving?"

"I got the day off. I figured I'd stick around and be insulted some more." She glared at Judy, who ignored her again. I rolled my eyes.

"Fine, just don't...bicker, all right? I have enough trouble without the two of you arguing over clothes." I accepted another augury slip and made my escape.

When I returned, book in hand, Judy was saying, "...and the line is all wrong. It should be—"

"Unbroken from the shoulder to the thigh, yeah," Viv said. "I don't know what he was thinking."

"What who was thinking?" I said.

"André Courrèges," Judy said. "The triangle shift, sure, but it was so overdone. I have an original Courrèges pantsuit I love, though."

"Ooh, jealous," Viv said. "It must have cost you a fortune."

"Who's André Courrèges, and why should I care?" I said, handing off the book to Judy.

The two gave me identical looks of amused disdain. "Only one of the great fashion designers of the '60s," Judy said. "Though I don't know whether to thank him or curse him for the go-go boot."

"Go-go boots really are for tall women," Viv agreed. "They'd just make you look like you were playing dress-up."

"What did I say about arguing?"

"It's true," Judy said, ignoring me. "I look better in platform heels or just plain old Mary Janes."

"I'm leaving," I said, taking another augury slip with a smile for the customer. At least they weren't fighting anymore. Anytime Viv and Judy were in the same room they tended to circle each other, growling like a couple of dogs challenging each other for the same bone (i.e., me). It was funny right up until it wasn't, and mostly I found it tiresome. Couldn't we all just be friends?

When I exited the oracle, I found the store empty except for my current customer and Viv and Judy, laughing their heads off over something. "What's so funny?"

"You had to be here," Viv said. "Oh, I feel better now. I really needed to laugh."

"I'm glad," I said, stifling a flash of irrational jealousy. "That will be $500, Mrs. Duclos, and your check is welcome here."

"Thank you," Mrs. Duclos said, eyeing Viv and Judy with some skepticism. Judy finished writing the receipt and accepted the woman's check. It was clear she was holding back more laughter. I'd never heard Judy laugh so unconstrainedly before.

When Mrs. Duclos was gone, Viv and Judy went back into peals of laughter. "I hope you weren't laughing at Mrs. Duclos," I said irritably. "She's a nice woman and a valued customer."

"No, nothing like that," Viv said, wiping her eyes. "Time for a rest?"

"I need to put a couch in the office," I grumbled.

"I'll get you a Diet Coke," Judy said. I stared at her retreating back. Judy had never volunteered to get anything just for me before.

"I might have guessed Judy understands clothes by the way she dresses," Viv said in a low voice. "We're totally going shopping later."

"At least you'll have someone along who appreciates it," I said, more snappishly than I'd intended.

"Hey, I like shopping with you! It's like having a disgruntled Barbie to dress."

"I am *not* disgruntled." I leaned against the counter and rubbed my forehead. "So who else came to the funeral?"

Viv's face lost its characteristic animation. "Lots of people. Amie, Sheridan, Poppy. Dave and Linda. Markus and Jerret. It was a really long day. There was the funeral, and then the graveside service, and then we all went back to the Alcocks' for a sort of luncheon. Not that anyone could eat anything. Mostly we stood around holding punch glasses and talking about how natural she looked. How peaceful."

Judy returned from the break room with a cold bottle which she handed to me. "It's amazing what morticians can do," she said. "Or are they called funeral directors these days? I can't remember."

"I don't want to think about it," I said, "what they'd have to do to make someone who'd died like that look natural instead of terrified."

Viv gave me a funny look. "What do you mean, died like that? Tiffany had an undiscovered heart condition."

Judy and I exchanged glances. "You didn't tell her," Judy said.

"I forgot. It's been busy."

"Tell me what?"

I set my bottle on the glass top of the counter. "Tiffany was killed by an invader."

"She was not! It was a..." Viv grabbed my bottle and took a long drink. "But those don't leave you looking peaceful."

"Yeah, which is why we said—"

"No, no, listen, Hel," Viv said, taking another drink. "I talked to Mrs. Alcock for a little while, a very uncomfortable little while, and she said—she was the one who found Tiffany, you know. It sounds like you know a lot more about this than I do. But you know she was found in the backyard, right? And Mrs. Alcock said she looked peaceful, like she'd died happy. Not terrified. I'm pretty sure Mrs. Alcock would have noticed if her only daughter had died of fright."

I gently removed my drink from Viv's hand and finished it off. "That's impossible."

"Or maybe not," Judy said. "You said when you were attacked, it left you euphoric rather than in agonized terror. Maybe Tiffany was like you."

"That's...actually, it's a little frightening," I said, "considering I don't know why I reacted the way I did, and it's too late to see what Tiffany and I had in common."

"What I don't understand is why my father hasn't been pursuing this," Judy said. "He had to know she didn't die in fear."

"Maybe not," said Viv. "Doesn't rigor mortis wear off after a few hours? I don't know how many, but if it took long enough between Tiffany's death and the time some magus figured out how she was killed, maybe her face might have relaxed out of that...fear rictus, or whatever you call it."

I looked at Judy. "Dibs on not calling your father."

"Oh, no," Judy said. "I'm not going to relay this third hand. This is a job for the custodian."

I grumbled, "Fine," and headed for the office. "Call me if anyone comes in."

In the office, I debated between using the office phone, a putty-colored lump so old it had square push buttons and a handset connected to the base with a long curly wire, and using my own phone, which carried with it the possibility that Rasmussen would see my number on his caller ID and ignore my call. In the end, I opted for the office phone. I punched in Rasmussen's number and waited. After a handful of rings, someone said, "William Rasmussen's office."

"This is Helena Davies at Abernathy's. Could I speak to Mr. Rasmussen, please? It's official business."

There was a long pause. Then Rasmussen's familiar smooth voice said, "Ms. Davies."

"Mr. Rasmussen, I'm calling about Tiffany Alcock. Were you aware she didn't die in fright?"

There was a longer pause. I kept from tapping my fingernails restlessly on the desk. Finally, Rasmussen said, "How do you know?"

"A friend spoke to Tiffany's mother at the funeral. She looked peaceful—the mother said it was like she'd died happy. Could that have something to do with the anomalous nature of the invader attack?"

Another pause. It was starting to feel like I was talking to Rasmussen on a taped delay or something. "It could," Rasmussen said. "Thank you for the information." He disconnected before I could say anything else. I stared at the handset, now emitting a droning whine, then hung up. It wasn't like I'd expected Rasmussen to suddenly become cooperative, but I'd hoped to at least learn *something*.

I met Judy in the hall, heading my way. "Campbell's here," she said. My heart did a funny little leap I scolded it for. I managed to keep my pace sedate instead of running to greet him.

Malcolm and Viv were having a conversation that cut off when we arrived. "I'm here for an augury," he said, handing me a slip of paper with a smile that set my foolish heart racing again.

"You haven't decided to be conventional, have you? Coming in the afternoon?" I unfolded the paper and glanced at it, then took a second, longer look: *Where is the creature who killed Martin Wellman?*

"I was busy this morning. My team has been in the field since nine o'clock last night." He did look tired, his dark eyes shadowed and his face unshaven. Combined with the suit, it made him look more like a male model than a businessman. I wondered why he'd taken the time to change but not bothered to shave. *Focus, Helena.*

The augury was so close to the one Rasmussen had asked for I almost asked him about it. But that would be unprofessional, so instead I smiled at him and entered the oracle.

I'd half expected a storm, but the light merely went bluish as usual, and I smelled freesias. I wandered among the bookcases, searching for the augury. Derrick was a pediatrician; surely he couldn't just call in sick when the team needed to be out all night and into the next day. Or maybe I was wrong about that. For all I knew, Derrick's practice catered exclusively to Wardens, the men and women magical and not who fought the Long War against the monstrous invaders. They would understand if fighting invaders took him away from his day job. From what I knew of my customers, the Wardens who hunted invaders saw that as their true jobs, and their mundane employment was just something that paid the bills.

I rounded a corner and found the book, outlined in a blue glow, and took it back to Malcolm. "$650," I said, handing it over. "Can I ask you something about it? We can go in the office if you're concerned about privacy."

Malcolm paused in the act of removing a tube of *sanguinis sapiens* from his inner pocket. "Ask away," he said, but he looked wary.

"It's nothing dire. Just—" I glanced at Judy, who was scowling. It was past time to forget about secrecy. "It's almost word for word the same as one I had a few days ago."

"Really?" He handed the tube to Judy, who set it on the counter with a *clink* and began fiercely writing up a receipt. "I won't ask you to violate the Accords by telling me whose augury that was."

"No, and I wouldn't tell you. But I can tell you that the subject of that augury was killed by invaders, but in an anomalous way."

Malcolm's eyes narrowed. "Anomalous how?"

"There were no invaders found in the area of her body. And she looked like she died happy."

"Hmm. That matches what the team and I have been seeing."

"And I thought...you know how the touch of an invader makes me euphoric? I wondered if there was some relationship between the two cases."

"It's an interesting notion. I hadn't thought of it, but it's possible." Malcolm leaned against the counter and tapped his fingers on the glass in a rhythmic one-two-three-four. "We have encountered three deaths matching that pattern. So far we have had no luck in tracking the killer, but I am convinced we are looking for a single invader rather than three. I hope this augury—" he tapped the book's glossy cover—"will give us more specific guidance. Thank you."

"Wait!" He turned around at the door. "Is Olivia well?"

"She is fully restored. I'm afraid I allowed an invader to slip past me and attack her." A shadow crossed his face. "But we had plenty of *sanguinis sapiens* to replace what the monster stole. I'll tell her you asked after her."

"Thank you."

When he was gone, Judy said, "You were *really* close to the edge there, Helena."

"I know. But I don't think I crossed over, do you? And I didn't tell him about the second augury, the one that had no result even though only one word was changed. That would have definitely crossed the line."

"I think all this secrecy is bad for you," Viv said. "It's only a couple of hours until closing. Let's go get dinner afterward."

"Sounds good," I said. Then I closed my eyes and swore. "No. I promised Cynthia I'd go shopping with her."

"We could come along."

"Thanks, Viv, but she said she wanted it to be 'just us.'" I groaned and rubbed my temples. "What's the incubation period for bubonic plague?"

"Two to six days," Judy said.

"I'm scared that you knew that right off. I'm not going to ask how."

Judy smirked. "You shouldn't. Besides, if you're going to fake a disease you should fake one that's not so disfiguring. Like colitis."

"What's colitis?"

"An inflammation of the colon."

I made a face. "Remind me to stop asking you questions."

6

$\mathcal{I}$ held my hands perfectly still and let the manicurist have her way with them. I'd never had a manicure before and I still wasn't convinced it was a good idea, what with handling books all day. I could imagine my beautifully polished nails (light pink, like the curve of a rose petal) getting chipped on the edge of a bookshelf. But Cynthia had been enthusiastic, and I hadn't been able to say no.

Now I endured the final buffing and watched Cynthia receive the last touches on her acrylic nails. I'd politely turned them down for myself—it just didn't feel like me—but Cynthia's turned out so nice it was hard not to reconsider, just a little bit. Her nails were square-cut and French-tipped, with little rhinestones on the ring fingers. She managed to make everything she wore look perfect.

Cynthia saw me watching and smiled. "I think the maintenance is worth the end result, don't you? And yours look so pretty! I can't believe you've never done this before."

"Pedicures, sure, but not my hands." I held them up and examined how my nails shone in the lights. "This is...fun, actually."

"Don't sound so astonished." Cynthia leaned forward to address the lady in the mask working on her nails. "My sister can't believe we're having fun together, isn't that awful?"

I smiled weakly. She was right; I couldn't believe it. I'd gotten into Cynthia's BMW tense, worried about what torment she might unload on me. But we drove to the mall (my New York City sister, going to a mall in Happy Valley?) and she hadn't said anything more insulting than calling me Hellie once or twice. She hadn't made fun of the stores or the people. The manicure had relaxed me further, and while I was still wary—this *was* Cynthia, after all—I wasn't mentally braced for the worst anymore.

"You really ought to do this more often, you have such pretty, small hands," Cynthia said after we'd paid and exited the salon. She took hold of my right hand and brought it up in front of her face. "See how elegant they look?"

"I guess," I said, retrieving my hand without jerking it away. "So now what?"

"End of the Rainbow. Mom raves about it."

"Oh. The accessory place."

"Don't sound so enthusiastic. People will think you want to be here."

"Sorry. I haven't been there either."

"I'm starting to wonder why you hang out with Viv, if you never go anywhere. End of the Rainbow seems just like her thing."

"I'm just not a fan of shopping, that's all."

Cynthia hooked her arm through mine and pulled me along. "Then you're doing it wrong."

The accessory store turned out to be a rainbow assembly of color —big swathes of it, because everything was grouped by color, purses, jewelry, everything. I wandered over to the turquoise blue section to browse. My favorite color, and here it all was in one place.

"Check it out," Cynthia said. She held a pair of ruby red chandelier earrings up to her ear. "My thing, or what?"

"I like them."

"I may get them." She ostentatiously looked around, then mimed putting them into her purse.

"Cynthia!"

"Oh, don't worry, I don't shoplift. Not like you, back in the day."

She picked up a necklace that matched the earrings and looked at herself in the tiny shelf mirror.

"I never shoplifted! That was you!"

"It was not. You totally took that bracelet and then acted like I'd put you up to it."

The tension built behind my eyes again. "Cynthia, *you* told them I'd planted it on you. I can't believe you don't remember!"

"Whatever. The point is, I never stole anything in my life and I'm not about to start now. You should try on that bracelet. But not blue. You ought to wear amber and gold. Warm colors."

I picked up a coil of turquoise beads that wrapped five times around my wrist and admired it defiantly. "I like this one."

Cynthia shrugged. "Suit yourself. But Viv will tell you it's wrong for you."

I bought the bracelet just to piss her off, but she didn't say anything else about it. I left the store feeling irritated, my earlier pleasure gone. "Jamba Juice?" Cynthia said.

"Sure." I spun my new bracelet on my wrist. I didn't have anything I could wear it with. That would teach me to buy things out of spite. Well, Viv might like it. Or, more likely, she'd make me buy something to go with it.

We sat in the food court and sipped our drinks and watched the other shoppers. "That woman shouldn't have gone with the orange hair," Cynthia murmured, pointing discreetly. "She looks like she had an accident in a paint factory."

I sputtered with laughter I tried to contain. "That's mean."

"It's true! It's not like I think she's a bad person, I just believe in being honest about things like that. It's why I have the job I do. I'm willing to say the hard truths."

"Yeah, but that woman probably thinks she looks beautiful, or she wouldn't have chosen that color. You'd just hurt her feelings."

"Better a little pain now than a lifetime of people looking at you and going 'where did you hide your pot of gold?'" Cynthia said in an exaggerated Irish accent.

I snorted and had to suck down some of my smoothie to conceal it. "You're awful."

"Just honest." Cynthia leaned back in her seat. "What's that?"

I looked off down the promenade, well-lit and crowded with shoppers. Something was coming our way fast, something low to the ground that scurried like an animal on a well-waxed floor. It was shoving people out of the way, and cries of fear and anger drifted toward us. Apprehension gripped me, and I stood. "We should move."

"Why? It looks like a dog. A big dog." Cynthia stood and watched the oncoming creature. It glittered under the soft lighting of the mall like a beetle, and its many legs scrabbled at the floor, sending up impossible sparks like metal on stone.

Following behind it at a dead run were several people dressed in military fatigues and carrying long knives. They passed the people knocked down by the creature without provoking any more cries of astonishment. They were fast, but the invader was outpacing them.

I grabbed Cynthia's arm. "We have to get out of the way," I said.

It seemed everyone else in the food court had the same idea. We shoved through the crowd of shouting, screaming people, back in the direction of Jamba Juice. Cynthia fought me, and I yanked hard on her arm, begging her to move.

"It's just a frightened dog!" she shouted over the din. "Nothing to be afraid of!"

I couldn't see the illusion the invader had put on itself to blend in, the better to isolate and kill a victim, but I was pretty damn sure it looked scarier than a frightened dog. "Let Animal Control handle it!" I said. "It probably has rabies."

Cynthia succeeded in pulling away from me. I darted after her. She emerged from the crowd right in front of the thing, which instantly focused on her. Cynthia knelt down and put out her hand toward it. Its mandibles clacked as it barreled down upon her. I screamed and flung myself at her, knocking her over, and the thing missed its strike and tumbled over both of us.

"Stay down!" a woman commanded, and I put all my weight into keeping Cynthia down. She struggled, shoved me aside, and I fell on my butt. The creature had come up against a wall of frightened people and turned around. The hunting team was between it and us now, and I sucked in air and tried to calm myself. What illusion were they under, those paramilitary types with their knives? Animal Control? If they killed the thing in full view of everyone in the food court, so much for keeping a low profile.

I grabbed Cynthia's leg to keep her from crawling away. "Don't get in their way!"

"They're going to kill it!"

"They'll just...subdue it..."

The *pop* of a tranquilizer gun went off, provoking more screams, and the thing collapsed. The woman who'd told us to stay down, an Ambrosite I knew named Allie, went forward to pick the invader up in a fireman's carry. "It's all right," she said in a loud voice. "No one was injured. We apologize for not capturing it sooner." She looked at me, and her eyes widened. I jerked my head in Cynthia's direction, hoping Allie would take the hint and not address me in public.

She did. She and her team turned around and went back the way they'd come. They were gone so rapidly no one had time to do more than gape. Excited conversations started up all around us, strangers brought together by a near-crisis. I stood and brushed myself off. "Well, that was exciting."

"Are you kidding me? Those people should be fired, if not arrested. Letting an animal like that run loose in a populated area," Cynthia said, pushing herself to her feet. "And why did she look at you like she knew you?"

Damn. "I've never seen her before," I lied. "Maybe she thought I was someone she knew."

"And it came right at us. Like it was looking for us. Helena, what's going on?"

I couldn't tell her that as custodian of a Neutrality, I was just enough different from the average non-magical human to draw the attention of invaders. They didn't come after me often, but when they had before, there had always been a team or a warded area I could be safe in. "I told you we were in its way. That's why I wanted you to move. I read somewhere that rabid animals move in a straight line."

"It looked at me. Like it knew me."

"I think you're overwrought. Come on, let's just go home."

Cynthia gathered up her purse and said nothing more. I was so relieved at not having to evade any more questions I didn't think to worry about her silence until we were nearly at my door. "You have seen her before," she said as I was getting out of the car.

"Seen who?"

"That woman Animal Control officer. She was in the bookstore the other day. You sold her an expensive book. How does someone working for the city make that kind of money? Because I doubt they pay Animal Control people very well."

"Good memory. I don't remember her at all," I said, laughing weakly.

"I just think it's weird, that's all," Cynthia said.

"If I get attacked by another dog, I'll agree with you," I said, and ran for my door.

Once inside, I leaned against the heavy steel door and cursed. Cynthia might be superficial and mean, but she wasn't stupid. I couldn't have guessed she could identify Allie from one quick meeting. Well, it didn't matter. The number of invader attacks in the city might be higher than usual, but the odds of me running into another one, let alone while I was with Cynthia, were in my favor. And she'd be gone by the end of the week.

I went upstairs and let myself into my apartment, kicked my sandals off and dropped my purse on my kitchen counter. I spun the turquoise bracelet around my wrist again. It was pretty, and I didn't care if it didn't suit me.

My phone buzzed. I dug it out of my purse.

ARE YOU ALL RIGHT?

Malcolm. Allie must have told him about the attack. I'M FINE. MY SISTER SUSPECTS SOMETHING WEIRD.

No response. I poured myself a glass of water and stared out the window at the busy street below, bathed in the warm light of the setting sun. Cynthia had done a good job of acting like a human being today, which only made me wonder what she wanted from me. She couldn't possibly believe that a couple of hours shopping and a manicure could fix what was broken between us. Well, I had the advantage of her: I didn't care if we were friends. She'd been absent for years and I hadn't missed her, and I wasn't going to miss her when she went back to New York.

My phone rang, and I snatched it up. "Yes?"

"When you say she suspects something weird," Malcolm said, "how seriously should I take that?"

"I don't know. Not very. She noticed the invader came straight for us, and she recognized Allie as an Abernathy's customer. She doesn't know enough to put those things together and come up with anything dangerous."

"I'm sorry you had to be involved in that chase. Sanford tells me the invader escaped containment a quarter mile from the mall. At that range, it couldn't have been pursuing you. It was just coincidence that it reached a point where it could scent you. I assure you, you were never in any danger."

"I know. Tell Allie I'm not upset, okay? I've never seen anyone chase an invader into a mall before."

"Invader attacks increase every day. We don't know what's causing it, but I suspect it to be deliberate."

"Deliberate?"

"I think the increased numbers of invaders are intended to conceal some other purpose. Possibly this creature we have been pursuing the last several days. It kills, then disappears only to strike elsewhere. We have very few records of such a monster, and none on how to effectively hunt it. Saying that I am frustrated understates the issue by several miles."

"I can imagine. Do you think it's the invader that killed Tiffany Alcock?"

"Was she the victim you referred to the other day?"

I closed my eyes and silently cursed. "Um. I probably shouldn't have told you that."

"She's not one of my prey's victims. And I'm grateful you slipped. Knowing there is more than one of this type of invader out there will help my search."

"Just don't tell anyone—as if I needed to warn *you* to be discreet."

He laughed, a warm sound that thrilled through me. "Your secrets are safe with me."

"I know."

He fell silent, but before it could become awkward, he said, "Even so, it's possible you should not contact me about things that are the province of both factions. I would not want to put you in an untenable position."

My heart constricted. "I...that occurred to me," I lied. "But I don't know anyone else well enough for that, and sometimes people have to be told."

"You ought to contact Ryan Parish."

Ryan Parish, leader of the Ambrosites and Malcolm's putative boss, didn't like me any more than I liked him. In a world without Rasmussen in it, he'd be my enemy. "I should. I will."

"Very well. I will likely see you tomorrow. Good night, Helena."

"Good night."

I clutched my phone for a few moments after Malcolm hung up, fighting an urge to cry. This was *stupid*. Malcolm was right; I kept leaning on him, going out of my way to tell him things, and I ought to be telling his faction leader instead. But it still felt like a rejection. Which was also stupid, because we weren't together, couldn't be together, and I owed it to Jason not to be emotionally attached to another man. Even if we were only friends.

The sun had set, and lights came on up and down the street. I put on my pajamas and crawled into bed, then called Viv. It went to voicemail. Right, she'd gone out with Judy, and they were no doubt having more fun than I had. Though I'd been having fun right up until the end, I had to admit. Fun with my sister.

Irritated at Viv's unavailability, I slapped my phone down on the nightstand. I should be happy that they were becoming friends, that they'd finally discovered something in common that had nothing to do with me, but I felt jealous and angry and depressed.

I picked up the phone again and scrolled through my contacts to Jason's name, then let my finger hover over it for a few seconds. I didn't want him to come over, because what I needed was someone to tell about the evening, and half of it was a secret. And for the other half, I wasn't sure Jason would listen sympathetically when I complained about Cynthia. Frankly, there wasn't much to complain about, which made me suspicious. If there was any weird behavior in the vicinity, it was hers.

I got out my diary, then sat cross-legged on the bed to write down what had happened—the bit about the invader, not the manicure. *Someday an invader will catch me where I'm defenseless,* I wrote, *and that will be it for me. At least I know I'll die free from pain.* I put the pen down and re-read those lines. Disgust filled me like a bad taste in my mouth. Defeatist much? I crossed out the lines fiercely enough to leave a mark on the previous page.

Maybe it was time to start going armed, though guns made me uncomfortable. Hector Canales should be able to hook me up with an invader-fighting weapon, and Malcolm—no, Olivia and Derrick would teach me how to use it. I had to stop thinking of Malcolm first when I needed something.

I let the street noises soothe me to sleep, and fell into a dream in which Malcolm and Jason fought a series of duels for me and Jason won every time.

7

I pushed the wide-headed broom through the aisles of Abernathy's. It was exactly wide enough to fit between the shelves that were closest together, the ones where if you met someone coming the other way, one of you would have to back up. Abernathy's never got really dirty, but all those books shed dust, and I sometimes felt half my job was keeping up with it.

The store was quiet that morning, a stillness almost reaching that of the oracle, though the oracle's quiet had a deeper hush to it. I reveled in the stillness. Soon enough the place would be thronged with Nicolliens, and possibly Malcolm, and though most of my customers were as quiet in Abernathy's as they would be in church, a lot of people all in one place made noise even when they were trying not to.

"Helena?"

"Back here."

Judy came around a corner, her arms full of books. "I found these in the back of the office. Do you want them shelved?"

"Oh. Those were left over from Mr. Hallstrom's last augury. They're the ones the store wouldn't give credit for. I don't think we ought to shelve them if the oracle doesn't want them."

Judy snorted irritably. "And yet we're supposed to dispose of them. I think we should charge Hallstrom rent."

"I wonder where he's getting these books. Do you think Abernathy's would reject them if they were stolen? Or does it care?"

"You'd know that better than me." Judy hefted the books into a less awkward position. "I'll put them back and they can gather dust until we figure out what to do with them. Take them to a thrift store, probably."

"That makes sense." Casually, my eyes on the broom, I said, "Is that what you and Viv did last night? Thrift store shopping?"

"Vintage stores, yes. It was fun. I didn't realize Viv actually knew anything about the clothes she wears. We had a good time."

I pushed away feelings of jealousy. "That sounds nice."

"What about you and your sister? Was she the demon from hell you expected?"

"Not really. We were attacked by an invader that nearly took a bite out of her because she thought it was a dog."

Judy laughed. "Invaders never look like the cute and cuddly kind of dog. Your sister is crazy."

"Tell me about it. And she recognized Allie Sanford. It took some fast talking to keep her from thinking there was some plot going on involving me and this bookstore."

Judy stopped laughing. "That's serious. You can't let her know the truth."

"She doesn't even know there's a truth. I'm not worried. Malcolm wasn't worried."

"When did Campbell get involved?"

"We, um, spoke after the attack."

"You, um, spoke?" Judy rolled her eyes. "When are you going to learn—"

"*He* called *me*, Judy. Allie told him about the attack."

"Even so, it's not healthy for you to stay so close."

"I know!" I leaned the broom handle up against the nearest bookcase. "I'm trying, I swear."

"I believe you." Judy focused on my new bracelet. I'd worn it even though it didn't match my outfit. "Where did you get that? The color's all wrong for you."

I scowled and swept my way out of the stacks. My peaceful mood had evaporated like morning mist. Now I just wanted the Nicolliens to arrive so I could busy myself with the oracle and stop thinking about my life as a burden. I was so tired of feeling cranky all the time.

I put the broom away in the basement and came trotting back up the splintery steps, worn in the middle from generations of feet. Judy passed me on her way into the office. "They're lining up already," she said. I groaned. It was going to be another busy day.

I checked my phone for the time. 9:53. I could open a little early if there were customers already waiting. And there were—two men and a woman, peering through the front windows with their eyes shielded against the morning light.

I crossed to the front door, opened it, and shrieked, recoiling. Two nasty-looking creatures, one black with a spiked carapace, the other blood red with writhing tentacles growing out of its back, lunged for me. I slammed the door and leaned against it, breathing heavily. Damn Nicolliens and their damn familiars.

I heard knocking. Someone, his voice muffled by the door, said, "Ms. Davies? We're so sorry about that. They're leashed now—you can open the door."

I released a deep breath and opened the door. Both familiars were tied to a nearby lamp post. When they saw me, they sent up an awful keening howl and strained at their leashes, trying to reach me. A whiff of paint thinner, the usual smell of a familiar, came to my nose. I retreated to beyond the countertop, which wasn't much reassurance because I could still see their awful shapes through the plate glass window with ABERNATHY'S stenciled across the top.

"They won't hurt you," the man said, hurrying in past his companions and shutting the door.

"They give a good impression otherwise," I said, shuffling around so I didn't have to look at the creatures.

"It's just that you're a custodian. They do it to Lucia, too, or would if she'd let us bring them anywhere near her."

Lucia was smart and nasty enough to enforce that. I was just too much of a pushover. "Let's just get this over with," I said. "Augury?"

"Safe deposit box."

I escorted the man to the basement, with its wall of silver safe deposit boxes, and returned upstairs to find the front of the store thronged with Wardens. A quick glance outside showed not only that the familiars were still there, but there were more of them. They circled one another, sniffing as if they were the dogs everyone else saw. "What is this, Bring Your Monster to Work Day?" I asked the next woman in line.

"It's these threats from the Ambrosites," she said, handing over her augury slip. "The idiots think our familiars are behind the increase in invader attacks. As if that was even possible."

"I hadn't heard that." I glanced through the window at the familiars. One multi-segmented monster had climbed up on something with too much grass-green fur and was either trying to mate with it or eat it. "I admit that sounds unlikely."

"It's just an excuse to bring up the old challenge, to force us to stop using familiars. They'd rather we lose the Long War than use every advantage we have. No familiar has hurt a human in any way in over seventy years."

"But you have to admit they're terrifying. I can see why people would think they're dangerous."

The woman shrugged. "No more dangerous than keeping a Rottweiler. Those are perfectly safe—they just look terrifying. Bad press."

I felt her judgment was compromised by not seeing her familiar in its true guise—the illusions magi placed on them affected everyone except me, as Abernathy's custodian—but just nodded and walked away into the oracle. I'd seen a familiar take down an invader, preventing harm to its team and to innocent bystanders, so I couldn't say the risk of capturing invaders and forcing them to work against their own kind wasn't worth it. But hard as I tried for impartiality, it was something I had trouble accepting.

I came out of the oracle and handed over the book. "That doesn't explain—"

The door flew open, and a man in a polo shirt and pressed khakis came through, preceded by a stinking whirlwind of tiny clawed limbs and an oversized head with slavering jaws. I screamed and put the counter between me and it as fast as possible. "I'm here for an augury," the man said, yanking on the leash to bring his familiar to heel. It ran around behind him and flung itself at me.

The crowd murmured, shifting to allow the man plenty of space. "Get out!" I shrieked. "And take that thing with you!"

"I'm entitled to an augury. And Venom would never harm—"

I tried to calm my agitated, rapid breathing. "No familiars on the premises," I said. "The Accords clearly state that. Get out. And don't come back."

"You can't do that!"

"Want to bet I can?" I pulled out my phone and called Lucia, though I knew she wouldn't answer. She let all calls go straight to voice mail. "If you leash your monster outside with the rest, I'll give you a pass this once. But don't you dare try to make your business more important than the oracle's."

The familiar made another lunge for me. I stood my ground, though I wanted to cower behind the counter. If I did that, I wouldn't know where the thing was, whether it was coming for me. The man looked around, for sympathy, I thought, and found none forthcoming. He yanked on his familiar's leash and left the store. I watched him walk away down the sidewalk and sighed. My legs were shaking and I needed the support of the counter to stand.

"I'm sorry about that," said one of the waiting customers. "He knows the rules. He probably hoped you didn't, being as new as you are."

"Why did you all bring them?" I tried to take a step and found I was still too shaky with nerves and adrenalin. "I've never seen so many." I'd never seen any at Abernathy's, to be honest, but then I rarely had time to look out the windows while the store was open.

"There have already been attacks on familiars," said the woman waiting for her augury. "We want to keep them close, just in case."

"Bad idea parking them all outside, then," said Judy. She had the receipt book in hand and was looking out the window at the familiars. "Just one disgruntled Ambrosite and you're all out your familiars, not to mention the costs of keeping them in check."

A murmur went up. Two men silently left the store, taking up guard positions near the familiars. I handed the book to the woman and said, "$500. I'm sorry people have been attacking familiars."

"Thanks. I'm determined it's not going to happen to Panic. I've had it for seventeen years and it's like family now."

I suppressed a shudder and turned to accept the next augury slip.

It was twelve-thirty by the time everyone cleared out. I leaned against the counter and scrubbed my eyes. "I know your father's a Nicollien, but you can't tell me you don't find familiars a little unsettling."

"I grew up with Shard and Shatter. They were just like big dogs," Judy said, putting the ledger away.

"How do they make familiars, anyway? I've seen invaders captured, but there's got to be more to it than putting them on a leash."

"It's complicated magic. You need a bone magus for the binding, and a paper magus for the illusion—it has to be an origami illusion for it to last—"

The door swung open. "I hope you haven't had lunch yet," Jason said. His hands were full of a couple of bags containing takeout cartons. They smelled deliciously of hot meat and vegetables. "I know how you like ginger walnut shrimp."

"I do. That's so sweet of you!" I went to kiss him, feeling cheered by his presence.

"I brought enough for all of us—"

"That's okay, I brought lunch," Judy said swiftly. I opened my mouth to protest that she'd done no such thing, but was silenced by her glare. "Why don't you eat upstairs, and I'll let you know if anyone comes in who needs help." Her glare broadened to include clearly the unspoken words *spend time with your boyfriend and stop pining after the unobtainable.*

"Sounds good to me," Jason said. "Where's this mysterious apartment I keep hearing about?"

Jason was suitably impressed by my home, which was decorated in the style of seventy years before. "Does this work?" he asked, running his fingers along the cabinet of the antique radio that sat below my very modern television.

"No, unfortunately. I keep meaning to see if I can have it fixed, but that takes time."

"Which you have little of, I know." He smiled to let me know it wasn't a jab. "The place smells like sunshine."

"And motor exhaust. That's what you get when you live above a busy street."

"I'd think zoning laws would prevent you living here. How'd you get around that?"

"Oh, there's some exemption or something," I said airily. I didn't actually know how the Wardens had arranged things so I could live here, and I was afraid to think too much about it for fear of breaking the magic. "Come look at the kitchen."

Jason wandered past the white painted cabinets to my antique refrigerator, opening it to look inside. He ran a finger along the stove top, with its gas burners, and flicked one on and off again before I could smell more than a whiff of gas. "Wow. Makes me wish I knew how to cook."

"My mother keeps hoping it will rub off on me."

"She would. Want to eat? There's chopsticks."

I brought out napkins and then, after a moment's reflection, a couple of cold bottles of beer. We sat and ate in peaceful contemplation. Jason caught my eye and winked, making me smile. This wasn't so bad. In fact, I couldn't remember why I'd been so opposed to having him up here.

"Thanks for doing this," I said when I was mostly finished. I never was able to eat an entire carton of ginger walnut shrimp. "I needed a break. It's been a busy morning."

"Anything for you, hon." Jason pushed back from the table, taking his bottle with him. "Mind if we sit for a while?"

We sat snuggled together on my maroon velvet couch, sipping beer in silence. I leaned against Jason and closed my eyes. He was a good man, and I liked being with him, and I needed to stop wishing for what I couldn't have.

I felt Jason remove the bottle from my hand and lean down to put it on the hardwood floor with a *clink*. His other arm tightened around me, his fingers stroking my sleeve. "I hate to disagree with you," he said in a low voice, "but your apartment is much nicer than mine."

"Yours is bigger."

"Don't need a lot of space for this." He drew me close and kissed me. I put my arms around his neck and kissed him back. He smelled of Old Spice and a hint of sharp, minty soap. His hand slid down my back and tugged at my blouse, untucking it from the waistband of my skirt.

"Jason, we don't have time—"

"Just relax, Hel. Take a moment." He kissed me again, more deeply, and his fingers worked their way under my blouse and onto my skin. It tickled, and I shivered involuntarily. His other hand came to rest on my knee, pushing my skirt up slightly. He made a pleased sound deep in his throat. I pulled him closer, putting my hand over his and squeezing just a little.

"I should get back—"

"We have plenty of time. Us naked on this velvet—tell me you haven't thought about it."

I wasn't about to tell him he wasn't the one I'd fantasized having naked on the couch. Ruthlessly pushing away those thoughts, I ran my fingers through the soft hair at the base of his neck and let him push my skirt higher. This was—

Footsteps sounded on the stairs, distantly, then there was a knock at the door. "Helena?" Judy said. "*Mr. Campbell* is here and needs your assistance."

It was like a gallon of ice water to my body. I shot away from Jason too rapidly to be strictly polite and saw his hurt expression seconds after I realized what I'd done. "Sorry. I was just startled."

"I get it." He didn't look like he did.

I rapidly tucked in my blouse and straightened my skirt. Then I took his hand and lifted it to my cheek. "Rain check?"

He smiled. "Probably best. I don't have a lot of time myself. I just thought we could...anyway."

He'd brought me lunch just so he could get into my pants? I managed a smile and let go his hand. "I have to go. This is an important customer."

"Well, walk me to the door at least."

It took all my willpower to walk down the stairs and through the stacks without dragging Jason along and shoving him out the door. Malcolm waited by the cash register, looking unbearably handsome in a pale gray suit and goldenrod waistcoat, his tie fastened by a pearl the size of my thumbnail only a few shades lighter than the suit. His eyes came to rest on Jason with polite indifference. I was sure my head was going to burst into flame from sheer embarrassment. It couldn't possibly be obvious what we'd been doing just moments before. Besides, by his expression, Malcolm didn't care even if it was.

At the door, Jason kissed me, a long, lingering, sexy kiss I tried to enjoy, but my sense of Malcolm's presence made me uncomfortable. I hoped Jason wouldn't notice my reluctance. But he smiled at me, said, "See you later," and was gone without showing any sign that he thought my behavior was abnormal. I stayed at the door, watching him get into his car and drive away, until my cheeks felt their normal color.

Malcolm didn't seem bothered by the interplay. "I hope I didn't interrupt your lunch," he said.

"Oh! No, we were...finished eating...did you need an augury?"

He handed over the slip of paper. "I would be interested in your opinion of this augury," he said.

I unfolded the paper. *What creature killed Martin Wellman?* "I think it will reject this one," I said. "It's awfully close to asking 'who?'"

"Nevertheless, I would like to try, if you don't mind."

"I don't mind." I should mind, on the oracle's behalf—should steer my customers away from wasting the oracle's time. But I trusted Malcolm, and if he thought this was an augury I should try, I was willing to go along with it. I refused to think about whether this made me partisan.

I braced myself as I stepped into the oracle's stillness and found, as I'd expected, a howling, whirling storm. "No augury!" I shouted, and the storm faded. I paused for a minute. "You know, we ought to be able to work out a better system," I said. "That storm can't be comfortable for you. Isn't there some other way you can signal when there's no augury?"

Silence. Dust motes gleamed gold in the sunbeams. I sighed and left.

"Nothing," Malcolm said. He and Judy were standing side by side in a way that told me their strained silence hadn't been broken while I was gone.

"No. As I thought. I'm sorry."

Malcolm accepted the augury slip. "I have another I'd like to try, as long as the store remains quiet."

I looked at the second slip. *Where is the invader that killed Martin Wellman?* "I think—" I shut my mouth tight. No talking about other people's auguries, even the failed ones.

"You think this one will fail as well," Malcolm said. "So do I. Please try, anyway."

I nodded and returned to the oracle. To my surprise, it was still and quiet, not roaring with a windstorm. The light, however, was blood red, the light of a dying sun. My pulse pounded in my ears like a distant sea beating on the shore. There was no blue light anywhere, not even the purple light I might have expected where blue met red. I paced through the aisles, searching until I was certain there was no augury anywhere. "Is this your compromise? No augury?" I said.

The light went faintly blue in an instant. I searched again—still no blue-limned book. "Huh," I said. "I like it. It's less definitive than the storm, but I think we're both happier." I found my way out of the warren, musing on what this meant for my theory that the oracle was alive in some way. If it could understand me on that level, maybe there were other things I might be able to communicate.

"No augury," I said when I emerged.

Malcolm let out a long, deep breath and leaned on the counter with both hands. "One more," he said.

"You're wasting the oracle's time," Judy said.

"This one, I expect to see fulfilled," Malcolm said. "I apologize for taking up your time."

"It's no problem," I said, glaring at Judy, who glared back. "What is it?"

He handed over a third augury slip, and I carried it into the oracle before unfolding it and reading it. *Where will the killer strike next?*

It sent a chill through me. It sounded so ominous, like we were dealing with some agency beyond human comprehension. I held the slip in both hands as I searched the stacks for the augury. This time it was a thick volume of *Architectural Digest* from five or so years back. I admired the house shown on the cover, which reminded me a little of my friends the Kellers' home, blocky in a style that had been ultra-modern forty years ago and was still attractive.

"This is it," I said. "$700."

"Thank you." He gave Judy two small tubes of *sanguinis sapiens*. I wondered if I'd ever feel comfortable asking him why he seemed to have an unlimited supply of the stuff.

"Can I ask...how the hunt progresses?"

He looked grim. "Not well. This augury both gives my team guidance in its search and fills me with foreboding. I think—" He shut his mouth, looked off toward the front door.

"What?"

"I don't want to burden you."

"Malcolm, don't be stupid. If there's something I can do to help—"

"There may be nothing." But he looked indecisive, something I'd never seen on him before. "And yet—" He looked at Judy. "This is something Rasmussen should know. You should tell him. He and I aren't on speaking terms."

"What is it?" The chill I'd felt was back, and it had brought friends. I felt tense again, poised to bear whatever Malcolm might say.

"The worst news," Malcolm said. "We're not looking for an invader. Those murders were the work of a human being."

8

"Impossible," Judy said. "No human would kill like that."

"But a human could," Malcolm said. "The only thing preventing someone from murdering in that fashion is a sense of morality, not an inability to drain magic from someone. We do it every time a Warden dies—harvest their remaining magic for use in the Long War. And I have compelling evidence that I'm right."

"What evidence?" I tried to picture a human attacking someone the way invaders did and came up blank.

"The fact that none of the victims displayed the symptoms of an invader attack, and the absence of invaders in the vicinity of the murders." Malcolm had his eyes fixed on Judy, who looked belligerent. "Some abnormalities in the bodies Tinsley has been unable to explain away. My team has documented it thoroughly, and we're convinced this is the correct explanation."

"I don't believe it. I want to see your evidence."

"At the risk of sounding uncivil, you're not the one we need to convince. Now that I have the results of this augury, I'm going to turn my information over to Lucia and let her decide what to do with it. My team will continue hunting the killer, but we need more manpower."

"Do you have any idea who the killer might be?" I asked.

Malcolm looked grim. "I'm not even certain we're dealing with only one person. When I believed it to be invaders, I knew there were at least two victims who were not killed by the creature my team was tracking. Now I must re-evaluate my investigation. If there is more than one person...I should not have mentioned it to you. Don't tell anyone else about this possibility."

"I'm calling my father," Judy said, pulling out her phone. "Let me tell him before you talk to Lucia. He deserves to know before the witch hunt starts."

"I agree. He wasn't who I had in mind when I hoped you would keep this to yourselves."

"Witch hunt?" I said. "But..." Understanding dawned. "It could be anyone, right? Which means everyone will suspect everyone else."

"More to the point, Nicolliens will blame Ambrosites, and vice versa," Malcolm said. "Relations never returned to normal after the threats against Abernathy's two months ago, and this will only make things worse."

"Father?" Judy said. "I've learned something you need to know. No, it can't wait." She rolled her eyes and tapped her toe in its black patent leather shoe that probably had a designer name. After a few seconds, she said, "Malcolm Campbell says the deaths are being caused by a human, not an invader. Yes, that's what I said." Another pause. "He has evidence and he's taking it to Lucia. I thought you should know. Actually, so did he."

"I have trouble picturing what it was like for Judy to grow up in that household," I murmured to Malcolm. He smiled a little, but said nothing.

"Father, I don't know what his evidence is. You'll have to—yes, he is. I know he shouldn't be here yet, but I—no, Father, I can't make Helena do what I want. That's not my job." A tinny cascade of speech too distant to be intelligible poured out of her phone. Judy just stood there, nodding silently and rolling her eyes again. Then she said, "You'll just start an argument. Arrange to meet at the Gunther Node and you and Campbell and Lucia can work it out." Another pause. "I don't know if fair is really what we should be worried about now, if there's a serial killer magus running around loose. I'll see you at dinnertime." She hung up.

"Thank you," Malcolm said. "Please excuse me. I have to meet with Lucia and, apparently, with Rasmussen as well. I'm sure I'll see the two of you again soon, and often." He nodded and left the store with his augury.

"Serial killer?" I said.

"What else would you call it? There've been at least five deaths, and those are just the ones we know about because Campbell tells you everything. All with the same M.O., all displaying the same symptoms, or whatever you call how someone dies."

I shivered and straightened my skirt. "Serial killer."

"Don't take this the wrong way, but at least we don't have to worry —the killer is only going after non-Wardens."

"Unless he's only going after non-magi, which would make both of us vulnerable."

We looked at one another for a long, silent moment. "I'm going upstairs to put away the leftovers," I said. "I'll be right back."

"Sorry I interrupted your 'lunch,'" Judy said with a smirk. "Feel better? Or just disappointed?"

"Conflicted," I said, and trudged back upstairs, where I put away the rest of the shrimp and half a carton of white rice for later. I threw away the empty cartons and wiped the table. I couldn't help feeling like Jason had manipulated me into letting him into my apartment— but he was my boyfriend, so he shouldn't have had to resort to manipulation. I was being stupid, and worse, I was being distant. I had to stop holding Jason at arm's length when it came to this apartment. Or everything, really.

No one came into the store until the afternoon rush. I took a turn doing data entry and tried not to feel angry at Jason or guilty over feeling angry at Jason. By two o'clock I was ready to run screaming into the streets, anything to get away from my thoughts. I almost wanted Cynthia to come in so I could pick a fight with her. I was so tired of the complicated relationships in my life.

It wasn't until the third augury of the afternoon that I heard Malcolm's theory repeated. "It's a human killer," said Doug Schrote. I knew him well as a treasure hunter who came into the store frequently, wanting auguries that would give him clues to their locations. "That is, it's a human who's doing the killing, not that they're killing humans...except they *are* killing humans, so I guess it's true however you mean it."

"How do you know?" I said, gripping his augury slip tightly.

"Everyone's talking about it. Ryan Parish denied it, but he'd say that just to keep people from panicking. I think it's better to be open about these things, don't you? We need real information, not lies."

"But if there's no information, isn't it better people not speculate?"

"How can they not? I told Ms. Pontarelli it had to be a Nicollien— someone with a familiar he could sic on the victim."

"I don't—" I shut my mouth. I wasn't sure how much of what I knew was privileged information. Lucia would tear me a new one if she found out I'd given away facts about what was now her case. "I don't think it's a good idea to make accusations without evidence," I said instead.

"It's hardly an accusation to state the truth," Doug said.

I shook my head and turned away. Doug wasn't terribly bright, so maybe it was natural for him to think of something so ridiculous, but what if other people, intelligent and reasonable people, let their emotions carry them away into making accusations that made sense?

All the Ambrosites had theories. Most of them had to do with a Nicollien being the murderer. All of those centered on familiars doing the killing, which told me the information about the victims' condition, that they hadn't died in agony, hadn't gotten out. Either that, or my customers didn't care about logic.

Around four, just after the last Warden left, Derrick Tinsley came through the door, and my heart lightened. I hadn't realized how tense I'd become until I saw his familiar stocky form in the doorway. "How are you?"

"I'm headed home for a few hours' sleep, but Campbell sent me with an augury request for tonight." He waved a torn piece of paper at me.

"Then I'll be quick." I accepted the paper and tried not to feel disappointed Malcolm hadn't been the one to come.

As I searched the shelves, I contemplated the augury request: *Where will the killer strike tomorrow?* What had been Malcolm's augury just a few hours before? Something about where the killer would strike next. It seemed a slim difference, but I wasn't a monster hunter, so what did I know? At least they were getting some rest. I could appreciate Malcolm's desire to catch the killer, but surely even he couldn't go forever on no sleep?

"How's Olivia?" I asked when I returned, augury in hand. "It's $450."

"Better. When you lose magic and have it restored, the physical effects are immediately cured. It's not like breaking a bone—or even breaking a bone and having it magically healed, which still hurts for a while." He pulled out a wallet and riffled through the bills inside. "It's your facility with magic that's depleted. Takes a while for you to be a fully functional magus again. Good thing steel magi like Campbell are immune to having their magic drained, because we can't afford to have them sidelined. And Campbell in particular is a crappy patient. Never can sit still for very long."

"I can imagine." I accepted his payment. "Do you think you're close to finding the killer?"

Derrick's face went grim. "Wish I could say we were. We're closer than we were yesterday, that's for sure, but who knows what that means overall? At least there are more teams working on it—but you know Campbell. He won't be happy unless we're the ones who catch the bastard."

"I know. Tell everyone hi from me, okay? And stay safe."

"You stay out of trouble," Derrick said with a smile that transformed his rather bulldog-like face, and left the store with a wave for Judy.

"I can't believe he's a pediatrician," Judy said. "You'd think he'd scare the kids, with a face like that."

"I think he looks nice," I said, loyally if not truthfully.

"Whatever. I'm going to work on the database. I think we're only a few hours from having it finished."

I sat behind the counter and massaged the small of my back. A complete database of Abernathy's customers would be nice, though I couldn't immediately think how I'd use it aside from no longer having to write a repeat customer's address every single time. Judy would probably have some ideas.

I stretched and kneaded out a particularly vicious knot just beside my spine. This afternoon hadn't been too bad. Maybe good sense would win out, and everyone would stay calm, and Malcolm would catch the killer. He might even catch the guy tonight.

I was getting really good at optimism.

I CAME SWIMMING out of a dream of dancing at prom with a faceless stranger to find the music hadn't been just in my head. My phone was ringing in my bedside table drawer. I fumbled around in the darkness until I found it. Groggily, I said, "Hello?"

"Samantha Bannister is dead," Judy said.

I fumbled my phone and peered at it, but couldn't see the display clearly. "What time is it?"

"Who cares? Did you hear what I said?"

"I don't know who that is."

"She's a magus. An Ambrosite paper magus. Brittany and her team found her outside her house about an hour ago, drained of her magic."

That woke me up fully. "Did they catch the killer?"

"If they had, I would've led with that." Judy sounded exasperated with my slowness. "Don't you see what this means?"

"The killer's begun striking at magi."

"And the Ambrosites are going to go crazy blaming the Nicolliens. It's going to be war."

"They wouldn't be so stupid."

"Of course they would. People don't think with their brains when they're angry. I wanted you to know in advance."

I turned the clock on the nightstand to face me. "Judy, it's not even six o'clock!"

"I'm sorry. I'm...honestly, I'm scared. I've never seen my father this furious. He and Brittany nearly came to blows, and I'm not totally sure she'd pull her punches. It's not like it was her fault."

"I bet she's mad about it." Brittany Spinelli was the Nicolliens' top hunter, a steel magus nearly as good a fighter as Malcolm. At least, I thought Malcolm was better, but that could be my attraction talking.

"I think she was angrier with herself than anything else. I hope they catch the guy soon."

"Me too. Is it cowardly for me to admit I'm grateful now the leaders imposed those time restrictions on their people? I don't want to referee any fights."

Judy sighed. "Let's just hope Campbell is sensible enough to stay away."

"He will," I said, though I wasn't sure. Malcolm's singlemindedness when it came to hunting invaders meant he put his own safety second. I didn't think he was in much danger, but I also didn't want to see him torn apart by a mob even he couldn't fight.

"I'm sorry I woke you. I needed to talk to someone who's on the outside of all this."

"Aren't you on the outside, too?"

She let out a single *hah* of laughter. "Not as far as my father is concerned. He thinks he knows where my loyalties lie, but I'm trying to see both sides. Is it bad to wish the killer would take out a Nicollien magus next?"

"You don't really think that."

"No, I don't. Not at all. But it would be nice for this not to be faction against faction."

I sat up and leaned against my headboard. "I wonder if that's the point."

"What?"

79

"Maybe the killer is trying to build tension between the factions. Turn this into a civil war."

Judy was silent for a moment. "It does look like that's what's happening, doesn't it?"

"It's a thought, anyway. I don't know anything about the investigation to know if it's likely."

"I have to go," Judy said. "I'm going to suggest the idea to my father. He's so angry about the idiocy of the Ambrosites he's not thinking clearly. He might be able to make use of this."

"I'll call Mal—" I squeezed my eyes shut until I saw spots. "I'll call Mr. Parish and let him know. Maybe they can work together."

"Good luck convincing Parish," Judy said, and hung up.

I turned on my lamp and dropped my phone back into the drawer. Should I try calling Parish immediately? It was awfully early. I scowled and picked up my phone. Putting off an unpleasant task didn't do anything but make it more miserable, and I was sure Parish was already awake, dealing with the death of one of his faction.

Parish picked up almost immediately. "Do you have good news?" he said, as if he'd been waiting for my call.

"Um...I don't have an augury, if that's what you mean. But I heard about Ms. Bannister's murder and I—"

"I don't have time for this, Ms. Davies."

"Just listen! What if the killer is trying to increase tension between the factions? Start a war?"

"Nicolliens don't need an excuse to fight."

"Mr. Parish, most of them don't hate Ambrosites. They're able to get along with them. I've seen it in Abernathy's"—*or I did before you and your asinine policy*—"and until this killer came along, everything was mostly peaceful. Doesn't it look like someone's going out of his way to make the Nicolliens into the enemy?"

"I think the Nicolliens aren't sufficiently interested in rooting out the evil in their midst. That makes them the enemy. Thanks for your help, Ms. Davies. I'll be by for an augury this afternoon."

He disconnected, leaving me holding my phone to my ear with a rising desire to scream. So the entire faction was the enemy because

THE BOOK OF MAYHEM

of one rogue magus? For all Parish knew, it was a rogue Ambrosite with a hatred of Nicolliens who wanted to make them look like villains. I was leaning toward that theory myself. In either case, though, the killer was getting what he wanted—a war between magi. And I had no idea what that would look like.

I put away my phone and wearily dressed. There was no way I was getting back to sleep after that. I'd have breakfast, and then I'd... sit around waiting for the mail and the first rush of customers. There had to be something else I could do.

My phone rang again at about seven-thirty. "Hey, Hellie, I didn't wake you, did I?"

"No, Cynthia. What's up?"

"Why should something have to be up for me to call my baby sister to chat?"

"Isn't it a little early for a heart-to-heart?" I gritted my teeth at "baby sister."

"I'm still mentally on east coast time. Anyway, I wanted to have dinner with you, just the two of us. Nothing fancy."

"I...okay." She'd have to leave soon, right? And then all these awkward attempts at bonding could end. "Where?"

"I'll pick you up at seven. Wear something nice, but not too nice, all right?"

"Okay. Thanks."

"It'll be fun!"

I stared at my phone for a bit after she hung up. What did she think she was accomplishing? I caught sight of my manicured nails and sighed. She was trying, I'd give her that.

By eight thirty I was bored and frustrated. I'd cleaned every surface I could think of, had counted the cash in the till twice, reorganized the stash of *sanguinis sapiens*, and scrubbed the sink in the basement (wearing long purple rubber gloves to protect my beautiful nails). I eyed the remaining stack of paperwork sitting beside the computer, waiting to be entered. To hell with it. I called Malcolm.

"This is Campbell. Leave a message."

"Hi, it's Helena," I said. The abruptness momentarily scattered my thoughts. "Um. I was thinking—suppose the killer is trying to start a war between the factions? I mean—you've probably already thought of that, but it sounds like nobody else has, so I thought...anyway, that's all." I hung up before I could make the call more personal. It was business between us, nothing else.

I called Jason. "Hey, hon," he said. "I'm almost to work, so I can't chat."

"Oh." I felt deflated and relieved at the same time. "I just wanted to say hi."

"Just hearing your voice cheers me up. Want to get together tonight?"

"Sure, I—no, wait, I forgot my sister wants to have dinner tonight, just the two of us."

He laughed. "Don't sound so thrilled."

"I'd rather be with you."

"And that cheers me up further. I wish we could do lunch again, but it's the weekly get-together where the guys from the office tempt fate by going out to eat without any women present. Someday some-one's going to sue for sexual discrimination, but until then it's beer and brats down at the pub."

"Have fun. I'll talk to you later."

With Viv at work and Judy probably still busy with her father, that exhausted my range of conversational possibilities. I could call my mother, but she'd just want to praise me for making friends with my sister, and I didn't think I could stay civil for that. So I went into the stacks and picked a book at random, settled behind the counter, and read. It was a manual for refinishing bathrooms, boring and soothing, and following the instructions and diagrams, which were small and poorly printed, kept my mind occupied until Judy blew in at ten minutes to ten.

"Father sent me with instructions," she said.

"I don't take instructions from William Rasmussen," I said, slamming my book closed.

"I know. I told him that. But some of his ideas make sense, and I thought it was worth showing them to you, let you decide if you wanted to use any of them." Judy handed me a folded sheet of paper. "Also, he's throwing a party tonight and you're invited. It's to show there's no animosity toward Ambrosites on the part of the Nicolliens."

"Who else is he inviting? Not Mr. Parish?"

"Yes, absolutely Mr. Parish, and a dozen other prominent Ambrosites. And Lucia, and some of the other neutrals who work for her."

I unfolded the sheet of paper. "Oh, there is no way in hell I'm doing *that*," I said. "Or that. And I don't know if I should ban people just because they're saying bad things about the other faction. Isn't that a First Amendment right?"

"It's up to you as custodian what kind of speech to allow." Judy came around and read over my arm, being too short to see over my shoulder. "But I think reminding them that we're all working for the same ultimate goal is a good idea."

"I agree. I'm not good at making speeches, though." I tossed the paper at the counter, where it slid across the glass and fluttered to the floor beside the stool.

"You are if you get riled enough. And I'm pretty sure they'll rile you today."

Memory struck. "Oh, no. The party's tonight? I told my sister I'd have dinner with her."

"Then you've got a good excuse to get out of it, haven't you?"

"But I accepted her invitation first."

Judy grabbed my forearm. "Helena, you *have* to come to this. Aside from Lucia, you're the most prominent neutral power in the Pacific Northwest. If you don't come, it's like saying you agree with the Ambrosites. It will make things worse."

I glanced at the front door. People were already lining up outside. I groaned. "You're right. I'll just have to put Cynthia off until tomorrow." I pulled out my phone and texted her quickly, surprised at how guilty I felt about telling her no. I saw people tethering their familiars to the light post outside and groaned again, inwardly this time. Stupid as the theory that a familiar had done the killing was, I could sympathize with the Ambrosites who wanted to outlaw all of them.

Almost nobody wanted an augury. What they wanted was to talk —about the death of Bannister, about the threats many of them had received, about what Rasmussen was doing about it. It frightened me, how many of them had been threatened personally and not just about their familiars. All anonymous, of course, the cowards, but I couldn't imagine that some of those letters didn't come from magi who knew these Nicolliens and had been friendly to them up until now. Staying impartial was harder than ever when they wanted me to join in their damning of the Ambrosite faction.

"They've always hated us," one man shouted to be heard over the others. "This is some Ambrosite with a grudge against Nicolliens, trying to make us all look bad. As if possessing a familiar makes someone evil enough to commit murder!"

"We need to do something about it!" cried another man. "Take the fight to them!"

There was general agreement to this. I felt the mood of the crowd grow angrier, verging on becoming a mob. Outside, familiars under the watchful gaze of two Nicollien steel magi howled.

"Stop it!" I shouted. "Hasn't it occurred to you that you're giving the killer exactly what he wants—discord between the factions?" I no longer cared whether my theory was true; at the moment, it made perfect sense. "There's only one villain here, and the hunters will track him down. And then we'll know for sure. But all the rest of you, Nicolliens and Ambrosites, you're all innocent of everything except blaming each other."

"The Ambrosites have been threatening us," the first man said. "That's not innocent."

"Don't expect me to believe Nicolliens haven't done their share of threatening," I said. "And before you go on, let me point out that I don't care who started it. You're all adults. You don't have to respond to those threats. Let the hunters and Lucia deal with the problem."

"You're young, and you're idealistic," said an older woman near the back of the crowd. "You don't understand this conflict."

"Don't I?" I felt anger rising within me. "I listen to you people—both factions—every day. Until two months ago you all came in here and mingled and got along just fine. If it's idealistic to believe you're capable of behaving like reasonable people, fine, I'm an idealist. But my way isn't the one that will leave people bloody on the killing fields."

"I'm not going to wait for someone to attack Belial," said the first man. "I have a right to defend myself."

"I agree," I said. "But I'm not going to support you if you strike preemptively. And I'm not going to make Abernathy's a place where you can stir each other up to violence. So unless you have an augury request, I'm going to have to ask you all to leave."

Muttering, the crowd dispersed, leaving me with just one man holding an augury slip. When I returned with his book, the store was empty except for him. He was thin and short, wearing a T-shirt with a bulbous-looking spaceship on it and a really old pair of Birkenstocks, but his smile was unexpectedly charming and it comforted me.

"You're doing the right thing," he said, reaching for his wallet.

"Which part?"

"Not letting them get away with believing they're justified in holding on to their anger. They're good people, for the most part, but they're scared, and scared people can do a lot of damage if they let their fears take over."

"You're sensible. Why don't you tell them that?"

"I do. But I'm one of them. The Neutralities and their custodians have tremendous influence on the magical community in part because they stand outside the factionalism. I think secretly most people on both sides wish the conflict could end. But now that there's almost no one left who remembers what it was like before Marie Nicollier and Frank Ambrose went to war over familiars, it's easy to think this is all it will ever be." He smiled ruefully. "And to think Nicollier and Ambrose were the best of friends once."

"Sometimes best friends make the worst enemies."

"That's well said. I may steal it from you." His smile went mischievous, and I laughed and waved goodbye to him.

"Jeremiah's a good guy, even if he does have weird ideas about his familiar," Judy said from behind me. I startled. She was nearly as good at sneaking up on people as Malcolm.

"What weird ideas?"

"Hmm, not so much weird as uncommon. He treats his like a tool instead of a pet, like most Nicolliens."

"I don't think that's weird at all. It's how I'd look at them, if I had to have one. There won't be any familiars at the party tonight, will there?"

Judy shook her head. "No. Father wants to downplay their existence for now. No sense rubbing in the key point of contention."

"That's a relief." My phone buzzed. THANK YOU, Malcolm texted. That was all. I tried not to feel disappointed. "Now, why don't we see if we can finish that database and take it for a spin?"

9

The Rasmussens' home was a white two-story antebellum structure, complete with pillars, that would have looked more comfortable in the center of a plantation. It wasn't large enough to be overwhelmingly grand, and the long cracks in the driveway made it seem more human, but it still dominated its corner of the block. I parked my car a few places down the street and walked back along the sidewalk to the front door. Several other cars, most of them much nicer than my ancient Honda Civic, were parked in front of the house and in the driveway. I rang the doorbell and waited.

Immediately the door opened. A white-haired gentleman in a conservative suit and white gloves far too warm for this weather greeted me with a gracious nod. "Please go through the hall and past the sitting room to the patio."

Awed, I did as he said. A staircase circled the round entry to the second floor, and past that was a long hall extending through the house. The hall was tiled in giant squares of granite and rose two stories above my head. Impressionist paintings I hoped were reproductions hung along the walls, bright blotches of color against the stark white.

I passed an opening that led to a sunken living room done in contemporary Scandinavian décor except for a black baby grand piano in the far corner. Did Judy play, or had it belonged to her mother, who'd died seven years ago? Judy never talked about her, so all I knew was her death had been of illness and not anything connected to the Long War. I couldn't imagine Rasmussen doing anything so nonviolent and tranquil as playing the piano.

I'd thought the Scandinavian room was the sitting room the man had mentioned, but when I reached the end of the hall I found myself in a vast space filled with chairs and sofas and low tables perfect for setting drinks on. A family portrait of Rasmussen, his wife, and Judy hung over the slabs of river rock the fireplace was made of. In the portrait, Judy was about ten, but the painter had perfectly captured her habitual scowl when confronted with something stupid, like having her picture painted instead of photographed. The warm mahogany and russet and brown combined with rich leather made me want to sink into one of the chairs, but the room was empty, and I could hear muffled conversation coming from beyond the French doors, which stood ajar.

I pushed open the door and stepped onto the patio, which was an enclosed space almost big enough to be called a sun room. More chairs, these of wrought iron with sage green cushions, stood unused around a matching table. Strands of white Christmas lights circled the top of the white vinyl fence surrounding the yard beyond. The patio's sliding door was open, so I went through to where the rest of the guests had gathered on the lawn. More lights outlined the roof of the patio, giving the yard a fairyland look.

One glance at the guests told me if this was fairyland, it was a fairyland at war. Two largish groups stood at opposite sides of the yard, sipping from wine glasses and glaring at each other. Smaller groups of two or three stood in the center of the yard, seeming oblivious to the hostility of the others. I couldn't see Rasmussen anywhere. Nervous, I trotted toward the one familiar face I saw, but I was intercepted by a smiling young woman bearing a tray of drinks. I took a glass of white wine—I could just picture myself spilling red all over my cute flowery summer dress—and continued on my way, hoping no one else would accost me.

"I haven't missed any hostilities, have I?" I asked Lucia Pontarelli, who was dressed, for once, not in yoga pants and T-shirt but in loose capris and a button-down blouse. "Not that I want there to be hostilities."

"I understood you, Davies." Lucia took a healthy swig from her glass. She was brave enough to dare the red wine. "And no, nobody's challenged anyone else to a duel. Yet."

"Where's Mr. Rasmussen?"

"Went inside to take a call. This party was a terrible idea. Nobody's mingling. The Ambrosites keep looking at the Nicolliens as if they've got their familiars tucked inside their back pockets. The Nicolliens keep *not* looking at the Ambrosites and are pretending they don't exist. I'm about two minutes away from taking my people and leaving."

"Ms. Davies! Thanks for coming," Rasmussen said from behind me. I turned to greet him. "Have you met Amber Guittard, my right hand?"

"I have. It's good to see you, Ms. Guittard."

"Likewise," Guittard said. She was a gangly woman whose wide smile displayed prominent front teeth, but she had beautiful eyes and dressed more fashionably even than Judy. "I hope Abernathy's hasn't suffered because of these unfortunate events?"

"No, though things have been strained."

"It's fortunate we arranged to divide Abernathy's time between the factions, don't you think?" said Rasmussen with a smile that came just close enough to smug that I couldn't call him on it.

"I still say it's too bad it's the only solution you and Mr. Parish could come up with, but it's helped," I said.

"And speaking of Mr. Parish—Ryan. Thanks for coming." Rasmussen extended his hand to the big, well-muscled man who came through the patio door at that moment.

Ryan Parish shook it with no sign of distaste. "Will. I hope this isn't a mistake."

"Of course not." Rasmussen raised his voice. "We're all united in wanting to find this killer."

"And prove Nicolliens don't support his actions," Brittany Spinelli said. Even across the yard from me, she was striking with her short red hair and lean, muscular frame. She wore black combat fatigues that bulged in places, suggesting she had concealed weapons on her.

The sight of her made me wonder why Malcolm wasn't there. Surely Rasmussen would have invited him if he'd asked Brittany to come? They disliked each other, of course, but Rasmussen couldn't afford to exclude the Ambrosites' most skilled fighter in the Long War if he wanted to look like an egalitarian. I suppressed my disappointment and kept scanning the crowd for Judy.

"So why are Ambrosites the only ones being targeted?" a man I vaguely recognized from the store said.

"One murder doesn't make a trend," Lucia drawled. "Let's not exaggerate."

"Ms. Pontarelli is correct," Rasmussen said. "I've invited you all here to remind you that we have the same goals, however we may differ in achieving them. I'd like to think that the fact you've accepted my invitation means you're not lost to reason. Talk to each other. Discuss the facts. If you come to any conclusions, Ms. Pontarelli would be happy to listen." Lucia snorted and drank more wine. "But most importantly, remember that we are all magi together, not faceless enemies." He put his hand on Parish's arm and drew him aside, speaking quietly.

"And that speech should remind you why he's the Nicollien leader," Judy said quietly.

I jumped a little and nearly lost control of my wine glass. "It was good. I almost forgot I don't like him. Sorry."

"It's all right. Father's good at making enemies. He sees you as an impediment to his plans and doesn't waste time pretending otherwise. At least he's honest." She shrugged and took a drink from her own glass. She'd chosen a rosy pink that matched her blouse.

"True." Rasmussen was an enemy who'd challenge me to my face. I sipped some wine and said, "What should we do?"

"Talk to everyone. Don't spend a lot of time with one faction or the other. Good thing Campbell's not here for you to moon over. That would screw everything up."

"Why isn't he here?"

Judy shrugged. "I don't know. He was invited, but he politely turned it down. Probably out hunting. I know Brittany resents being here instead of in the field—notice her subtlety in dressing for work?"

"I noticed. Brittany's not a subtle person." I liked Brittany, but in the way you might like a tiger: it's pretty, and powerful, but get too close and it will rip your head off. "Let's go talk to her. She might tell us something about the hunt."

Brittany turned away from the woman she was talking to when we approached. "Helena, Judy. I can see why Judy'd have to be here, but what made you come, Helena?"

"I'm just trying to help ease tensions. How goes the search?"

"It would be better," Brittany said with a feline smile, "if I didn't have to stand around here making small talk. I told Rasmussen I'm giving him half an hour and then my team and I are out of here."

"I have to agree with you," I said. "Catching this killer is the most important thing you could do."

The smile vanished. "I want to beat Campbell to it. He's getting arrogant beyond belief, just because he was the first to guess we were looking for a human. His selfishness is going to lose us the Long War."

"I don't think the Long War hinges on one man," I said, suppressing a desire to shout at her in Malcolm's defense.

Brittany made a dismissive noise. "I'm just tired of him lording it over the rest of us. As if anyone cares who his father was or how many steel magi there are in his family tree. What matters is what you do here, now. I've killed or captured more invaders than he has."

"Aren't there several teams working on finding this killer?" Judy said, overriding my ill-judged retort. "What matters is that he's caught, not who does the catching."

"Sure, just so long as it's me," Brittany said with a laugh. "Hey,

91

your father is giving you the stink-eye. You'd better go chat with someone else before you get into trouble." She turned away and grabbed another Nicollien by the arm, pulling him in to speak to him in a low voice. I marched away without waiting for Judy. The nerve—!

"Slow down and take a breath," Judy said, taking my arm and bringing me to a halt. "You know what Brittany's like."

"I don't care what she says, Malcolm is *not* arrogant!"

"You and I know that, but you have to admit he's got that air about him that says he thinks he's superior to everyone else."

"You just don't like him."

"No, I don't. But I figure if you do, there must be something worthwhile about him."

I gaped at her. "That's...an unexpectedly nice thing to say."

Judy shrugged. "Friends should support each other, right?" She wasn't quite meeting my eyes, and now her cheeks matched her blouse and her wine.

"Yeah," I said. "They should."

Judy tugged on my arm. "Let's go talk to some of the Ambrosites. And hope none of them try to take my head off because of my last name."

We bounced between groups for nearly an hour, by which time I was in despair and wishing I'd gone to dinner with Cynthia instead. Neither faction was speaking to the other regardless of Rasmussen and Parish's hinting. Judy and I were at our most eloquent, urging, cajoling, sometimes even pleading with people to see sense. I had no idea if it was working, but it felt like it wasn't. The magi were determined to hate each other, and there wasn't anything I could do to change that.

We met up with Lucia briefly. She gave us a cynical smile that was just loose enough to show she was tipsy, though otherwise she displayed no symptoms. "Still happy you came?"

"I think this was pointless," I said. "Nice idea, but no one's willing to listen."

Lucia surveyed the backyard with a slow turn of her head. "Oh, they're listening. They don't like it, but you and Judy make some good points. And they know neither of you has an axe to grind. Good work distancing yourself from your father, Rasmussen."

Judy scowled. "I just wish they weren't all so stupid. It's not rocket science. There's a killer out there and he's not representative of either faction. The End."

"You're the one who told me conflict between the factions is inevitable," I said. "They don't trust each other at the best of times. This is just an excuse to hold onto that."

Lucia nodded. Then she stilled, one hand on my arm. "That doesn't look good," she said, jerking her chin in the direction of the patio. A young man dressed in hunter's fatigues stood in the doorway, talking to Rasmussen. Rasmussen had one fist clenched at his side and was leaning toward the young man. He glanced around, caught my eye briefly, then looked at Lucia. Lucia let go of me and headed toward Rasmussen. After a few seconds, Judy and I drifted after her.

"—don't tell them now," Rasmussen was saying when I was near enough to hear his words to Lucia.

"They need to know," Lucia said angrily. "Better here in controlled circumstances than from rumor later."

"It will—" Rasmussen saw me standing nearby. "This is a private conversation."

"Sorry," I said, not that I was. "But it sounds like Lucia wants everyone to know, whatever it is."

"This is not Lucia's call."

"Actually, it is, Rasmussen. But I'm sorry about it. You got farther than I frankly thought you could." Lucia turned away and called out, "Everyone, we've had some bad news, and I'm counting on you to stay calm and use your influence to keep others from reacting badly. Mike Lavern was killed about an hour ago, drained of his magic—"

An uproar cut off the rest of her words. Judy gripped my arm so tightly it hurt. "An Ambrosite," she whispered in my ear. Nicolliens and Ambrosites who had been drawing closer to one another now backed away toward their opposite sides of the yard, yelling threats and profanities. Two women emerged from the groups and ran at each other, clawing and punching until they were pulled apart by others of their factions.

Parish stood aloof from the fight, his dark, handsome face set like stone. Rasmussen was shouting, his face bright red, but no one listened to him until he made a complicated gesture and everyone covered their ears, wincing in pain. Rasmussen, a paper magus skilled at illusions affecting all the senses, had never displayed his talent where I could see it before—or, rather, see the effect, as my position as Abernathy's custodian made me able to see through illusions. Or hear through them, apparently. Now it shut the crowd up.

"That is *enough!*" he roared. "There is no Nicollien conspiracy to murder Ambrosites. Ambrosites are not using this as a pretext for outlawing Nicollien familiars. Use *sense*, people! All we know is that someone is killing magi by draining their magic. If you allow this to drive a wedge further between our people, you will only be helping this killer do his foul work. Now. Go back to your homes. You are all influential within the community; use that influence to keep the peace. Mr. Parish and I will speak with you tomorrow."

There was embarrassed silence for a few moments. Then people began filing through the patio door, though I noticed the Ambrosites all waited for the Nicolliens to leave before exiting. Lucia, Judy, and I were the last to walk through the door. "So much for that," Judy said.

"It was worth trying," Lucia said. "Go home, Davies. Get some rest. I'll be sending people over for auguries in the morning. Not that I expect to get any sleep tonight."

"I'll be ready. See you in the morning, Judy."

Lucia was parked a few spaces down from me, and we walked back to my car together. The night was clear for once, clear and cool, with a few stars visible against the glow of the street lights. "Do you really think it was worth trying?" I said.

Lucia shrugged. "I know you think I always go for the aggressive solution first because of my custodianship," she said, "but I prefer talking my way through a situation before I resort to violence. Rasmussen gets on my last nerve, but he's a strong force for good in this community. So's Parish."

"I can't believe you can say that about Mr. Rasmussen, given how he invoked the Accords against you!"

"You don't see everything that goes on here, Davies. Rasmussen and I...we're never going to be friends, but we've come to an understanding. The point is, Rasmussen and Parish are at least trying to do damage control. Imagine what things would be like if either of them were egging on their people to hostility."

"Have you ever seen the factions fight each other? I mean, literally fight?"

"Once, at a distance. About twenty years ago in Chicago. The Ambrosite leader for the Midwest hated Nicolliens so much he encouraged his people to outright violence against them. The two Archmagi had to step in, and the Ambrosite was removed from power. But for five days there was undeclared war in the streets. Several people died, lots more were injured, and I don't think magery has ever come as close to being discovered as it was during that time. If it happens again..." Lucia paused with her hand on the roof of my car. "Let's just hope it doesn't happen again."

"Is there anything I can do?"

"What you've been doing. Talk sense to people. Be a force for reason in this nightmare." She turned away, then said, over her shoulder, "And if you see Campbell, warn him to stay away from Spinelli. She's just looking for an excuse to fight him."

I watched her walk away, then got into my car and drove home. Malcolm fighting Brittany...he was good, and I was loyally certain he could defeat her, but it wouldn't be a bloodless victory. Then I remembered the look in Lucia's eyes when she'd said it, how amused she'd been, and I flushed hotly. So she knew I cared about Malcolm. That didn't give her the right to tease me about something that could never happen—that she ought to know better than anyone would never happen.

Back in my apartment, I sat at my kitchen table with my phone in front of me and debated. I should warn Malcolm about Brittany. I should maybe even tell him about the murder. I scowled and picked up my phone between thumb and forefinger like it was a dead rat.

Malcolm probably already knew about the murder, and he didn't need my warning about Brittany because he also already knew she hated him. It was time I stopped going to him for every little thing, because it was just making my life harder.

I checked the time. Too late to call Jason. I plugged my phone in and got into my pajamas, then took out Silas Abernathy's book on his travels as a stone magus. I sometimes read from it when I was too keyed up to sleep, random excerpts here and there rather than reading it straight through.

Tonight, I read: *Setting a new ward is less difficult than renewing an existing one. At first, this seems illogical, but a moment's thought makes it clear that this is only obvious. An existing ward can't be snuffed out, so its renewal is a matter of matching one's will and power to the remnants of the old one. I found this most challenging in Lumbini, which is one of the larger warded sites in the world. Its constant stream of visitors, not all of whom have good intent, means its wards are constantly in need of renewal. I found the place soothing to the spirit, but challenging to my aegis, which responded poorly to its fractures. I understand now why an individual stone magus is not allowed to renew the wards there more than twice in five years.*

I set the book down. The aegis, the sliver of matter embedded in a magus's heart to allow him to manipulate magic, was something I still didn't understand well. It had physical and metaphysical properties, but the idea of having a sliver of glass or paper or steel stuck into my heart, even if it was only partially there, made me cringe. I'd been told that back in the earliest days of magery, only one in ten people survived the Damerel rites, the ritual that implanted the aegis. How desperate they must have been to take that risk.

I tried reading more, but my eyes weren't staying focused, and eventually I laid the book aside and turned off my light. What I wouldn't give to have Silas's other book, the journal about his time as custodian. I only guessed it existed, because Silas was too methodical not to have kept a diary when he was in charge of Abernathy's, but it was a guess I felt confident about. *Maybe the Athenaeum knows about it,* I thought muzzily, and slid into sleep.

$\mathcal{T}$en o'clock rolled around the next morning without a single person entering the store. It was so weird I checked my phone several times, wondering if the display was right. "I don't know why no one's here," Judy said irritably when my wonderings became verbal. "Just be grateful there isn't anyone to start a war."

I did the day's mail-in auguries, which took until just after noon, and still no one came. I found Judy sitting at the desk in the office, typing rapidly. "You're sure it's not Sunday?" I said, only half joking.

Judy blew out her breath in exasperation. "Come over here and look at this," she said. I came around to her side of the desk. She brought up the database interface, clicked on the Search field, and typed BLACK. Seven records came up in the center of the screen. "These are all the people with the surname Black who've done business with Abernathy's. Actually—" She double clicked on one name. "This one's a duplicate. I'll have to merge it with the other. But see how easy it was to find that mistake? And it's even easier to fix it."

"I'm impressed. Now what do we do with it?"

"What *don't* we do? We can generate mailing labels for the day's auguries, search on someone's history, quickly look up a customer's records...it's going to speed up a lot of our processes."

"That's great! Especially the mailing labels. I've got a stack of books that need to go out in the mail."

"Okay, but lunch first. I'm starving."

Two o'clock came, and again the store stayed empty. I was starting to worry. The spectators, the ones who came by just to chat, I could see staying away, but the hunters? They needed auguries more than ever now that the killer had stepped up his game. And Lucia had said she'd be sending someone over for an augury, so where was that person?

Judy and I finished packaging the auguries, and Judy took them to the post office. While she was gone, I sat behind the front counter and idly picked at the flaws in the glass top with my thumbnail. I remembered Cynthia doing the same thing several days ago. She was picking me up for dinner tonight, and I was trying not to resent having to go. Not that I had anything better to do, since no one was banging down my door looking for an augury.

The door swung open, and I sat upright. "Oh! Olivia!"

"Surprise," Olivia Quincy said. She looked perfectly healthy, not at all as if she'd had half her magic sucked out of her body only days before. "How are you?"

"Better, now that you're here." I came around the counter to hug her. "Do you need an augury, or is this a personal visit?"

"Augury." She held out a slip of paper. "Everyone says hi. It's been crazy the last few days, but we're so close. At least, Campbell thinks we're close. I've never seen him drive himself to the brink like this before. I think he's taking these murders personally."

"Why would he do that?"

Olivia shrugged. "He feels guilty that he, in his words, 'wasted' so much time pursuing invaders that didn't exist. Samantha Bannister was a close friend of his mother's and someone he grew up calling Aunt. He has issues with responsibility."

"I see." No wonder he'd been so short with me. "Hang on, and I'll get this for you."

The bluish light of the oracle comforted me. I unfolded the slip. *Where will the killer strike next?* I'd seen so many variations on this I wondered if the oracle was tired of providing answers to it, even the cryptic half-answers embedded in the books it selected. I came up with a battered copy of *The House With a Clock in its Walls* and returned to Olivia, who was doing something with her phone she shut off when I appeared. "I used to love this book when I was a kid," I said, handing it over.

"I've never read it. Maybe I'll get a chance now, once its oracular power is exhausted." Olivia handed over a tube of *sanguinis sapiens*. "I hope Campbell's right, and we're close. Or someone's close. I don't care who so long as the killer is stopped. But I'm exhausted. We all are."

"I'm sorry. Good luck." I waved goodbye, then went back to my stool. I'd done my little bit toward finding and stopping the killer. I just wished it could be more.

Lucia's messenger came by at nearly six, when I was getting ready to close up shop. The augury was easy to find, which felt like an undramatic end to a strangely quiet day. I handed it over, accepted $7000 in hundreds from the woman, and locked the door behind her. Judy had left early, citing a message from her father requesting her presence, so I was alone as I wandered through the store, picking up scraps of paper and straightening shelves and generally tidying up.

As I got ready for dinner with Cynthia, I couldn't help wondering what Lucia would make of her augury. Maybe she had learned something new about the killer, something that would give the Wardens an advantage. Lucia was right; it was remarkable that Parish and Rasmussen were able to handle this as well as they had, without personal animosities getting in the way. It made me respect them more, though I didn't like them any better, since they both wanted me out of their way. We were never going to be friends, but we could probably work together.

I put on a strappy dress made of something silky and rose-colored (*warm colors, happy now, sis?*) and a pair of white sandals, put my things into a purse that matched the dress, and kicked back on my velvet couch to wait for Cynthia's text. Warm evening sunlight poured through the windows until I felt drenched in honey, perfectly relaxed and ready for anything my sister might throw at me tonight.

I ran my fingers across the back of the couch, enjoying how the maroon velvet was smooth in one direction and resistant in the other. It reminded me of kissing Jason, and I dug in my purse for my phone. I'd text him, see what he was doing tomorrow night. We hadn't had a real date in over a week, unless you counted dinner with my family, which was sort of like a date in the same way honeymooning with your mother-in-law was a wedding trip.

As I pulled out my phone, it buzzed with an incoming text. Cynthia was downstairs. I dithered briefly, then put my phone away and gathered up my purse. I'd text Jason later. Right now I didn't want to keep Cynthia waiting. Who knew what she might come up with, left to her own devices?

The little BMW was comfortable and its engine purred just at the edge of hearing. "I love leather seats, don't you?" Cynthia said. "These don't even hold onto the heat of the day. I don't know why. German engineering, probably."

"It's nice," I said, running my fingers over the smooth contours of the seat. "Where are we going?"

"A little place I heard about from some of the guys in the conference. It's called Giuseppe's and the linguini is supposed to be divine."

"I love Italian food."

"I know."

"How do you know that?"

"I do know things about you, Hellie. We grew up together, remember?"

You don't know I hate being called Hellie, apparently. I thought about mentioning it, then discarded the notion. "I just didn't think you paid all that much attention. We didn't have a lot in common, growing up."

"You're three years younger than me. That's a big gap when you're young. Not so much when you're twenty-two and twenty-five."

There were nine years between me and Malcolm. I turned to look out the window so Cynthia wouldn't see me blush. "I guess that's true. We're closer to being in the same stage of life now."

"Exactly. We're both employed, we're both dating seriously, we're both living on our own...we understand each other's lives better now." Cynthia swung into a driveway and pulled up in front of the valet stand. "Or at least, I think we should."

I couldn't think of anything to say to that. A liveried attendant helped me out of the car, and I followed Cynthia into the restaurant.

Once we were past the foyer, the restaurant was dimly lit, with a bunch of little round tables each with its own tiny lamp. The maroon carpet and the deep red of the walls gave it a cozy, intimate look. Men and women spoke in hushed tones, filling the room with murmuring sound like flowing water. But more striking than all of that was the aroma of marinara sauce, a dozen different cheeses, and freshly cooked pasta. I drew in a deep breath, and my stomach rumbled. Cynthia laughed. "I can already see this is a hit."

"If the food tastes as good as it smells, I may come here all the time."

"I'm glad you like it. I wanted tonight to be memorable."

The waiter ushered us to a table near the left side of the room. "Any reason why?" I asked as I took my seat.

Cynthia shrugged. "I'm leaving in a few days, and I don't know when I'll be back. This may be the last chance we have to spend time together for a long time."

"Well, that's reason enough."

We spent some time looking over the menu, though I already knew what I was going to have: every time I tried a new Italian place, I ordered its lasagna to see if it measured up to my mother's. The waiter came by and filled up our water glasses, took our orders and our menus, and walked away again. Cynthia's phone beeped, and she began texting someone. I sat and fidgeted. What could I possibly say to Cynthia that I hadn't failed to say a hundred times before?

"Sorry," Cynthia said, putting away her phone. "Business. Sometimes I don't know how they get on without me."

"Do you ever have trouble with the glass ceiling, or stuff like that?" I asked.

Cynthia laughed. "It's all about tradeoffs. If you're willing to work like a man, you're more likely to be treated like a man. Though I won't say it's not hard. There aren't a lot of women in my position and there'll be fewer as I get older and get promoted. Not something you need to worry about, in your job, is it?"

"What's that supposed to mean?"

"Why are you upset? I meant you don't have to worry about pleasing your bosses so they won't pass you over for some up and coming young man. Or have I misunderstood your job?"

I flushed. "Sorry. I don't know where that came from."

"I do."

"Really?"

Cynthia unfolded her napkin and spread it on her lap, but her eyes never left my face. "You've always felt insecure when it comes to your successes. Didn't help that I won all the prizes and took all the acclaim in high school, did it?"

"I see you're still as arrogant as you used to be." If she was going to be a bitch, I wasn't going to hold back.

"That's not bragging, it's just true. I'm not going to apologize for being successful, Hellie."

"Would you *not* call me that!" I said. "It's like you think I'm some kind of pet!"

She looked surprised. "I didn't know it bothered you."

"Right, because the last hundred times I told you not to do it wasn't enough of a warning."

"I don't remember you ever telling me you hated it. Sorry."

She sounded so taken aback I felt guilty. "That's okay. Just...don't." Had I ever told her not to call me that? Or had I just thought it all those times? "And I'd rather not talk about your successes."

"I don't want to, either. We were talking about you. I'm just saying that whenever you did succeed at something, it wasn't big by comparison to what I was doing and Mom and Dad never acknowledged it. I didn't think about it at the time, but in hindsight, it bothers me."

"Yeah, because you were the golden child."

"I know," Cynthia said without a trace of either humility or arrogance. She might have been commenting on the weather. "It probably sucked to be you sometimes."

Her candor made me uncomfortable. "Can we talk about something else? How about your conference? How's that going?"

She smiled and shook her head. "It's fine. I've already sent information back to my bosses and we should have a deal ready by the time the weekend's over. But you don't care about that."

It's better than talking about what a failure I am. "You made an effort to learn about my work, I figure I can return the favor."

"I envy you. You seem so confident, running your store, and all those people like you...I can't think of more than four of my coworkers who think of me more fondly than as a brass-balled bitch. I wish I had what you have."

My discomfort grew. "I...I'm sure more people than that—"

"No, it's pretty much just those four. And two of them only like me because I buy lunch once a week. You're so lucky."

I leaned back in my chair as the waiter deposited my lasagna in front of me. "I guess I am. Though Judy despised me when we first met."

"That's the little one, right? She's so cute. Why did she despise you?"

"She thought she was going to get to run the store. She has experience I don't. But I'm the one they hired, and she eventually realized she was better off helping than sniping at me from the sidelines."

Cynthia laughed. "How's the lasagna?"

I cut off a small bite and blew on it before popping it into my mouth. "Mmm," I said, savoring the blend of flavors. "Almost as good as Mom's. She uses more cheese."

"I keep telling her it's too bad she never became a chef. She's good enough she could do it."

"She liked feeding us more."

"I know." Cynthia forked up a mouthful of linguini. "I don't know if I could do what she did. Stay home and raise kids."

"She did a lot of other things, too."

"Yeah, but it's not the same as having a job outside the home."

Cynthia took another bite, smaller than the first, swallowed, and put down her fork. "Helena, I'm pregnant."

Stunned, I lowered my fork to my plate. *"What?"*

"I'm pregnant. Seven weeks."

"But...how?"

Cynthia gave me a wry smile. "The usual way."

"I mean...you don't want kids. Do you? You said you didn't."

"I don't. It was an accident. Ethan doesn't even know."

"What are you going to do?"

"I don't know. I don't even know if I'm going to keep it." Cynthia nudged her fork to lie parallel with her knife. She looked suddenly old in the dim light of the lamp. "I haven't told anyone but you."

"Not even Mom?"

"I'm not telling her until I've made a decision. I don't want her getting all excited if...anyway. But I had to tell someone. And you're my sister."

She said it so simply—*you're my sister*—and yet with such feeling I was struck mute. All the resentment I'd harbored against her vanished, leaving only regret and a trace of guilt. "I'm not much of a sister," I finally said.

"Don't say that. You're a great sister."

"I mean—Cynthia, I hated you when we were younger. You stole all my boyfriends and you made fun of the way I dressed—"

"I'm sorry. I was full of myself back then and it was fun to tease you because you got so mad you couldn't speak—"

"See? Even now you think that's funny!"

Cynthia shook her head. "I was laughing at myself, how stupid I was. We're really different, I know that, and in some ways that's never going to change. But we're both older now, and I hoped—" She had tears in her eyes. "I hoped we could get past that."

"How do you expect that to happen if you've never once apologized for what you did?"

"I just did. Hellie—I mean, Helena, if you want me to apologize for every little slight, we'll be here until next Tuesday. I'm sorry I treated you so poorly and I'm sorry I didn't appreciate you when we were younger. But right now—" Her voice broke. "Right now I could really use a friend."

I scrubbed away tears from my eyes. "Admit it was you who stole the bracelet."

"If I'd seriously tried to steal it, one or both of us would have gone to jail. The manager knew it was a gag. I was trying to get you to lighten up a little. You were always so *serious*, all the time. I just wanted us to have a shared experience."

"The shared experience of nearly going to jail?"

"It's brought us closer together right now, hasn't it?"

I laughed and wiped away more tears. "Cynthia, I'm sorry I resented you. I would have been a jerk to you even if you hadn't teased me so much. I was so jealous."

"And I never stole your boyfriends, though I admit I did flirt with them. But I flirted with everyone back then."

"What about Tyler Grant?"

"Tyler who?"

"In drama club? You were starring in *The Importance of Being Earnest* and I was on stage crew with him? I liked him so much, and you just swooped in—"

"*Oh.* Come on, Helena. You weren't dating him, you just wanted him to ask you out. And you didn't want him. He made fun of you to me—you were so gawky as a freshman—and besides, he dumped me after two weeks for some girl on the student council."

I reached across and took her hand. "Then I owe you thanks."

She squeezed my hand in return. "You'd better eat that before it gets cold."

"You, too." I took another bite to give myself time to think. I felt so stupid. What was I supposed to say? I'd never given pregnancy any thought, never considered what I might do or what advice to give someone else. "So...what *are* you going to do?"

Cynthia retrieved her fork, but didn't do more than poke at her linguini. "I really don't know. This couldn't have come at a worse time. Being pregnant, and then having a baby to care for...I won't be able to do what I've been doing at work. But the worst part is I don't know what Ethan will think. He's talked often about how nice it is that we aren't tied down to a baby like some of our friends. I don't even know if he wants to marry me—not that we have to be married to raise a baby, but it's the same kind of commitment."

"I think he ought to know, don't you?"

Cynthia sighed. "Yes. But I'm a coward. I don't want him to dump me."

"I don't think that's a good reason for an abortion."

"No. It's not." She sighed again. "And part of me pictures being a mom and thinks, how the hell am I supposed to do that? I'm not the most maternal person in the world."

"Mom always said it's different when it's your own kids."

"I know. Helena, how did I get into this mess?"

I grinned, and intoned, "Well, when a mommy and a daddy love each other *very much*—"

"Shut up." She grinned back at me. "I didn't realize how much of a burden this was until I told you. Thank you."

"Well, I *am* your sister." I laid down my fork. "Look, Cynthia, I don't know what to tell you. I've never really thought about being pregnant, or how you make that kind of decision. I just don't know. But...if you want my opinion, you've never backed down from a challenge in your life, and I can't imagine a bigger challenge than motherhood."

"I...think you're right." She took another bite of linguini, chewed and swallowed. "I can't—"

My phone rang. I ignored it. "Can't what?"

"I can't believe I'm going to be a mother."

My heart tried to swell out of my body. "I'm going to be an aunt. The cool kind of aunt who spoils her niece rotten."

"It could be a boy."

"Then I'll spoil him rotten too. You have to tell Mom. No, you have to tell Ethan first." My phone rang again. "What are you going to do if he..."

"Then I'll have to be a single mother." She didn't look as brave as she sounded. "But this is the right thing to do, and I'm—"

My phone rang yet again. I swore and pulled it out. Judy. "I'm sorry, let me take this and find out what's got her panties in a twist." I half-turned away from Cynthia, as if that would give me privacy. "Judy, what is it?"

"Helena, I'm sorry," Judy said, "but this is important. Malcolm Campbell just murdered Amber Guittard."

"*What?*" The room seemed to swell, everything receding from my vision. "Judy, that can't be true."

"It's true. He was seen by three magi. Stabbed her through the heart."

"They must have made a mistake. It's—" I glanced at Cynthia, who was looking at me with concern. "It's someone trying to make trouble."

"Two of the witnesses were Ambrosites, a couple of Parish's people. There's no question. He killed her." Judy was crying. "That bastard killed her."

"There has to be some reason, Judy. He wouldn't—"

"Don't make excuses for him, Helena. Just don't. I loved Amber like an older sister. I've known her all my life. And he just walked up to her and stabbed her."

I swallowed my own tears. "What does Lucia say?"

"*Lucia* says we don't have all the evidence." Judy's bitterness was almost palpable. "I don't know what other evidence she wants."

I looked at Cynthia again. "It just doesn't make sense."

"Well, I guess you didn't know him as well as you thought." She disconnected so abruptly I felt dizzy again. I lowered the phone to my lap and stared at the remains of my lasagna.

"What's wrong?" Cynthia said. "That sounded dire."

What can I tell her? "I, um, that was Judy. Her boyfriend just broke up with her and she was really upset. They'd been together a long time and he just did it out of nowhere."

"That sounded worse than a breakup. Your face...you look like someone died."

"No, nothing like that," I lied. "It was just completely unexpected. Sorry to interrupt dinner."

"That's all right." She still looked skeptical. I smiled and took a last bite of lasagna. I wanted dinner to be over so I could go home and try to reach Malcolm. I had no doubt, if he'd killed someone like Amber Guittard, he had a good reason.

"I'm leaving Monday evening, but I...actually, this is something I should tell Ethan in person, don't you think?" Cynthia pushed her plate away. "Do you want dessert?"

"I'm full. But thanks."

"I don't know what my boss is going to say. He'll probably flip out, but he can't fire me."

"Is that because you're too valuable?"

"That, and I'll sue him for discrimination. I don't intend to let this affect the quality of my work."

"You're going to be fine."

Cynthia leaned across the table. "Are you sure you're all right? You look really shaken."

"It's been an emotional evening."

"I can tell. How about we take you home?"

We drove in silence until we reached my door, when Cynthia grabbed my hand and squeezed it. "Thanks. For everything."

"I'm sorry it took us this long to be able to really talk."

"We both had some growing up to do. Me more than you." She smiled briefly. "You know," she added, "if there's something going on, you can tell me."

"There's nothing going on."

"I'm not sure about that, but it's your life." She looked disappointed. I smiled weakly. *You wouldn't believe it if I told you.*

I waved goodbye and went inside, locking the steel door behind me and setting the alarm. I had my phone out and was calling Malcolm before I even made it up the stairs. It rang, and rang, and finally went to voice mail. I hung up without leaving a message. What could I say? I needed to speak to him, not his voice mail.

Once inside, I tried calling Judy, but she didn't answer either. I scrolled through my contacts. Who else would know what was going on?

I tapped a name. "Lucia, it's Helena. Call me." She'd know what it was about. I sat on my couch clutching my phone and stared at the dark room. I'd forgotten to turn on the lights, and now it seemed like too much trouble to get up and find the switch. Malcolm had killed the Nicollien second-in-command. I couldn't think of anything more likely to start a war than if Rasmussen killed Parish. What was Malcolm thinking? It must have something to do with the murders, but Guittard hadn't even been in Portland when the first murder happened. *Unless he's snapped. Olivia said he was under pressure.* No. Malcolm would never let his work change who he was, and who he was didn't go around killing innocent people.

I got into my pajamas and went back to sitting on the couch. I couldn't sleep now. I tried Judy again and left a message this time. It sounded like Judy's loyalties had been tested and she'd come down on the side of the Nicolliens. Well, I could hardly blame her for hating Malcolm.

I stood and paced the living room, bumping into the nonfunctional, ancient radio cabinet and rubbing my sore hip. There was nothing I could do but wait. It made me furious and miserable and heartbroken all at once.

My phone rang, and I pounced on it. "Hello?"

"Campbell hasn't contacted you, has he?" Lucia said.

"No. His phone's not picking up either."

"He probably ditched it so we couldn't trace him that way. Damn. He needs to turn himself in."

"Lucia, *what happened?*"

"I don't know." Lucia's voice was tight and angry. "Witnesses say he went in to see Guittard in private. They heard shouting, and when they entered Guittard's office, she was slumped over her desk and Campbell had a bloody knife in his hand. He fought his way free and disappeared. Injured five more in his flight."

"But that's circumstantial! He might have discovered the real killer. It might not have been his knife."

"That sort of thing only happens in movies, Davies. There wasn't anyone else in the office and no one was spotted entering or leaving while he was there. He did it. I just want to know why."

"He must have had a reason."

"Which is why I haven't issued a kill on sight order. My people will find him, and bring him in, and we'll discover the truth."

"You're not telling me everything."

There was a long silence. "I'm not the only one looking for him. The Nicolliens are furious. I hear Spinelli has sworn to take his head. She wasn't speaking metaphorically."

"You can't let her do that!"

"You may be overestimating what I'm capable of. The best I can do is see Spinelli in front of a tribunal for murder if she succeeds. Not that I expect Campbell to go without a fight—for all I know I'll be trying him for two murders if there's a confrontation."

"Lucia, this is ridiculous!"

"Like I said, Campbell needs to turn himself in so I can put him in protective custody. His team hasn't heard anything from him either." She blew out an exasperated breath. "I don't have the resources to pursue our killer *and* find Campbell. Not to mention the explosion that will happen as soon as this becomes public. Who told you? Judy?"

"Yes."

"Rasmussen is ready to kill Campbell himself. I guess his daughter wasn't as far from being a Nicollien as I thought."

"She's just grieving. She'll see sense soon." I hoped it was true. If Judy couldn't stay impartial, I couldn't keep her on as my assistant.

"If Campbell contacts you," Lucia said, "tell me immediately. And for God's sake convince him to be sensible."

"He won't contact me."

"You sure about that?" Lucia cut the connection and my phone beeped to indicate the end of the call. I set my phone down and closed my eyes. If Malcolm hadn't contacted his team, he certainly wasn't going to call me. There wasn't anything I could do if he did but urge him to turn himself in.

I trudged down the hall toward my bedroom, clutching my phone. Sleeping was out of the question. I'd read Silas's book and see if that calmed me.

Snuggled into bed with the window open a crack for the cool breezes, I tried to focus on my book. The sounds of the street below, the smells of exhaust and popcorn, filled my senses until the words on the page made no sense no matter how often I read them. Finally, I set it aside and stretched. I'd left that book on bathroom remodeling downstairs. It was probably an excellent cure for insomnia.

I padded barefoot down the stairs without turning on the lights and opened the office door, took two steps inside, and was rooted to the spot. Malcolm, the phone receiver held to his ear, stared at me, looking as stunned as I felt.

My hand gripped the doorknob so tightly my knuckles were white. Malcolm's stunned expression gave way to impassivity. He said, "That works for me," and it took me a second to realize he was talking to whoever was on the other end of the line. "I'll meet you there," he added, then paused. "Don't worry about me, just be ready. Tomorrow at noon." He hung up the phone with a *click* that felt like it should echo in the quiet room.

We stared at each other for a long moment in which I searched desperately for something to say that wasn't inane or accusatory. Malcolm still looked impassive. I wondered what he saw when he looked at me. Whether he thought my silence covered fear.

Malcolm said, "I'm sorry. Yours is the only phone I could safely reach that can't be traced."

"It's all right," I said, and silence fell again like a storm cloud, waiting for the deluge.

Finally, Malcolm said, "By your expression, I can tell you know I killed Ms. Guittard."

"I know. Malcolm, why?"

He shook his head and took a step toward me. "You need to stay out of this. It will all be over, one way or another, in a few days."

I wanted to close the distance between us, but I was afraid that would just make Malcolm leave. "Lucia wants you to turn yourself in."

"If I do, Ms. Guittard's colleague will certainly have me killed. I'm safer free."

"Her colleague? Malcolm, just tell me—what happened?"

He smiled, a bitter, self-mocking expression. "I have to go."

"Where?"

"You're safer not knowing." He took a few more steps toward me.

I moved backward to get between him and the outer door. "You'll go to Derrick?"

"And mix him and his family up in this? Not a chance."

His face was haggard, bone-weary, and my heart went out to him. "Have you eaten?"

He smiled, a grim, mirthless expression. "I can't exactly stop at McDonald's."

"Come upstairs, and I'll fix you something."

"I won't drag you into this." He made a move in my direction that I once again blocked. That would only work so long as he was reluctant to physically move me aside, and I had no idea when that would happen.

"You used my phone. It's too late for that. Or did you think I could just go back upstairs and pretend I didn't see you?"

Malcolm shook his head. "Just give me ten minutes' head start before you call Lucia."

"I'm not calling Lucia. Come upstairs with me." I held out my hand to him, feeling like I was trying to coax a wounded animal to trust me. Malcolm still stood lightly on the balls of his feet, poised to run.

"What happened to impartiality?"

"This isn't about being impartial. It's about helping you. I have faith in you, Malcolm, and whatever your reasons, I'm sure they were valid ones."

Malcolm shook his head ruefully. "I'm going to regret this. *You're* going to regret this."

"'Maybe not today, maybe not tomorrow, but'—"

"This isn't the time for games, Helena."

"I'm sorry. I thought we both could use some levity." I held the door open for him. "Do you like pot roast?"

I served him one of my mother's leftover meals and sat opposite him at the tiny table, watching him eat. His black fatigues were filthy, as if he'd rolled around in the parking lot, and he had a shallow cut over one eyebrow. His hair was ruffled in back, and I controlled an impulse to run my fingers through it to straighten it.

Malcolm ate like he hadn't seen food in weeks. "This is incredibly good," he said.

"My mother is an excellent cook, and she's afraid I'll starve to death if she doesn't provide me with home-cooked meals. It's better than frozen dinners."

He smiled, flashing his dimple, and the room shrank down until it was just the two of us sitting companionably around the table. "Much better. Though at this point I'd be happy with Lean Cuisine."

I cleared his plate and silverware, then returned to sit across from him. "Please tell me what happened. I don't care if that makes me involved. I just need to know why you did it."

Malcolm leaned back in his chair, a contemplative look on his face. "I killed Ms. Guittard," he said, "because she was the accomplice of our serial killer."

"Impossible. How could she—and why—"

"I was able to trace her because she carried out two of the murders herself. When I confronted her, she denied everything, of course. Then I laid out my evidence against her, and told her I would take it to Lucia. She attacked me, and I defended myself, which came down to a choice between her life and mine. But I think she chose not to be taken alive, given how easy it was for me to kill her. She might even have wanted to bring tensions to a boil by letting an Ambrosite kill a high-ranking Nicollien. And I played into her trap."

"Don't sound so bitter. You can't be expected to see everything."

"Can't I?" He laced his fingers together and rested them on the table. "I shouldn't have confronted her, not when I'm so close to finding the killer, but I hoped to coerce her into giving up her accomplice. I was impatient, and see what it's gotten me."

"Do you really think the killer can have you murdered in protective custody?"

"Indirectly, yes. Spinelli probably wants my head, and she'd fight Lucia's people if it meant killing me. And then there would be war."

I shivered. He'd said those words like they were a dire prophecy, some black and tarnished book produced by the oracle as an augury for all of magery. "So you have to stay free long enough to find and capture the killer, and induce him to tell everyone Ms. Guittard was working with him. I just can't believe it. I really liked her."

"So did a lot of people. I don't know what caused her to start killing, or how she came into contact with our second killer. Another reason to regret killing her. It's been a long several days."

Now that I had a good look at him, I saw he looked exhausted as well as haggard. "Do you have a safe place to sleep?"

"As safe as anywhere."

"Is it as safe as here?"

Startled, Malcolm said, "Helena, I can't sleep here."

"Why not? It's probably the best-warded building in Portland. And no one will think to look for you here."

"I won't put you in danger."

"What danger? The worst that can happen is Lucia will yell at me."

"If the killer finds me—"

"He doesn't want any contact with you, Malcolm. *You're* hunting *him*, remember? I can make you a bed on the couch. You can leave early in the morning. Just...let me help you. Please."

Malcolm pushed away from the table and went to the kitchen window. He put his hand to the curtain, but let it fall without touching it. "I shouldn't," he said.

I got up and went to the hall closet where I kept my spare linens, such as they were. I had some sheets and a microfleece blanket, probably not sufficient in the winter, but plenty for a nice summer evening. I spread sheets over the velvet couch and laid out the blanket, then went to my bedroom for a pillow. "There," I said. "Now, are you seriously hurt? You can clean that cut in the bathroom."

"Helena," Malcolm said, then fell silent. "Thank you."

"It's no problem. There's English muffins in the bread basket in case you leave before I'm up, and you can make coffee if you want. Just—don't let them catch you."

"I don't intend to be caught."

I smiled at him and retreated to my bedroom. Faintly, I heard the bathroom door open and close. I should have shown him where the towels were, though I doubted he wanted a bath at a time like this. I'd never regretted not having a shower until that moment.

The apartment was as still and silent as if I were the only one in it. I lay on my bed and stared blindly at the ceiling. I'd been too cavalier about all this. If Lucia found out, I was going to be in so much trouble I'd need an industrial backhoe to dig myself out. But I couldn't help it. I believed in Malcolm, he needed my help, and I couldn't not give it to him.

I rolled onto my side and clutched my pillow to me, cuddling it for comfort. I didn't see any good way out of this. Malcolm hadn't said it, but he didn't need to—even if he caught the killer, he'd still need to get his evidence in front of a tribunal, or at the very least to Lucia, and Brittany and the other Nicolliens were still out for his blood. I had no doubt Brittany, for one, wouldn't hesitate to try to kill him no matter what Lucia said. The idea of Malcolm dying at Brittany's hands made me clench my pillow tighter.

Restlessly, I shifted position to my back and squeezed my eyes shut. I wasn't going to fall asleep any time soon. I still didn't have a book to read, but I was fairly certain I couldn't focus on anything I might find on the shelves downstairs. Usually when I got this way, I turned on the television or an old movie, but I couldn't do that with Malcolm occupying my living room.

I groaned and sat up, thrusting my pillow aside. Maybe some tea would help, something hot and herbal. I'd just have to be quiet to avoid disturbing Malcolm, who might be asleep already, as tired as he was.

1 2

I opened my door quietly and tiptoed down the hall, avoiding the spots that creaked. The living room was dark, dark enough I couldn't see Malcolm on the couch, though I knew he was there with a burning awareness that touched every part of me. I turned on the little light over the stove and set the kettle on to boil. One of my canisters, the kind that were supposed to hold flour and sugar, contained chamomile tea bags, and I fished one out and dropped it into a mug Judy had bought me for a gag last month that said WORLD'S BEST BOSS.

"Can't sleep?" Malcolm said, and I shrieked and spun around. He lounged in the doorway, wearing a tight-fitting black T-shirt that showed off his chest and some very wrinkled black boxer shorts. *Malcolm Campbell, in my kitchen, in his underwear* shot through my mind like the solution to a game of Erotic Clue, and I made myself stop staring.

"Some nights are like this," I said, hoping he couldn't hear my heart hammering. "I can feel how tired my body is, but my mind won't let me sleep."

"I understand. Any chance of me getting some of that tea?"

I took out another mug, this one with a picture of a tiara and the words SELF-RESCUING PRINCESS that had been a gift from Viv. All my most interesting stuff had been given me by someone else. Why didn't I do things like that for myself? For the briefest moment, I felt sorry for myself. Ruthlessly I pushed the feeling away. I was interesting. I just had even more interesting friends.

Malcolm examined the mug and smiled, once again flashing the dimple. I wondered whether he knew just how devastating it was. "As opposed to all the princesses who have to be rescued?" he said.

"I guess. Viv liked the sentiment. She said it was to remind me I don't need to wait around for anyone to save me. I don't know that I get into trouble all that often."

He glanced up from the mug. "There was the invader that tried to destroy Abernathy's. And that magus kidnapped you and locked you in a warehouse to be killed by a swarm of monsters."

"Two times in twenty-two years. I think that qualifies as not very often."

"True. And you rescued yourself both times."

I smiled. "With some help from you. I would have died if you hadn't been in the store that day, or if you hadn't been captured with me."

"And vice versa." He smiled back at me.

"So we're both self-rescuing princesses?" I said, laughing. The kettle whistled, and I filled both mugs.

"Apparently."

I got out a spoon and poked my tea bag, watching ribbons of brown thread their way through the water. "I should let you get to sleep."

"Every time I close my eyes, I see Ms. Guittard's astonished face as I stab her through the heart. I'd rather be awake."

"I'm sorry. Do you...does it always bother you, when you kill someone?"

Malcolm laughed and set down his mug to clasp my hand, briefly but firmly. "Not counting my military service, I've only killed two people before this, and both of them were accidental deaths," he said. "The look on your face, bravely trying to pretend it's nothing that I've killed other humans...I've never seen anything so heart-warming."

"I told you, if you killed someone I know there had to be a reason."

Malcolm picked up his mug again and took a sip. "The first one truly was accidental. We were sparring, and she was careless, and so was I. I still have nightmares about it, the way she looked...anyway. The second was in the killing fields, in a duel, and I didn't intend for him to do anything but suffer. I inadvertently struck an artery, and he bled out before anyone could save him. Amber Guittard is the first person I've killed intentionally, and I'm going to carry that memory to my grave."

"You all talk about the killing fields like it's nothing. What are they?"

"The official name is the Palaestra. It's named for an ancient Greek wrestling school. We go there for weapons training and to resolve matters of honor that can't be handled publicly. The killing fields is what we call it when we need a reminder that the Long War is deadly not just because of the enemy we fight, but for the challenges we pose each other. It used to be people were quicker to take their disagreements to the Palaestra. Mr. Parish, for one, dueled often and I know he took lives."

"That seems so wasteful, when both Ambrosites and Nicolliens are fighting the same war."

"It's easy to forget the other side is human, and then it's a short step to believing 'not human' means 'enemy.' I know for many years I hated Nicolliens for what they've done to my people."

I wanted to ask him what that was, but his face looked grim, looking back into dark memories, so instead I asked, "And now you don't hate them? Why is that?"

He focused on me. "I learned to see them through your eyes."

I wanted to turn away from his gaze, but felt pinned there like a captive butterfly. "You want to watch a movie?" I said, desperately reaching for equilibrium.

He raised his eyebrows. "At this hour?"

"It's how I get to sleep when I feel this restless."

"All right. Did you have something in mind?"

"I don't know. *Casablanca?*"

"Isn't that a little heavy?"

"I can't bear watching something light and frivolous when everything around me is so dark. It just feels wrong."

"Then *Casablanca* it is."

I left Malcolm to figure out my DVD player and got out some microwave popcorn. Tradition was tradition, even if Malcolm was still in his underwear and acting like that was no big thing. Really, I couldn't expect him to sleep in those filthy fatigues. So if it didn't bother him, it wouldn't bother me. I'd just have to ignore my burning awareness of him, of his lean, well-muscled body and his tousled hair and...

I closed my eyes and gripped the edge of the counter just below the microwave until the sharp line cut into my palms. Just a friend.

I heard the music of the title screen playing just as the microwave beeped. I poured the popcorn into a big bowl and went into the living room, where Malcolm was sitting on the couch with my pillow under one arm. I sat next to him—not too close, but close enough to share popcorn.

"Why don't you own digital copies of these movies?" he said. "It's more convenient."

"I started collecting these before digital was a thing, and now it's habit. Besides, if you own physical copies, you're not at the mercy of the internet."

"Or you could lose all your DVDs in a fire."

I scowled at him. "Just start the movie, heathen."

I caught him smiling as he pushed Play. The Warner Bros. logo filled the screen, then faded to the familiar outline map of Africa. I couldn't count how many times I'd seen this movie that I knew every detail.

I took a handful of popcorn and nibbled it, wanting to make it last so I wouldn't have to reach into the bowl again and possibly brush against Malcolm's fingers, doing the same thing. I stealthily watched him out of the corner of my eye. He was leaning on the arm of the couch, which meant his body was angled away from mine, and despite myself, I felt a pang that he was so determined not to touch me, even by accident.

I made myself focus on the film. It has a slow, measured pace to the first few minutes, laying the essential background, and I started relaxing even before the action picked up at Rick's Café Américain. "I don't know what it is about watching an old favorite," I murmured. "You'd think I'd get bored of it, but I never do."

"I know," Malcolm said. "There's something comforting about it."

I yawned. "Excuse me. I feel...not better, exactly, but as if my troubles are at a distance. I know it's probably not the same for you."

"No. But I'm better able to ignore my problems for an hour and a half than I was when I was lying here staring up at your ceiling."

"I'm glad." I wanted to ask him what he was going to do next, but Victor Laszlo and Ilsa Lund had just walked into the night club, and that would have ruined the mood. I took some more popcorn and settled myself more comfortably on the couch. "As Time Goes By"... was it a melancholy tune all by itself, or just by association with Rick and Ilsa's doomed love affair?

"Sam's not actually playing the piano," I observed dreamily.

"I noticed that. I doubt we're supposed to be looking at his hands."

Malcolm's last words were swallowed up in a yawn that triggered one of my own. I felt so relaxed my eyelids were drooping. I heard Humphrey Bogart's voice coming from very far away, saying "Here's looking at you, kid," and then the Germans were marching on Paris. I was falling asleep. I ought to go to my own bed and leave Malcolm to his, even if his bed was just my couch with a couple of sheets on it, but I felt so comfortable I didn't want to move.

A clap of thunder, then an enormous rattle startled me out of sleep I didn't remember entering. I was lying on something hard but yielding, and something heavy was draped over my shoulder. The scent of Malcolm's woody aftershave, and the faint smell of masculine sweat, surrounded me. I blinked, and sat up. Malcolm reclined in the corner of my couch, deeply asleep, his head thrown back and his arm just coming to rest on his lap from where it had lain across my shoulders. I'd had my face pressed against his chest and could still feel the warmth of his body where I'd slept against him. Malcolm looked so peaceful in sleep, younger and more vulnerable than he did when he was awake, and looking at him made my heart ache with longing.

I focused on the screen. There was the plane that would take Ilsa and Laszlo to Lisbon, taxiing across the runway. The propeller noise must have wakened me. Malcolm had to be truly exhausted not to have heard it.

I shook his shoulder, gently, and said his name. He came awake in an instant, his expression hard and fierce, grabbing my wrist and twisting my arm so I cried out. As swiftly as he'd grabbed me, he let go, looking aghast. "Helena, I'm sorry. I didn't know it was you."

"I'm not hurt," I lied, rubbing my wrist.

He took my arm, gently this time, and examined it. "A remnant of my time in the military," he said. "I'm used to coming awake under attack."

I just as gently removed my arm from his hold. His touch reminded me once again of how close we were, how informally dressed, and the urge to snuggle back into his arms struck with such force I couldn't breathe. "I'll have to remember that," I said, then blushed hotly at how I'd implied I might have reason to wake him in the future.

He didn't respond. On the screen, Ilsa and Rick were having their final scene together, and he was telling her she'd regret not leaving with her husband. "'Maybe not today, maybe not tomorrow, but soon, and for the rest of your life,'" I murmured along with Bogie. I glanced at Malcolm to find he was looking not at the television, but at me, and the intensity of his dark gaze unnerved me. "Do you think he was right?" I stammered. "That Ilsa would have regretted leaving her husband, even for love?"

"I suppose it depends on how important her duty was. Sometimes there are compensations, when you give up the possibility of love for your responsibilities." Malcolm leaned forward, resting his elbows on his knees. "What do you think?"

I felt as if our conversation were happening on two levels at once, one on the surface and another flowing deep beneath the first. "I think duty is a cold companion," I said.

He smiled, the briefest twitch of his lips. "That's almost poetry."

"A sad and terrible poetry. You don't...stop caring about someone just because you can't have him. Or her."

Malcolm nodded. "Even if that might be easier."

The music swelled with the closing credits, and the screen faded to black, leaving us in darkness lit only by the gray radiance of the television. Malcolm shifted his position, bringing him closer to me. "I'll get the lights," I said, and fumbled my way off the couch, brushing his leg as I went. I found the table lamp at the other end of the couch and turned it on, blinking in the sudden brightness, then turned to look back at Malcolm.

He still had his eyes on me. As I turned, his lips curved in the faintest of smiles. It was an expression of pure and simple pleasure, and my heart ached at being on its receiving end. I sank down onto the couch next to him. "I...think I could sleep now," I said, shyly, not sure if he could hear what I was asking.

"I think we already have," he said, his smile turning amused. "But a few more hours would be nice."

"Then I'll leave you to it." But I didn't move.

"Thank you again for giving me shelter," Malcolm said. "I owe you a debt."

"I didn't do it to be thanked. I...you needed help, and I couldn't abandon you."

"If you knew the condition of the place I'd intended to spend the night, you'd understand how truly grateful I am."

"Worse than a couple of sheets on a couch?"

"Much worse." He shifted position. "And the company is much less pleasant."

He smiled at me, flashing the devastating dimple, and my heart did a little flip-flop. Without thinking, I scooted closer, took his face in my hands, and kissed him.

It was like kissing a wall. Malcolm didn't respond in the slightest to my kiss, not even to move away. He just sat there and...*endured*. I pulled away from him and searched his face for some clue as to how I'd misread him, some reaction, even if it was disgust. Nothing. I might as well have been shadow, or stone, something unimportant and easily ignored.

Gently, Malcolm laid his hand on my shoulder. "Go to bed, Helena," he said, completely expressionless.

I snatched my arm away from his grasp and fled to my room without a word.

Safely inside, I flung myself on my bed and let humiliation burn through me. How could I have been so stupid? Nothing had changed. We still couldn't be together, and I'd made such a fool of myself. I'd never be able to face him again, ever. I was too embarrassed to cry. My brain insisted on replaying those few seconds, my lips pressed to his unresponsive ones, his voice telling me to go to bed, over and over until I wanted to stab myself in the ear with a carving fork to get it to shut up. Why had I believed things could be otherwise, no matter what I felt for him?

Because I loved Malcolm Campbell. And duty was a poor substitute for that.

I crawled under the covers and squeezed my eyes shut, curling into a ball, as if that would make the pain go away. I wished I could call Viv, tell her everything. What would Viv say? She'd tell me what she had two months ago when Malcolm had revealed how he felt about me—

Oh. Oh no. *Jason.*

My humiliation was overridden by massive, crushing guilt. I had a boyfriend. I hadn't thought about him this evening, not even as a reminder to stay away from Malcolm. I hadn't thought about Jason at all, which made me the most selfish woman on the planet. I thought more about Malcolm than I did about him. Holding him at a distance, denying him access to my apartment...I'd been cheating on Jason emotionally the whole time we'd been dating and never realized it. I groaned into my pillow and punched it a few times. Despicable, selfish, stupid woman. I didn't deserve someone as nice as Jason. Didn't deserve anyone at all.

I lay there berating myself for my stupidity until I jerked awake, only then realizing I'd been asleep. The world outside my window was light, and I checked my clock—9:22. Swearing, I rolled out of bed and hurried to the door, where I stopped, hand on the knob. Suppose Malcolm was still here? I couldn't face him. No, he'd have to leave before dawn.

I slowly opened the door and peered out. I couldn't hear any noises of someone moving around. I tiptoed down the hall and peeked into the living room. The sheets and blanket were neatly folded on the couch, with the pillow balanced atop the stack. I walked to the couch and saw a small piece of paper atop the pillow. *Thank you,* it read in Malcolm's elegant script. I clutched it and burst into noisy, irrational sobs.

When my tears ran out, I went into the kitchen and made coffee, which was about all I felt I could stomach. Then I dressed and did my hair, brushing it until my scalp ached. My eyes were red-rimmed, and my cheeks had two blotches high on my cheekbones, but otherwise I didn't look like a woman who'd had a crying fit. I put on makeup anyway. The bookstore would be full of Wardens today, and I didn't want anyone thinking I'd had a moment's weakness and helped a wanted fugitive.

I checked my phone. 9:52. I still had things to do, and maybe they'd make me late, but the Nicolliens could wait a few minutes. I texted Viv, though I wasn't sure what to say. In the end, I asked her to come by when she got off work. Immediately I got the response SATURDAY NO WORK 2DAY WHAT'S UP

I texted back EVERYTHING. COME FOR LUNCH?

I realized after getting her YES reply that I couldn't talk to her freely in front of Judy—couldn't tell Judy Malcolm had been here at all—but I needed comfort and reassurance so desperately I was willing to think of ways to get Judy out of the store for even a few minutes. Because my evening was going to be full.

I took a deep breath and tapped Jason's name. I would give anything not to have this conversation tonight, but it was past time I was honest with both of us. CAN I MEET YOU AT YOUR PLACE AFTER WORK? I typed. WE HAVE TO TALK.

13

*A*bernathy's felt colder than usual, with a wintry chill in the air that matched the chill in my heart. I should have been grateful for it; it was going to be an unusually hot day. I trudged through the store to the front door, wishing I'd dressed more warmly. There was already a line outside of people peering through the store window. Someone banged impatiently on the door. I felt like flipping her off, but tensions were already high and I didn't want to antagonize my customers further.

I flipped the sign to OPEN and unlocked the door. "Finally," said Brittany Spinelli, pushing past me. "Don't you understand what's at stake?"

"I'm sorry for the delay," I said, and held out my hand for her augury slip. "Everyone please form an orderly line, and we'll do this as quickly as possible."

"You'd better," Brittany said. "That bastard could have fled the country already."

"Campbell's not that sensible," said a man farther back in the line. "He'll want Will Rasmussen next."

I felt tears prick my eyes, and fled into the oracle before they could betray me. Once inside, I unfolded the paper. *How do I kill Malcolm Campbell?*

I'd known what they were all here for, but seeing it laid out so baldly in sharp, pointed black letters made me feel even colder. I looked around. This was a question the oracle shouldn't answer, and to my relief the oracle's light was blood-red like the light of a dying sun. No augury. I blotted my eyes and waited a few minutes to regain my composure, then went back into the store.

"There's no augury," I told Brittany, handing back her slip.

"What?" Brittany's eyes narrowed. "You're lying."

"The oracle won't tell you how to kill someone," I said, pitching my voice to carry over the low murmurs of conversation. "So don't bother asking."

The noise swelled into shouting, some yelling at each other, some yelling at me. I stood my ground until someone called out, "You're defending him, aren't you? I'll see you before a tribunal for violating the Accords!"

"I'm sworn to be impartial, and to carry out the will of the oracle," I said. "It's true I think you're wrong to try to enact vigilante justice when Lucia is carrying out the investigation. But I'll serve as I've promised no matter what those auguries say." I felt my throat close up on those last words and swallowed hard.

"Campbell deserves death for what he's done," Brittany said. "Amber was a good woman, and he slaughtered her like an animal."

"Then the investigation will prove that. Unless you think Lucia Pontarelli should go before a tribunal for not finding the results you've already decided are true. Now—if you have a valid request, I'll take it. Otherwise, get out of my store."

Brittany stared me down. She was several inches taller than me and muscled like a bodybuilder, and I had a moment's fear that she might attack me, she looked that furious. I kept my expression calm and determined, ignoring how sweaty my palms felt. What would I do if she hit me? Lie on the floor bleeding, probably. That angered me, that knowledge that I was helpless against her, helpless to save myself or to help Malcolm. My anger buoyed me up, and I stared back at her, daring her to strike.

Finally, she spat out a blistering curse and turned away. "I want another augury," she said.

"You'll have to go to the end of the line," I said. Fury flashed across her face again, but she stormed off, shoving people out of her way. I took the augury slip from the next man in line. *Where do I find Malcolm Campbell?* I ignored the despair filling my heart and walked into the oracle.

All morning, the requests were variations on a theme:

Where is Campbell?

What do I do to find Malcolm Campbell?

Where is Campbell hiding?

When will Campbell kill next?

After the third augury, I was numb with fear and horror. With my barely-formed faith I prayed, every time I entered the oracle, to see the blood-red glow of no augury. The blue-tinged light that had formerly filled me with such joy now seemed a harbinger of doom. Every book I took from the shelves bore the potential for Malcolm's death.

By the seventh augury I wanted to break down and cry at how I was contributing to this deadly hunt for the man I loved. One of these hunters would interpret their augury, and find Malcolm, and then someone would die. And if it was him...

I leaned against a bookcase, pressed my face against the unfinished yellow wood, and breathed in the smell of pine and old paper. "Why are you helping them?" I whispered. "They want to kill him. Isn't that crime enough for you to prevent?"

Silence. The oracle never spoke except through its auguries—and once when it was in extreme distress. Of course *my* turmoil meant nothing to it. "Answer me!" I screamed. "Say something that will help me make sense of this!"

The bookcases swallowed my voice. Motes of dust floated through the blue-tinged sunlight. Peace, unexpected and surprising, touched my heart. I shoved it away. I didn't want to feel peaceful. I wanted to rage and throw books and scream until my throat was raw. I flung the augury I held away to ricochet off a shelf, knocking three more books over. "I need an answer," I said. My words came out choked with tears. "Just one sign that I'm not contributing to a man's death."

I heard a sighing as of a great wind, though I felt nothing. A few more books toppled. Once again the feeling of peace came to me, easing my troubled heart. I closed my eyes and listened to the wind, imagining I could hear voices. They were unintelligible, speaking gibberish, but I felt less alone. "It's not enough," I whispered, wiping away more tears, but my fear for Malcolm and the pain I felt were draining away.

I opened my eyes and walked over to where the augury had fallen atop two other books I'd knocked off the shelf. One was a battered copy of a Julia Child cookbook, *Mastering the Art of French Cooking, Volume 2*. The other was much smaller, as big as my two palms side by side and as fat as Abernathy's instruction manual. Its spine was blank, and the numbers *1937-1939* were imprinted on the cover.

Curious, I opened the book at random. It was handwritten, not printed, and it seemed to be a diary. *December 17, 1937: The fad for aug. fam. prophecies continues. People are buying them as Christmas gifts for relatives, which strikes me as unorthodox and potentially frivolous. But the oracle fulfills their requests, so I must conclude it doesn't object to being used in this way. I like to pretend I feel its amusement every time one of these requests appears. Does the oracle understand our humanity, our frailties and flaws?*

I dropped the book in shock, then dove to retrieve it, hoping two impacts with the floor hadn't damaged it. Hands trembling, I turned to the first page. Written in very dark letters across the faint lines like notepaper were the words *The Diary of Silas Abernathy, 1937 to 1939*.

I clutched the book to my chest and closed my eyes again. "If this is an answer, thank you," I whispered. I wasn't allowed to request auguries on my own behalf, as that would violate the Accords, but there was nothing that said the oracle might not take pity on a custodian in extreme distress. *Or it's a coincidence. But some things are too big for coincidence.*

I retrieved the augury and brought it back to the customer, who had his arms crossed over his chest. "It's about time," he said, holding out his hand.

"Be polite, or I'll take it back."

"You can't do that."

All my fears for Malcolm, all my pain at my current situation, drifted at a distance. I was still heartsore, but something bigger than myself had taken hold of me and was buoying me up. "Watch me," I said, putting steel into my words, and was cheered further to see him recoil. Tentatively, he took the book from my hand and offered me an envelope full of twenties. Abernathy's was making good money off the Nicollien vendetta; I hadn't yet sold an augury for less than $2000. If they wanted to find Malcolm, they were going to have to work hard to do it.

The door slammed open. Judy blew through it, storming past people and forcing them to step aside. "Sorry I'm late," she said. Her voice was flat, lacking in its usual fire, and she looked as if she'd been crying. I could hardly blame her. She snatched the envelope out of my hand and grabbed the ledger and receipt book from where they lay on the counter. "I'll handle this. You do the next augury."

I set Silas's diary on the counter below the cash register and took the next augury slip. *Where is Campbell hiding?* It wasn't as emotionally difficult to read as the last one. I had Silas's diary. Everything was going to be all right.

I did nearly forty auguries before one o'clock, when the last Nicollien went away satisfied. It felt as if the oracle was trying to get rid of them as quickly as possible, though I couldn't imagine why. It was surely as indifferent to Malcolm's fate as it was to every other inquiry. Or was I wrong about that? If it was alive, as I suspected, it might have hopes and fears the way every sapient creature did.

I slumped against the counter and picked up Silas's book. It was covered in textured tan suede with little gold brackets capping the corners, and the words were imprinted in gold the way his other book, *Reflections*, was. I stroked the cover. It was like petting a mouse.

It even felt warm to the touch, warmer than the shelf it had been lying on.

"That's the last of them," Judy said, emerging from the back hall. "I hope one of them gets lucky."

"Don't say that."

"You'd better not defend him. I don't give a damn about your hopeless crush right now. He killed Amber and I want him to suffer."

The pain I'd been holding at a distance descended again. "Lucia will handle it."

"She's always liked Campbell. She won't stay impartial any more than you will."

"Shut up!" I shouted. Judy took a step backward in surprise. "Don't you *dare* accuse either of us of failing in our duty. I just spent three hours helping people who want to kill someone I...care about. You think it didn't occur to me to lie? To give them the wrong book?"

"I didn't mean—"

"You damn well did mean just that. If anyone's failing to stay impartial around here, it's you. You're hurt, and suddenly that means your promises fly out the window. I guess you were really a Nicollien all along, weren't you?"

Judy's lips compressed in a tight, angry line. "It's not the same."

"It's exactly the same."

The door swung open. "Hey," Viv said, "sorry I'm...is something wrong?"

"Judy was just leaving," I said. "She's going out to lunch, and she's going to think about what I said. And she might come back afterward."

Judy glared at me. "It's your store," she snarled, and pushed past Viv and out the door, making the bells jangle so hard I thought they might fly off. I slumped against the counter and buried my face in my hands.

"Wow, what did I walk into?" Viv put her enormous tote on the counter and leaned against the cash register.

"So much has happened, Viv, and I'm glad I fought with Judy because half of it I can't tell her."

"A story! I'd be more excited if I could see your face. You don't sound happy."

I lifted my head. "Malcolm killed someone. A powerful Nicollien."

Viv whistled. "He's an Ambrosite, right? I can't believe they're not all in here, wanting to find him."

"They were. It's been a busy morning. But that's not it. I gave Malcolm shelter last night, and he told—"

"What do you mean, gave him shelter? Did he sleep in your apartment?"

"On the couch. Stay focused. He told me he killed Ms. Guittard because she was one of the serial killers."

"She *what*? What do you mean, *one* of the killers?"

"Just that. Malcolm tracked her down and confronted her, and he had to kill her to defend himself. But nobody knows the truth, so he's on the run."

"What's Lucia doing?"

"Trying to find him before the Nicolliens do."

"You have to tell her what you learned."

"You have no idea how much trouble I'd be in for not calling her the second Malcolm showed up. Besides, I have no proof of Malcolm's story, just what he told me. It wouldn't make any difference. And the Nicolliens aren't listening to reason."

"Where did he go?"

"He wouldn't tell me. He was gone before I woke this morning." The memory of last night surfaced, and I cringed inside.

"What aren't you telling me?" Viv knew me too well.

"I did something stupid. I kissed Malcolm."

Viv gasped. "You did not. What did he do?"

"Sat there like a statue and then sent me away to my bed. Viv, I'm so embarrassed. I thought he...and I was so wrong."

"Helena, what about Jason?"

"That makes it a hundred times worse. I didn't think about him at all. I was ready to sleep with Malcolm and I totally forgot I have a boyfriend. What kind of awful person does that make me?"

"One who's in love with someone she can't have."

Tears slipped down my cheeks. "I thought I was over him because I had Jason, but the truth is I've never let Jason in the way I would if I really cared about him. I've been dreading the day he tells me he loves me, because I don't feel that way about him. And that's not going to change even though Malcolm and I can never be together."

"Are you sure about that?"

I remembered kissing Malcolm and the tears fell harder. "Positive."

Viv hugged me while I cried. "You're not an awful person," she said. "You made a mistake, that's all. Jason was your rebound guy, and we all know how badly those relationships can turn out."

I wiped my eyes with the tissue she handed me. "That's nice of you to say, but I think I knew on some level that I was using Jason as a substitute for what I couldn't have. I should never have done that."

"So what are you going to do?"

"What I have to. Break up with him. I'm so afraid, Viv. I don't want to hurt him."

"No way to avoid that. Get it over with quickly, that's the best way."

"I wish I could have you do it for me. You're experienced at letting a guy down easy."

Viv pulled an injured face. "I think there's an insult in there somewhere."

I laughed. "You know there isn't."

"Come on. Let's go upstairs and get something to eat. It's like raiding the refrigerator of the gods, what with all the food your mother gives you."

We collected our meals (veal parmigiana for me, baked ziti for Viv) and retreated to the break room in case someone came in. "So were you arguing with Judy over Malcolm?" Viv asked.

"She's siding with the Nicolliens and accused me of not being impartial."

"She's just upset. I'm sure she didn't mean it."

"Maybe, but she needs to remember as long as she's working

here, she can't take sides either. Ms. Guittard was a close friend of hers, and she's hurt and angry and wants vengeance."

"So you definitely can't tell her about Malcolm."

I forked up a bite and stuffed it into my mouth. "Nope," I said around my food.

"That's gross. I don't need to see what you're chewing."

"Then don't look."

I heard the door open, and quickly swallowed and rose from the table. "Can I help you?" I said to the short, thin man standing just inside the door. He wore a T-shirt with a Ravenclaw House crest and a really old pair of Birkenstocks. I vaguely remembered seeing him before.

"I'd like to use my safe deposit box," he said with a pleasant smile that warmed me. "It looks like I missed the rush."

"It was busy here just an hour ago," I said. "Please follow me."

In the basement, I looked up his name in the safe deposit ledger. "Jeremiah Washburn," I said. "Box G-243. That's one of the big ones."

"Probably too big, but I believe in being prepared." He inserted his key next to mine, and I pulled the box free and staggered under its weight. Washburn helped me get it onto the table. He was stronger than he looked.

"Thanks," he said. "I hope it's not an inconvenience."

"It's why Abernathy's is here. Well, not really. Abernathy's is here because of the oracle. But the safe deposit boxes are important to the magical community. So I don't mind."

Washburn put his hand on the lid of the box, and I turned away to give him some privacy. "Ms. Davies," he said, stopping me, "what do *you* think of all this? The murders?"

"I...don't know what to think," I stammered, caught off-guard by the question. "I know Mal—Mr. Campbell's team was close to catching the killer. At least, that's what they told me."

"Which makes Malcolm Campbell's killing of Amber Guittard mysterious, don't you think?"

"I...suppose so." How much could I reveal? I still felt bound to keep Malcolm's secrets, whatever else had passed between us.

"Very mysterious. I think it's unfortunate that so many magi have let anger and hatred blind them to pursuing our real enemy."

"I agree. This morning all of them wanted auguries so they could track down Mr. Campbell."

"Which you were forced to give them." Washburn smiled again. It was guileless, empty of hate, and it reminded me of Derrick's smile, though the two men couldn't be more dissimilar otherwise. "I honor you for it."

"Thanks, but I'm not sure I should accept praise just for doing what I swore I'd do."

"Keeping an oath under such circumstances is praiseworthy. Will it help at all if I tell you I'm convinced Campbell knew something no one else did?"

"If it means you're not out for his blood, then yes, it does."

"I think he was on the right track, and Ms. Guittard had something to do with his investigation. I don't know any more than that yet, but I intend to see if I can pick up the trail where he left off." He opened the box and took out an enormous gun, with a wide bore and a cartridge thicker than my hand. "Don't worry, this isn't a real gun," he said when he saw my shocked expression. "I think the Ambrosites are right to use tools to extend their fighting capabilities. This affects the nature of my familiar, altering its form to make it more effective against the invaders—and, now, against the serial killer."

"Can you turn a familiar against a human? I thought that was impossible."

"Impossible for a familiar to attack a human of its own free will. Commanding a familiar to attack...it's never done, but it's not impossible. I won't do it unless it's a matter of defending myself."

"Mr. Washburn, what kind of magus are you?"

He smiled again. "Wood," he said. "You won't have met many of my kind here in the city. We tend to work where there's plenty of material we have affinity to. But I've felt drawn to this fight, and I believe in never turning down a challenge when there's need."

Distantly, I heard the bells jingle. "I have to go," I said, "but... thank you. For not being irrational."

"I'm not sure I deserve thanks for doing what I swore I'd do," Washburn said with a wink. I laughed and ran up the stairs.

I met Judy at the break room door. "You came back," I said.

She nodded. "I'm...sorry. You were...right."

It sounded like something was dragging the words out of her. "Right about what?" I said, still feeling miffed.

Judy rolled her eyes. "About my not being impartial, all right? But I don't think you understand how much I cared about Amber. I want her killer brought to justice."

"And justice is a tribunal where Malcolm can give his reasons. Seriously, Judy, don't you think it's a little odd that Malcolm, who has almost no connection to Ms. Guittard, should just up and decide to kill her? I think we don't know the whole story yet."

"Amber would never hurt anyone. Are you suggesting she might have deserved death?"

"No, of course not." I couldn't tell her what Malcolm had said. "But a vendetta killing isn't the answer."

Judy sighed. "Don't think I won't pressure Lucia to do her job."

"I don't think she needs the reminder. But I agree. And maybe there's some way we can help."

"How can *we* help?"

"I don't know yet," I said, "but there has to be something."

14

I was impatient for two o'clock to arrive, bringing with it a rush of Ambrosites who, if nothing else, would not want auguries that would help them track down and kill Malcolm. But only a few Wardens showed up, all of them wanting the usual auguries about work and the future and even love. "Where is everyone?" I asked the last man, who was tall and fat and made me feel as if I'd shrunk.

"Staying home and out of the Nicolliens' way," he said in a bass rumble that felt like it should rattle the windows. "There's no guarantee a Nicollien might not attack an Ambrosite purely at random, just for being an Ambrosite."

"Surely they wouldn't do that. It's Malcolm they hate."

"Rumor is all us Ambrosites want to finally eliminate the Nicolliens, and this is the start of genocide. It's stupid, of course, but I can't say as I disagree with the sentiment. Get rid of them, with their deviant ideas and their evil familiars, make magery what it ought to be."

"Nicolliens aren't deviant," Judy said angrily.

The man glanced at Judy and dismissed her. "You're too young to understand the issues."

I grabbed Judy's arm and squeezed until she yelped. "Good luck with your augury," I said. I held onto Judy until the man left the store. "Sorry about that."

"You were right, I was going to start a fight with that goon." Judy rubbed her arm. "That's going to leave a mark."

"Maybe it can remind you to be self-controlled."

"I don't think I need that kind of reminder."

"Listen to this," Viv called out from somewhere inside the stacks. "'Thirty-two auguries this morning alone, most asking after matters of the heart. It seems springtime has roused our Wardens' appetite for love.' I love the way this guy talks."

"Are you reading Silas's diary? Stop that! It's my right as custodian."

"I think I'm falling in love with him. Was he cute? I bet he was cute."

"He was bald, Viv."

"Who says bald men can't be cute? Look at Jason Statham. Look at Dwayne Johnson."

"Yul Brynner," I volunteered.

"Who?"

I rolled my eyes. "*The Magnificent Seven*?"

"Nobody saw that but you."

"That is *so* not true."

"Anyway. The point is, bald men can be incredibly sexy." Viv came out from between a couple of bookcases and handed the diary to me. "Don't you have a picture of Silas somewhere?"

"In the office."

Viv darted away. Judy snorted with laughter. "She's odd," she said.

"Enthusiastic. Exuberant. Okay...odd too."

The bells jingled. "Hey, Helena," Derrick said. He was followed by Olivia and Hector.

"I'm so glad to see you! Has Malcolm contacted you?" I set the diary on the counter and gave Olivia a hug. She smelled like someone who'd slept rough for a couple of nights on the floor of a dirty garage.

"No. We were hoping...he hasn't contacted *you*, has he?"

"I haven't heard from him," I lied, hoping my face wouldn't give me away.

"Damn," Derrick said. "We're never going to find him if he doesn't want to be found. About all we know is he hasn't left the country, and that's only an educated guess."

"How can you be sure?"

"Because he hasn't caught this killer yet, and he'll stick to that no matter how it endangers him," Olivia said. "I wish he weren't so stubborn. He needs to go to Lucia and tell her what happened."

"So why hasn't he?" I asked. This duplicity thing was starting to grow on me.

Derrick shrugged. "Who knows? The last we heard from him, we were all going home for a few hours' rest. I should have known he had something else in mind from how quick he was to agree to that proposal. Then everything blew to hell and back. There's just no reason for him to attack Guittard. They barely knew each other."

"So you think it wasn't something personal?"

"*I* think it had something to do with the serial killer," Olivia said, flicking a glare at Derrick. "I just don't know what. Maybe an illusion that made him believe she was the killer?"

"Campbell wouldn't fall for that," Derrick said, in a weary tone that said they'd had this argument before.

"Illusions can be powerful. And he's good, but he's not infallible."

"Enough," Hector said. He handed me an augury slip. "We need a better lead than guesses."

The slip, as I could have predicted, read *Where is Malcolm Campbell?* "I hope it brings you luck," I said, and stepped into the oracle.

The book was right in front of me, as if the oracle was impatient with all the questions and wanted this one over with as soon as possible. I gathered it up, hugging the large atlas to my chest to feel the electric tingle spread through my body. "This could be good news," I said, offering the book to Hector. "$5000."

"It had better be, at that price," Hector said, reaching for his wallet. "Come on, you two, pony up."

141

"Judy will write you a receipt," I said. "Maybe it will be like Silas's augury, and open to the map that shows where he is."

"It's an atlas of South America, so I doubt it," Olivia said. She handed Judy a wad of cash. "This was easier when we had Campbell and his *sanguinis sapiens* fortune."

"I always wondered why he has so much of it."

"Wardens pay for his security services in raw magic, because it powers so many of the systems." Derrick watched Judy count the cash, but his attention was on me. "Campbell takes half his own salary in the same because it's a more universal medium of exchange in our community than cash. He pours a lot of resources into fighting invaders."

"Which is why I find it impossible to believe he just murdered Guittard," Olivia said. "He would never do something that would start a war between the factions. It would weaken our position in the Long War."

"I know he had a good reason for what he did," I declared.

"Let's hope you're right," Olivia said. "He's been under a lot of pressure lately. I guess it's not impossible that he just snapped. That's happened before."

"But not to someone like Campbell," Derrick said. "Canales, you have the augury?"

"I don't think we should study it on the premises," Hector said. "Don't want to put Helena in an awkward position."

"Thanks," I said. "You're probably right."

"We'll let you know when we learn something," Olivia said with a smile, and the three of them trooped out of the store, letting the door bang shut behind them.

"I think you know more than you're letting on," Judy said.

"What? Why would you say that?" I tried to keep my composure, but I was sure I looked guilty.

"You weren't nearly as frantic about Campbell as I thought you'd be. And you didn't demand details about what he seemed like when they saw him last. What aren't you saying?"

"I just...feel confident they'll find him, and the truth will vindicate him."

"Uh-*huh*," said Judy. She wore a skeptical expression and had her arms crossed over her chest. "I don't buy it."

"Well, there's nothing else for sale."

"I'm officially in love," Viv said, dancing past us and snatching Silas's diary off the counter. "Do you think he would go for a beautiful drummer with a colorful fashion sense and a gift for having fun?"

"Silas died fifty years ago, Viv. He probably would have thought you have crazy hair."

"I don't think so. He doesn't seem the conventional type. It's weird, reading his diary and knowing he's going to abdicate in a few years. He doesn't give any hint that he intends to."

"I wonder how soon he realized it? He abdicated in 1941, which isn't in this volume, but in *Reflections* he said the idea came to him on and off for months before he acted on it."

"I still think he was irresponsible to abdicate," Judy said. "He left the oracle vulnerable for weeks while they searched for a successor."

"You have to follow your dreams," Viv said, "otherwise what's the point of living?"

"I believe in being responsible."

"Boring."

The door jingled. "Thank you for interrupting that conversation," I said to the woman who entered. "Augury, or safe deposit box?"

The afternoon passed slowly and yet too quickly. Time dragged between customers, with none of us able to maintain a conversation for more than a minute at a time. I was painfully aware of what I couldn't tell Judy, and it hampered my desire to speak at all. Occasionally I dipped into Silas's diary, which despite its light, amused tone dwelt only on mundane matters. Silas's life as custodian was very much like mine, though he hadn't had to defend the oracle against giant monsters like puddles of black goo, or fight off a swarm of invaders armed only with a polearm made of rebar. 1937 had been a quiet year, with no hint of the war that was on the horizon, or none that Silas made note of, anyway.

And yet throughout this long, slow afternoon, I was conscious of six o'clock approaching inexorably, bringing with it the confrontation with Jason. I didn't know what to say to him. When I'd broken up with Chet, my only other serious boyfriend, he'd burst into tears and made an embarrassing scene, and all I'd done was told him I wasn't interested in him anymore. This was so much more difficult, and my sense of guilt complicated matters. I'd only been partially joking when I suggested Viv do the breaking up for me. She cared about the men she dated, even when the relationship was over, and she always knew what to say to make the blow less severe. I wasn't sure I wouldn't just trample on Jason's heart like some awkward foal, staggering to find its footing.

Finally, Judy came past, carrying her purse. "I'll see you Monday," she said. "And...thanks for setting me straight."

"Good night, Judy. I hope everything's settled soon. I want you to have justice." *And I want Malcolm vindicated.*

I went upstairs, where Viv was lounging on my couch watching television. "I have to go see Jason now," I said.

Viv sat up and turned off the TV. "You want to meet me afterward for dinner?"

"I...probably. I'll need someone to remind me I'm not a total bitch."

Viv put her arms around me. "You're not a bitch, and you care enough about Jason not to want him hurt. Just make sure he understands that. After that...you're not responsible for his reactions. If he gets upset—"

"And why wouldn't he?"

"If he gets upset, that's his business. Just don't do anything stupid, okay?"

"Like what?"

"Like agree to give it another shot just to make yourself feel less guilty and him feel better. You have this habit of making yourself into the woman your boyfriend thinks you should be. The best thing I can say about Malcolm Campbell is you've always been yourself around him. Not that I should encourage you to think about what you can't have."

I nodded. "I'll text you when it's over."

The drive to Jason's apartment went far too quickly. The grounds crew was busy trimming the hedges when I drove up. Some of the workers were shaping the topiaries on each end to look like bunnies sitting back on their haunches. Usually I found the sight pleasantly whimsical, but tonight all I could think was this was probably the last time I'd see it.

I knocked on Jason's door. We hadn't reached a point in our relationship where I had a key. Maybe that meant Jason wasn't that attached to me either. Maybe he wouldn't be too hurt. I felt relieved for about two seconds before guilt set in, guilt that I was trying to find ways to make this less awful. I wiped my hands on my pants. I would just have to be honest, and let Jason worry about his reaction.

The door opened. "Hey, hon," Jason said, and kissed me. "Come on in. I feel like I haven't seen you in forever."

"It's been a couple of days," I agreed. I followed Jason across the hardwood floor of his front room and sat beside him on his overstuffed couch. His living room was kind of bare, with just the couch and a television hung on the wall above a cabinet holding his cable receiver and an Xbox. He didn't even have curtains on the huge picture window that looked out on the parking lot, just white wooden slat blinds. Now that I knew what was behind my reluctance, I couldn't see how I'd ever fooled myself into thinking his place was nicer than mine. Bigger, and more modern, but it lacked heart.

"You want to go out to dinner?" Jason said. "Or we could stay in, if you'd rather. Order pizza, fool around—"

"Actually, there's something we need to talk about." He always referred to sex as "fooling around." Maybe that should have been a warning. "It's important."

"You look serious. What's up?"

I took a deep breath. Here it came. "We need to break up."

Jason blinked at me, blank and uncomprehending. I could see the moment he understood what I'd said. His eyes widened, and his mouth fell open. "Break up? Why?"

"Because…" I took another deep breath. "I'm in love with someone else."

"Wait—what? Who?"

"No one you know. A customer at the store. I just don't think it's fair to either of us if my heart's not in this relationship."

Jason shot to his feet. "I don't believe this. I thought we had something special."

"Jason, it's not like I don't like you. You're funny, and interesting—"

"But that's not enough for you."

"No. I'm sorry. You're a great guy."

His jaw went rigid briefly, as if he were swallowing a shout. "And that's supposed to make me feel better. I'm a great guy."

"I don't know if anything I could say would make you feel better about this. I'm sorry."

"How long have you been cheating on me?"

"What? I'm not cheating on you!" But my cheeks were rosy with memory. Did one kiss, one unreciprocated kiss, count as cheating?

"Like I'm supposed to believe that. Is he why you never wanted me to come to your apartment? That's where you meet him?"

"I don't meet him anywhere. I just can't lie to myself anymore."

"But you didn't care about lying to me." Jason took several angry steps toward the window.

"I didn't realize how I felt until last night. He and I aren't together."

"I don't care." Jason laughed again, a short mirthless bark. "It's not like I loved you, you know. You're cute, and you're a good lay, but that's all it ever was between us."

"Jason, don't be a jerk."

He spun around to face me. "Did you want me to beg you to change your mind? Take me back? I've got more self-respect than that."

"No, but don't act like that."

"You're so big on not lying, well, I'm not going to lie to you so you can get off on my pain. I'm upset, sure, but I'm not going to pretend I'm hurt worse than I am. I don't need you."

I stood. "I really am sorry, Jason. And I enjoyed being with you. I just don't love you, and that's not going to change."

"Get out."

I let myself out and went to my Honda Civic, then sat there staring at the dashboard for a minute before realizing Jason could probably see me, and who knew what he might think? So I drove around to the far side of the lot and parked, clutching the wheel and occasionally shaking. I hadn't expected Jason to be so vicious, and it hurt more than I'd thought it would. Not because of his cruel words —nothing he said mattered, and most of it probably came out of his pain and humiliation—but that he so easily made light of our relationship. I really had liked him, but I wondered if he'd ever liked me.

I pulled out my phone and texted Viv, IT'S OVER. NEED FOOD.

Her reply came so quickly I was sure she'd had her phone in hand, waiting. PICK ME UP.

I put the car in gear and headed toward the freeway. I felt empty inside, but in a good way, a freeing way. How long might that relationship have gone on without me knowing what kind of person Jason was? At least something good had come of kissing Malcolm.

The memory made me cringe again, but this time it was buried under my fears for him. I wondered how long he could stay ahead of dozens of hunters, all of them skilled at tracking their prey. And not only did he have to avoid them, he had to track his own prey, find the serial killer and bring him to Lucia. I clenched my hands on the steering wheel and sent up a silent prayer, though I wasn't a particularly religious person and I wasn't sure I was doing it right. I just hoped Malcolm could find the killer before anyone found him.

15

*T*he shrill beeping of my alarm clock jerked me out of a dream of running naked through a field of buttercups. I slapped it a couple of times until I found the snooze button. My head felt like someone had filled it with molten lead and given it a good stir, my eyes ached, and my mouth tasted like rotten meat. Why had I set my alarm for—I eyed it blearily—seven o'clock on a Sunday morning? Why had I set it at all? I was having dinner with my family later, but that was no reason to get up early. I closed my eyes against the pounding in my head. This was why I never got drunk: I got hangovers from hell.

It was coming back to me now. I'd gone to dinner with Viv, and then we'd gone for drinks, and sometime in there I'd told her I was going to save Malcolm's life. I'd had a plan for it, too, one I couldn't now remember. I'd been aware enough to call a cab to take me home, so I couldn't have been that drunk, but this hangover was making it hard for me to remember. It was probably a bad plan, like most things are when you think of them while drunk. Something about using my head.

Right. I was going to investigate Amber Guittard.

I pressed down on my lidded eyes, trying to keep them from

popping out of my head. My memory of the previous night was almost nonexistent. How had I intended to do that? And what was I hoping to achieve? Well, that was easy—I wanted to find evidence that she was connected to the serial killer. No one would be looking at her as anything but a victim. And if she'd actually killed two people, as Malcolm had said, there might be evidence of that.

I groaned and rolled out of bed, padded barefoot into the bathroom, and swallowed some pain pills. Then I went to the kitchen and made coffee. Now I remembered why I was up so early; I was going to visit the Athenaeum, greatest repository of knowledge both magical and mundane in the world. Probably it wouldn't be busy on a Sunday morning, but I had no idea how long this little quest was going to take. It was possible what I needed wasn't in the Athenaeum at all. But it was the only lead I had.

Fed, dressed, and with my teeth thoroughly brushed, I called a cab—I'd have to retrieve my car from the club later—and headed downtown.

The Athenaeum access point for Portland was in a florist's shop off Washington that looked like an old-time movie theater. I went inside and came face to face with a stranger, browsing the shelves and pots full of flowers and greenery. I reflexively smiled, but the man ignored me. I went around the other side of the display and pretended to be interested in the blooming poppies there. Was this guy a magus, or what? I couldn't enter the Athenaeum with him standing there if he wasn't.

A woman with blond dreadlocks and piercings in her nose and eyebrow pushed open a door behind me. I jerked my head in the direction of the man. Irina ignored me. This was typical of her; we'd never become friends. "Can I help you?" she asked the man.

I listened with half an ear to their discussion. The man was going to the hospital to visit a sick friend. *Why didn't he get flowers at the hospital gift shop?* I ran my fingers along the smooth curve of a poppy petal. I'd never seen poppies in a floral display before. Irina led the man around to my side of the display. "I think you'll find what you're looking for *on the far wall*," she said to me, emphasizing her words just slightly.

That was invitation enough for me. I crossed the room, avoiding the tall Greek vases that tipped if you brushed them even slightly, and with a final glance to see if the man was watching, ducked through a wall of green-and-yellow striped grass.

The room beyond smelled of loam, though aside from a couple of benches and tall tables it was empty. I moved one of the tables aside and pulled up on a black iron loop that blended with the dark floor, heaved the hatch aside, and knelt down to flip a switch. Lights bloomed beyond the hatch, revealing a shaft about three feet across lined with aluminum. I crawled over to the rungs mounted in one side and began my descent.

The passage to the Athenaeum felt shorter every time, probably because I knew better what to expect, and I never felt claustrophobic anymore, but it still was my least favorite part of the procedure. When I reached the bottom, I hurried through the arched doorway to the hall beyond, which was lined along the floor with the kind of emergency lighting you see on airplanes. The hall and floor looked like riveted sheet metal, but the floor was springy, like foam rubber, and I had to walk slowly to keep my balance.

I touched the first door I came to, and it slid open, revealing lights blossoming in pairs to illuminate the space beyond. Its egg shape always reminded me of a cheesy '70s science fiction movie, a pod in which the heroes escape the clutches of the evil space villain. There was no furniture, no seats, just a waist-high pillar of white ceramic. I inhaled the slightly warmer air that came from within and smelled the usual burnt-peanut aroma. Today it made my queasy stomach roil. I stepped inside and the door slid shut behind me.

I stepped up to the pillar and pushed open the sliding compartment near the center of the flat top, between two palm-sized rubbery disks embedded in its surface. Inside was a sharp hollow needle like a hypodermic. I opened my oversized purse and took out a miniature aluminum briefcase that looked like the sort a teddy bear would carry if it were a secret agent. I popped it open to reveal a foam honeycomb filled with vials of *sanguinis sapiens*, their bluish contents swirling in unseen currents. I hadn't known how much to bring for this, so I'd over-packed. This represented thousands of dollars of my own money, since I didn't think I could justify spending the store's funds on my personal business. Even if it ultimately served all of magery.

I took out a vial and pressed its rubberized seal against the tip of the needle until it touched the base of the recess. Letters flashed on the wall in front of me in dozens of languages, among which was English: PAYMENT ACCEPTED. YOU HAVE [21] CREDITS.

I placed my palms against the rubbery disks, and the wall cleared, the letters replaced by a pinpoint of white light that traced a spinning circle in the center of the wall. It spun fast enough to turn into a solid line, which blinked at me, faster and faster, until a silent "pop" sent silver glitter all across the screen. The glitter started forming letters, but I'd done this before. "I'd like to search in English, please," I said.

The room exploded with white light coming from deep within my own eyes, impossible to block out. I blinked a few times until my aching eyes adjusted, and pressed my palms more securely against the disks.

Welcome to the Athenaeum, a woman's voice said inside my head. I wasn't hearing her with my ears any more than I was seeing the light with my eyes. She sounded like the channel 2 weekend news anchor yelling at me. "Normalize volume," I said, wincing. This happened maybe every third time I came here, and I'd asked Irina and Guille, the access point attendants, if they could do anything about it. They'd said I was the only one who'd ever complained, like that was an answer.

Volume has been adjusted to your tolerances. Her voice was more comfortable now. *What would you like to learn about today?*

"Amber Guittard," I said. "From Seattle."

The whiteness whirled like a blizzard. Specks of gray appeared, whizzing about like dusky bees, hovering and then zipping away. They left right-angled lines like an Etch-a-Sketch that faded with time. *There are fifty-seven hundred records relevant to [Amber Guittard] +* *[Seattle]. How can I narrow your search?*

"Do you have any lists of her movements over the last ten days?"

The bees whirred about. *There are zero records relevant to your* *search. Would you like to try different search terms?*

Well, it had been a long shot. "How about...Amber Guittard and mysterious deaths."

There are seven records relevant to [Amber Guittard] + [mysterious *deaths]. Would you like to narrow your search further?*

"No. Display records visually."

An outline of a standard tablet appeared hovering midair in front of me. It had seven little rectangles like tiny book covers on it. I tapped one and the image swelled to fill the wall. It was a newspaper article about a heat wave in Chicago seven years ago in which fourteen people died. Guittard had given a statement to the newspaper about how to prevent heat-related death. I'd known she was a doctor, but I hadn't realized she hadn't always lived in Seattle. This didn't seem like a very mysterious death to me—unfortunate and sad, maybe. I moved on.

Three more newspaper articles had Guittard making some kind of statement about an unexpected death, but these really were mysterious, at least as far as the public was concerned. The individuals concerned were all high-profile, and they'd all died of stroke or something similar, but I knew from the descriptions that they'd all been killed by invaders. If someone were looking for a conspiracy, they might be suspicious at Guittard's involvement, but I wasn't sure this was evidence that Guittard was a killer. If she'd killed those three people, it was hard to imagine her being so openly involved with their autopsies. Or maybe that was part of her cover. I set those aside for later examination.

The fifth item was an article from a medical journal for magi, based on the title, which was "An Inquiry Into the Causes and Pathology of *Sanguinis sapiens* Extraction." The medical jargon was too complicated for me to follow, but the abstract summarized it as a study about how to most effectively extract *sanguinis sapiens* from a

THE BOOK OF MAYHEM

body. Amber Guittard's name was at the top of the study. It sounded gruesome, even if they were talking about removing it from a dead person and not a live one, but it was the first real piece of evidence I had: Guittard was an expert at extracting raw magic, and what little I did understand suggested the technique was the same whether the person was alive or dead. So I knew she was capable of committing that kind of murder. Unfortunately, there were a lot of other people who had the same ability. Guittard was different mainly because she wasn't a bone magus, as it was mostly bone magi who extracted *sanguinis sapiens* from dead Wardens. I closed that document and moved on.

The next document was Guittard's true death certificate, produced for the Athenaeum's records. It was different from her public death certificate, which would reflect the illusion Rasmussen's people placed on her to disguise her actual cause of death. I didn't know what they'd made it look like she died from, but it would be something that wouldn't look mysterious to the non-magical folk who handled her body. But the one in the Athenaeum was accurate. Cause of death: exsanguination due to a knife wound to the heart. *Oh, Malcolm.* I wondered why this had been tagged as mysterious. That might be Lucia's influence, refusing to condemn Malcolm out of hand, so the mystery would be the motive behind the murder.

I went to the last document feeling hopeless. Of course Guittard would have covered her tracks. What had made me think I could find what Malcolm couldn't?

It was a list of names:

Tiffany Alcock

Carlos Solorio

Johnathon Derleth

Aaron Hesse

Samantha Bannister (Ambrosite)

Mike Lavern (Ambrosite)

Shonna McNally (Ambrosite)

The victims—but what did this list have to do with Guittard? "Help," I said.

Accessing help files. Please state your request in the form of a question. The man's voice sounded like Robert Downey, Jr., which would comfort me if I weren't so distressed.

"How do I find out where a record came from?"

Say "display provenance."

"Exit help. Display provenance."

A new, smaller screen bordered in red and overlapping the document flashed into existence.

Document produced by Malcolm Campbell.

Seeing his name was a jolt to the chest. Malcolm had written this out, and submitted it to the Athenaeum, but why? He must have thought he would need it as evidence. And it looked off, somehow. "What is the connection between this document and Amber Guittard?"

Amber Guittard examined each of the bodies on this list for evidence of forcible extraction of sanguinis sapiens.

"Huh."

Please repeat your last input.

"Oh. Um...display a list of all people killed by extraction of *sanguinis sapiens* in Portland, Oregon—not by invaders—in the last ten days, in chronological order."

The screen cleared. A list of names appeared:

Tiffany Alcock
Carlos Solorio
Mary Gilbert
Johnathon Derleth
Aaron Hesse
Martin Wellman
Samantha Bannister
Mike Lavern
Shonna McNally

"Display this list side by side with the last document viewed."

There it was. There were two names missing from Malcolm's list. It was impossible that he'd mistakenly left them off. What had he said...that Guittard had killed two of the victims herself? Maybe those two were the ones she hadn't officially investigated, for fear of being linked to them. "Display as electronic files, but I'm not done searching."

What would you like to learn about today?

"I want to see any files submitted to the Athenaeum by Malcolm Campbell in the last ten days."

There are four records relevant to your search terms. Would you like to narrow your search further?

"No. Display visually."

You have insufficient credits to review all four records. Please apply another payment.

I popped another tube over the needle, and about half the liquid drained away. The virtual tablet appeared again, this time with four little rectangles. I prodded one with my finger. It was the list I'd just seen. I closed that and selected the next, and there was what I'd wanted: a map of Guittard's movements since she'd returned to Portland.

Malcolm had been thorough: the map was a detailed street map of the city and environs, color-coded with a key to the colors. He'd also scribbled notes in the margins in a much messier hand than I was used to seeing from him. There were times and dates next to all the red dots. I checked the key. The red dots were Guittard's location when the murders occurred. She'd been near every one of the victims except the two that weren't on Malcolm's list, when she disappeared from the map entirely.

Why did she kill them? read a note in the upper right, scrawled across the Columbia River. Looking at Malcolm's handwriting made me feel unexpectedly sentimental, longing to see him again. I swallowed tears and moved on to the next document. This one didn't make any sense to me; it was a sequence of numbers that looked like latitude and longitude, except bits of them were missing. A code, maybe? I set it aside to examine later.

The final document was a letter, written in Malcolm's usual elegant hand:

If you are reading this, it's likely I have failed in my attempt to wring a confession out of Ms. Amber Guittard. I have what I consider sufficient evidence that she is involved in the serial killings plaguing Portland over the last several days. What I do not have is the identity of her colleague, the man or woman who has committed most of the murders. I intend to leave this documentation in the Athenaeum to speak on my behalf, but I realize my confrontation of Ms. Guittard may result in my death. I can only hope that someone else will see what I have, for I fear the deaths will not stop until Ms. Guittard and her accomplice have achieved their mysterious goal.

He'd signed and dated it—the date was two days before. I read it over again, once more feeling a pang at seeing his handwriting. I was such a sap. "Display records to electronic files. Include information about provenance and dates the files were left in the Athenaeum."

Records saved. What would you like to learn about today?

"I'm done."

There was a whirring sound, and I bent to retrieve a flash drive from the compartment in the base of the pillar. "Thank you."

It was my pleasure, Helena Davies.

Shocked, I stopped where I was. "You know my name?"

Silence was my only answer.

"Can you speak to me?" Still nothing.

I took my half-empty vial of *sanguinis sapiens* and put it away in my briefcase. "Well, thanks again." I waved as I always did, feeling less self-conscious about it than usual. It made sense that the Athenaeum was partially aware, since it was a Neutrality like Abernathy's, but this was the first time it had shown that awareness toward me. It was unsettling.

I emerged from the access shaft to find Irina perched on one of the benches, wielding tiny pliers and a roll of green florist's tape. "Is he gone?" I said.

"No one's here but you and me," Irina said. She bit off the end of her tape and tucked it away somewhere within the blooms of her display.

"Oh. Well...thanks." I took a few steps toward the exit. "Um, does the Athenaeum ever talk to people?"

Irina looked at me as if I'd sprouted another head. "I've never been down there," she said, her faint accent growing briefly stronger.

"Ah. I see. Well...later."

I called another cab to take me to where I'd left my car last night, then drove home pondering what I'd learned. Nothing new, since it seemed Malcolm had followed the same path with rather more success. But I did have access to something he didn't: Abernathy's augury records. Maybe there was something the victims had in common, the magus victims at least. If I could figure out how to predict who'd be attacked next, maybe Lucia could set up an ambush or something. She could capture the killer, and force him to reveal that he'd been working with Guittard, and Malcolm would be exonerated. I'd just have to work quickly. Malcolm didn't have much time.

16

The first thing I did when I returned home was email Lucia, attaching copies of Malcolm's files from the Athenaeum. It wasn't enough to clear him of a crime, but it revealed his motives and I was certain Lucia could do something with the information. I didn't tell her I'd seen Malcolm, as I was still afraid she'd be furious with me if she knew, and I didn't want her yelling at me. Then I called and left a message. "It's Helena," I said. "I emailed you some documents I found in the Athenaeum. Malcolm didn't kill Ms. Guittard out of anger or a desire to start a war."

I hung up and tapped my fingers on my desk. My headache had almost faded away, and I felt energized by having made progress. What to do next?

I printed out the document that had all the victims' names on it and took it downstairs to the office. It was time to see if these magi had anything in common.

I pulled their augury records and sat at the melamine and chrome desk to go over them. The first thing they all had in common was that none of them had ever come in to Abernathy's for an augury. I opened Judy's database and brought up their customer records. Based on their addresses, they all lived within no more than ten minutes' drive of the store. I found a blank piece of paper and a pencil and made a note of this. Bannister and McNally had lived south of Foster Road, and Lavern lived off Deardorff. That made them virtually neighbors. Maybe the killer lived in that area.

Their auguries didn't tell me much. We didn't keep track of people's questions, just the books we sold them, so all I could tell was Bannister had requested only three auguries in the last fifteen years, while Lavern and McNally each had seven in the last twenty. None of them had requested auguries since I'd become custodian, so I'd never sent them anything and wouldn't be able to remember if their questions had been unusual or similar.

Discouraged, I filed the three folders away and sat staring at the computer monitor. *Hmm. Why not?* I typed in AMBER GUITTARD and pushed Enter. There was her file, with a series of addresses— she'd moved around a lot—and a thumbnail photo of her. I'd questioned whether this was necessary, and Judy had just said "The more information we enter, the more effective we'll be," and I'd shrugged and let her have her way. I looked at Guittard's face, open and smiling. No one would ever suspect her of being a murderer. But then, that was how people got away with crimes, by not looking like criminals. "Who is your accomplice?" I murmured. "What kind of man is he? Or woman, I suppose. Though I've heard most serial killers are men."

Guittard hadn't had many auguries, either. I checked her file and found that the last one she'd requested had gone out the day of the first murder. She'd come to Portland that night, so it was likely she never even saw that book, since we'd sent it to Seattle. *How to Win Friends and Influence People.* I wished I remembered her question. I couldn't imagine the outgoing and friendly Guittard needing that book for itself.

My phone rang. Lucia. I took a deep breath, bracing myself, and said, "Hello?"

"How in the hell did you find this?" Lucia shouted.

"I was looking for information on the killings and the list of names came up." A nice, safe, generic lie.

"You were, huh?" Lucia's voice went marginally quieter. "I guess it's not so weird that you'd care about this case."

"I don't want anyone else killed."

"Of course that's your reason. What else did you find?"

I leaned back in my chair, some of my tension draining away. "I gave you all the documents Malcolm submitted to the Athenaeum in the last ten days."

"No ideas about this list of numbers? Some kind of code?"

"I thought it was a code, yes, but I couldn't figure it out."

"I've got men working on it. We'll crack it, assuming there's something to be cracked."

It probably wasn't worth asking her to let me know when she solved it. "Did you know the three magi victims lived near each other?"

"Four victims, now. Sydney Eason was found dead early this morning. Another Ambrosite, like I need that kind of headache. And yes, Detective Poirot, I did know that. Eason lived east of Highland. Nowhere close to the other three. So that's another dead end."

"You did say you wanted anything else I'd found."

"True. Sorry, you can imagine I'm a bit touchy this morning. We're almost certain the killer was a wood magus, but other than that, the investigation is going slowly."

Cautiously, hoping my inquisitiveness wouldn't dry up her flow of information, I asked, "How do you know it's a wood magus?"

"Many facts that won't mean anything to you, Davies. And all the victims were killed outdoors, within a mile of their homes. Wood magi draw strength from nature the way steel magi draw it from metal. With as many victims as there are, it's a reasonable conclusion."

"I guess that narrows it down a bit. Mr. Washburn said there weren't many wood magi in the city."

"Washburn? Who's that?" She was back to sounding suspicious.

"A customer. He has a safe deposit box. Judy knows him."

"Really."

"You don't suspect *him*, do you?"

"I suspect everyone, Davies. I think I'll have a talk with your Mr. Washburn."

I wished I hadn't said anything. I liked the man. "I don't think he's the killer."

"Based on what evidence? Leave the investigating to me. Campbell hasn't contacted you?"

"I haven't seen him recently, no." A more dangerous lie, if she thought to analyze my words.

"You tell me as soon as he does, understand? And tell him to turn himself in."

"Are you really able to protect him?"

There was a pause. "I'll put my own life on the line to see he's unhurt," Lucia finally said. It sounded like a noble but potentially untenable sentiment.

"If I hear from him, I'll tell him that," I said.

Another pause. "You're not telling me everything you know, Davies."

"I'm telling you everything I can."

Lucia made a *hmph* sound. "Let's hope what you aren't telling me doesn't kill Campbell." She disconnected, leaving me with no one to deliver a scathing retort to.

I ruffled the pages in Guittard's file, then put it away. I didn't really know what I'd hoped to find. Maybe something in her file that screamed "I'm a serial killer, and here's who I'm working with." Still, Lucia now had Malcolm's information, and she could use that to prove Guittard had been working with the killer—not that that would put her closer to finding the killer, unless it did...

I rubbed my temples and yawned. Maybe I could take a nap before I headed out to see my family for one last dinner before Cynthia left tomorrow afternoon.

My phone rang when I was halfway up the stairs. "Did you see the news?" Judy demanded.

"No. What news?"

"Police had to stop a riot downtown. No one knows what started it

—no one outside the magical community, that is. Nicolliens and Ambrosites got into a fight and it spread from there."

"That's terrible! Did they use magic?"

"No magic. Just fists. But several people were arrested, and Lucia's refusing to bring magic to bear in bailing them out. She says they can sit in a cell for a while and think about what they've done."

I snorted with laughter. "I agree with her."

"So do I, for once. But my house is up in arms. Can I come to your place? I'm sick of my father repeating the same things in different combinations. It all amounts to how Lucia's not doing anything to keep the peace and we'd all have to be murdered in our beds for her to care."

"Okay, but I'm going to my parents' house for dinner in a few hours."

"Oh."

She sounded so forlorn I said, "You could come with me. My mom always makes enough food to feed an army."

"Could I? I mean, I don't want to intrude."

"I'll bring Viv too and then it won't be so much of an intrusion."

"Thanks. Let me in? I'm downstairs."

I hung up and, laughing, went back downstairs to open the door. "Come in and hear what I've learned."

"About what?"

"About why Malcolm killed Amber Guittard."

"What makes you think I'd want to hear anything about that?"

Too late I remembered Judy's connection to the dead woman. "We can talk about something else."

"No, now I have to know."

I threw open my apartment door and gestured for Judy to enter first. "You're not going to like it."

Judy scowled. "Tell me now or I'll spill *sanguinis sapiens* in your shoes."

"What would that do?"

"Nothing pleasant."

"All right. Malcolm had evidence that Ms. Guittard was an accomplice of the serial killer."

Judy had been about to sit on the couch, and now she froze, half-crouched. "You can't be serious."

"I found his evidence myself and turned it over to Lucia. She's taking it seriously." *I hope she's taking it seriously.*

Judy stood upright. "That's impossible. Amber would never do anything like that."

"Which is what Lucia's investigating. But you can see how, if Malcolm believed that, he might have confronted her and started a fight. Or she did."

"Don't defend him to me."

"Sorry. I'm just saying—"

"It's complicated. I know." She finally took a seat and clasped her hands in front of her. "It's not true."

"Lucia will find out if it is."

"I hope so. Helena, can you imagine what this will mean if it's true? A high-ranking Nicollien working with someone who's killing off Ambrosites?"

"I wish Malcolm hadn't killed her. He—I'm sure he wishes the same."

Judy gave me a suspicious look. "You've heard from him, haven't you."

"I'd have told Lucia if I had."

Judy sprang to her feet. "You *have* seen him! Helena, if you're abetting a fugitive—"

"I'm not!" I exclaimed, though I knew my face had to be giving me away.

She waved a hand dismissively. "Look, if you want to break the law, who am I to stop you?"

"It's not like that. I just let him sleep here. *On the couch,*" I added when Judy raised an eyebrow. "One night. And I've told Lucia everything he told me...just not that I've seen him."

"You are going to be in so much trouble when Lucia finds out."

"Which is why she's not going to find out."

In the face of my pleading expression, Judy threw up her hands. "Fine, I won't tell her. But if you see him again—"

"I swear I'll tell Lucia immediately. Now that she knows he didn't just kill Ms. Guittard for no reason, she'll be better able to protect him."

"His motives don't change anything. He could be wrong about Amber." Judy sat and leaned back, stroking the maroon velvet with one hand. "He *is* wrong about Amber."

"Lucia will find out."

"I can't believe I'm putting my faith in Lucia Pontarelli, of all people. But I have to admit, much as she irritates me, she does know her job."

I sat in an adjacent chair and pulled out my phone. "I'll text Viv, and we'll hang out here until it's time to go. We can watch a movie or something."

"Not one of those dire old black and white films you're so crazy about. You know I like action movies."

"And Viv likes rom-coms. How likely is it we can find something we all agree on?"

SPENDING SUNDAY with my family and Viv and Judy was the perfect way to relax and forget about everything related to magery—except, of course, for Malcolm's plight, which was never far from my mind. My parents made the appropriate unhappy noises when I told them I'd broken up with Jason, but didn't push for details. Mom thought Judy was wonderful and said a couple of times how nice it was that I had such nice friends, an underhanded dig at Viv, whom Mom only barely tolerated. It wasn't Viv's fault we'd gotten into trouble so many times when we were younger. Well, maybe it was, a little.

Cynthia remained as pleasant as she had at dinner the other night and didn't call me Hellie once. The subject of her pregnancy didn't come up, but I wasn't surprised she'd decided to let Ethan be the next to know. I hoped for her sake he'd be excited about the baby.

Though, since I knew practically nothing about him, maybe him *not* being excited was best for both of them.

But my pleasure didn't last. Judy woke me Monday morning at seven to tell me there'd been another murder, this one conventional. "Rachel Dawson killed Morena Smittis about an hour ago. Rachel's an Ambrosite and Morena's a Nicollien. It looks like an ordinary shooting, if there's anything ordinary about that."

"So it can't be linked to the magical world at all?"

"Not unless Rachel starts spouting off about magi and her aegis and the Long War. Which she won't, if she wants to live to see trial."

I shuddered. Magi could be brutal with each other in protection of their secrets. "What do the police think the motive was?"

"I don't know. They'll come up with something. Anyway, my father needs me this morning, so I'll be in a little late. Eleven o'clock or so."

"Thanks for the warning."

I wasn't looking forward to opening at ten. Saturday's auguries, the constant stream of people wanting to know how to find Malcolm so they could kill him, had been a nearly unbearable burden. I wished I could scream at all those Nicolliens, tell them what their beloved Amber Guittard really had been, but I had no idea what use Lucia had made of Malcolm's evidence and the last thing I wanted was to screw up her investigation.

I went through my morning routine, even checking my email in a vain hope that Malcolm might try to contact me that way. Nothing but spam. I really needed a better email filter. At nine thirty I went downstairs and busied myself tidying up, ignoring the growing line of Wardens outside the shop. Only a few of them brought their familiars, which I counted as a blessing, even as their presence horrified me. Maybe they wouldn't turn on a human on their own, but Washburn had said they could be directed to do so. Malcolm, with his steel aegis, might be immune to having his magic drained, but he could be torn to pieces by a pack of invaders as easily as anyone.

At ten o'clock precisely I opened the door and smiled pleasantly at the magus first in line. "Welcome to Abernathy's. Please form an orderly line and I'll take care of your requests."

"I'm not here for an augury," the man said. He and the next three people moved toward me as one, like a four-headed bull. "We're here for information on Malcolm Campbell's auguries."

I took an involuntary step backward. "You want what?"

"We want to know what his recent auguries were. The questions he asked."

"We don't keep those kind of records. And I wouldn't give them to you if we did. Talk about a breach of privacy!"

"So long as the custodian performs the augury, a customer can have no assurance of privacy," said the woman to his left. "*You* know what it is, therefore you can reveal it to others."

"I'm sworn not to do that."

"Custodians have given up privileged information in times of extreme need," said the shorter woman to his right. "There is precedent."

"What precedent?"

"In cases where the augury recipient had committed a crime, the custodian worked with the Gunther Node to disclose confidential information."

I shook my head. This conversation had a huge audience, all of them eager to see what I would do. "You're not with the Gunther Node. Lucia would have told me if she were sending someone."

"No. We're...an interested third party."

"Even if I agreed with you, which I don't, do you have any idea how many auguries I perform every day? I don't remember any of Mal—Mr. Campbell's."

"That's no problem. Our glass magus can do magic that will enhance your memory. It will only touch on Campbell's auguries. Everyone else's privacy will be protected."

Sweat prickled beneath my arms. "You can't force me to agree to that."

The four heads looked at one another. "No," the first man said.

"We were hoping to persuade you to be sensible. If Campbell is the serial killer—"

"*What?*"

"He was in the vicinity of several of the deaths. He probably killed Amber Guittard because she knew he was guilty."

"That's insane. Who came up with this theory?"

"It's common knowledge. Please, Ms. Davies. Your knowledge may be the key to stopping these murders."

I raised my chin and stared the man straight in the eye. "Malcolm Campbell is not the serial killer," I said. "Lucia's investigation will prove this. And I won't give up privileged information for any reason. Now, unless you want an augury, I suggest you take your common knowledge elsewhere."

The man glared at me. The woman on his left made a move as if she wanted to punch me, but the second man, the one who'd stood still during all of this, grabbed her wrist. "You'll regret this," the first man said, and led his team out the door.

I let out a long, slow breath, then turned to face the crowd. "Anybody else want to make insane requests of me? Then let's have the first augury."

The steady stream of variations on *Where is Malcolm Campbell?* became tedious after half an hour. "I wish you'd do something about this," I whispered to the oracle as I entered once again. "It's becoming unbearable. Do you know how I feel about him? Does it matter to you that I might be contributing to his death?"

The oracle kept its silence. I sighed and removed the augury, *The Wizard's Dilemma,* from the shelf. $3500. Not the most expensive augury I'd had all day, but it was up there. I wondered why, if the questions were all mostly the same, the prices for the books were so variant. Maybe some of these books easier to interpret than others, and if so, were the easy ones more or less expensive? I thought about comparing the prices and titles, which would be easy with the new database, but decided it was a bad idea. I didn't think the oracle liked people running tests on it.

Judy was there when I returned, chatting with the Nicollien at the head of the line. "Have you heard the rumor that Campbell is the serial killer?" she said.

"I have. It's idiotic."

"I agree. Campbell might be many things, but he's no serial killer."

"Then how do you explain that he was in the vicinity of most of the killings?" said the Nicollien.

Judy rolled her eyes. "He and his team were hunting the killer. Of course they'd be in the vicinity. Use your brain for something besides keeping your ears apart, Lucas."

I took Lucas's augury slip and smiled at Judy, warmed at her defense of Malcolm, whatever had prompted it. "Can I be compelled to submit to magic that will let me recall what someone's augury question was?"

"Of course not. Neutrality custodians are exempt because of confidentiality."

"That's what I thought," I said, and sailed away into the oracle.

The Nicolliens were all gone by twelve-thirty. I sank onto the rickety chair next to the front door and sighed deeply. "I'm hungry."

"I brought food from upstairs. You don't mind, right?" Judy had a couple of plastic containers in her hands and an uncharacteristically eager expression on her face.

"That's last night's dinner, isn't it? You just wanted more of the roast chicken."

"That's not a crime."

Judy retreated to the break room. I followed her, rubbing my eyes. I didn't know how much longer I could endure these auguries. Something had to change, and soon.

The door bells jangled before I'd taken more than two bites of my ravioli. I groaned and put down my fork. "Don't you dare eat that."

"I have chicken," Judy said with her mouth full.

"And you said *I* have bad table manners," I said.

Cynthia was standing inside the door, dressed down in business casual. "I'm on my way to the airport, but I wanted to stop in and say goodbye."

"Thanks for coming," I said, and gave her a hug that didn't feel at all forced. "I—excuse me." Two Wardens came through the door, past which I could see a tiny black ball of spite and despair, the smallest familiar I'd ever seen. "Let me help these two, and then we can talk for a minute."

The two Wardens glanced at Cynthia nervously, as if they were afraid she could see their aegises imprinted on their foreheads. Both were elderly, but unlike my friends the Kellers, they were frail and the man had a tremor in his hands. "I—would like to know if you have this book," the woman said.

"Why don't I look?" I said, and took a few steps into the silence of the oracle.

The question was *How should we divide our fortune?* and it was such a relief after the dozens of requests about Malcolm I took a little extra time savoring the feeling of being surrounded by thousands of books, any one of which could be the answer to their question. Eventually I spotted it high on a shelf and had to throw a few other books at it to dislodge it. I put my impromptu missiles back, patting them in apology, and headed back to the front of the store.

"Here you are—" I began.

Two men had entered while I was gone. One was tall and thin, the other bulkier, but both of them wore dark sunglasses and suit jackets, and both looked grim, as if they had bad news for me. This was almost certainly true.

"Ms. Davies?" said Detective Acosta. "We're here to ask you about some stolen books."

"Stolen books?" I said, clutching the augury to my chest. "We haven't had anything stolen."

"We believe you may have *received* stolen books recently," Acosta said, smiling unpleasantly. He reached inside his coat and pulled out a piece of paper. "Recognize this?"

I took the paper from his hand. It was one of our receipts, filled out by Judy, with a title, date, and purchase price written on it. Below the price was written "pd. in trade and cash." It was muddy on one corner as if it had been ground into the dirt. "It's an Abernathy's receipt," I said.

Acosta's smile broadened. I hated that smile. I'd met Acosta and his partner, Detective Green, when my old boss, Mr. Briggs, had been murdered, and Acosta had thought I was involved. Then he'd showed up when my ex-boyfriend Chet had "disappeared" and suggested I had something to do with that too. I was pretty sure he had me on some kind of watch list down at the precinct, or wherever he and his partner lurked when they weren't harassing innocent young women.

Except, this time, I might not be innocent. Paid in trade...we didn't have any way to prove the books our customers brought in weren't stolen, and if the oracle didn't care enough to reject stolen books, it was entirely possible I *had* received stolen goods and hadn't known it. "It means the customer paid partly in cash and partly in used books," I continued.

"Can you tell us the name of the customer?"

"Um...I think so." The number of the augury was in the upper left corner of the receipt. I got out the ledger from beneath the counter and flipped through the pages. The database would be faster, but I didn't like leaving these two unsupervised in my store. "Mitch Hallstrom." I remembered the smoky smell of the books he'd brought in. Desperate, eager Mitch Hallstrom.

"What else can you tell us about him?"

"Do you suspect him of stealing books?"

"We'll ask the questions, Ms. Davies. Anything else?"

I decided against antagonizing the man further. "He's been in two —no, three times. He always pays with trade and sometimes with a little cash. What is this about, detective?"

Acosta wasn't paying attention to me. He was scanning the room, taking an inventory with his eyes. "Mr. Hallstrom may have participated in several high-end book thefts. We believe he used this store to fence his stolen property."

"I had no idea any of Mr. Hallstrom's books were stolen."

"Let's hope that's true." Acosta took out his notebook and wrote a few words. "Do you have any of the books Mr. Hallstrom brought in?"

"I...don't know. We don't keep a very good inventory here."

"We'll have to take a look around."

"Do you have a search warrant?" Cynthia said.

Both detectives focused on her. I'd forgotten she was there. "We don't need a warrant to browse," Detective Green said. "This is a bookstore."

"But you need a warrant if you want anything you find to be legitimate evidence," Cynthia said. "And you certainly need a warrant if you want to do a full inventory of the store. So I suggest you come back when you have one."

The detectives turned their attention to me. "It would be better if you cooperated," Acosta said. "Better for you, certainly."

"I'll be happy to welcome you back when you have a search warrant," I said, trying to keep my voice from trembling the way my knees were.

Acosta gave me one final, long stare, then followed his partner out of the store. I slumped against the counter. "Why does this keep happening to me?"

"You can't let them inventory Abernathy's," my female customer said. "It would kill the oracle, oh dear, kill it dead."

"What oracle?" Cynthia said.

My face felt suddenly numb. "Um," I said, but my tired brain couldn't manage anything creative. The two elderly Nicolliens looked like they might have heart attacks right there on Abernathy's linoleum floor. "It's...um..."

"I know what an oracle is," Cynthia said. "But what was she talking about? Killing an oracle? That doesn't sound like something out of legend."

"She was talking about Abernathy's," Judy said, prompting all of us to turn around and look at her. "Abernathy's isn't a bookstore. It gives out prophecies to those who know to ask for them."

"*Judy!*" I exclaimed.

"Sometimes you have to cut your losses, Helena," Judy said, approaching us until she stood nose-to-chin with the much taller Cynthia. "And she's not going to tell anyone. Are you, Cynthia?"

"I don't even know what I'd say." Cynthia turned to me. "Is this true? You run a store that sells prophecies?"

"Yes. They're called auguries."

"That's what that man was talking about last week. Augury. Not a book series." Cynthia's eyes were gleaming. "Do they always come true?"

"Yes. Sort of. Cynthia—"

"No, I believe you. It's just amazing. Why doesn't everyone know about this?"

"Because most people wouldn't believe it," Judy said, "and it's not intended for frivolous purposes."

That was a lie, but I guessed Judy didn't want to go into details about magi and the Long War. Cutting our losses didn't mean giving everything away.

Cynthia smiled broadly. "Oh, I won't use it frivolously," she said.

"Wait—what? Cynthia, you can't—"

"Why not? I know about it now, so why can't I use it?"

"There's no reason she can't," Judy said. "Call it trade in exchange for her silence."

"No one would believe it if she started talking about it. And I know the Board of Neutralities have some way of shutting people up." The thought of how permanent that shutting-up might be made me wish I hadn't said anything.

"I won't tell," Cynthia said. She looked hurt that we'd even suggested she might. "I just want to use it. Can't I, Helena?"

Her expression was so imploring I sighed. "You can't tell anyone, all right?"

"I won't, honest! But you should help these nice people. Is this the prophecy? This book? I don't think *The Double Comfort Safari Club* is much of a prophecy."

I explained how auguries worked while Judy filled out the ledger and the receipt for the Nicollien couple. They scurried out the door as fast as they could, casting frightened glances at me as if they couldn't quite believe I wouldn't have them arrested for accidentally revealing the truth about Abernathy's. Maybe I should, but they were so scared, I felt bad about doing it. Besides, everything had worked out, and my sister knew some of the truth about my life...

...my rapacious, no-nonsense sister who had a take-no-prisoners attitude toward life and the steely determination to get her own way. New York might be doomed.

I didn't tell her anything about the Long War, or magi, reasoning that Judy was right and the details would only confuse her. Maybe it was something I could tell her some other time. I couldn't believe I was contemplating sharing secrets with Cynthia, who a week ago was my sworn enemy. Maybe things still weren't perfect between us, but I felt friendlier toward her now than I ever had.

Finally, Cynthia hugged me, and said, "Well. We've exchanged some pretty big secrets. Thank you for listening. And for being my sister."

"Good luck," I said, "and thanks for wanting to spend time with me. Maybe we don't have as many differences as I thought."

"I'll call you once I've talked to Ethan." She kissed my cheek and waved goodbye. "Sorry to hear about your boyfriend, Judy."

"Uh...thanks," Judy said, casting a confused look at me. I shrugged.

When she was gone, Judy said, "Well, hell. Now what do we do?"

"We just gave access to Abernathy's to a non-magus, non-Warden who doesn't even know about the Long War," I said. "Do you think Lucia will kill us slowly, or will she make it quick?"

"I don't think anyone needs to know about this. We handled it the best we could, and Lucia can't blame us for that. Besides, there's always Margie and George to throw under the bus if we have to. It was Margie's fault, after all."

"I feel bad about blaming them. It's not their fault if they forgot Cynthia wasn't a Warden. People come in here all the time who are strangers, and I never ask to see their Warden cards. There's no such thing as a Warden card, is there?"

"No. But I take your meaning."

"It's funny, but those detectives were asking about Mr. Hallstrom—"

"What detectives?"

"My old friends Acosta and Green. Apparently Mr. Hallstrom has been paying us in stolen books. I was just thinking it's weird that I'd never seen him before a week ago last Friday. Did you know him?"

"I'd never seen him before. But I don't know all the Nicolliens in the city. Lots of them, but not everyone."

I walked away toward the back of the store. "Let's see what he left behind."

The box of books the oracle had rejected was still in the office. "I wish I actually knew anything about old books," I said, sorting through them. "I should probably give these to the detectives. I'm sure, if the stolen books were valuable, they've got a list. Though they might insist on searching the entire inventory if there are more than just these. Which there are."

"They were going to search?" Judy sat back on her heels.

"Cynthia made them go get a search warrant."

Judy stood up. "Call the Board of Neutralities right now," she said. "Get their lawyers involved. We can't let anyone search Abernathy's that closely."

"But they wouldn't," I said, and closed my eyes. "They would." I whipped out my phone. "I don't have Mr. Ragsdale's number."

"I do." Judy recited it for me. I waited, listening to it ring.

Finally, a voice said, "Ragsdale's office." It was a nasally female voice with a slight Brooklyn accent, making me wonder just where Ragsdale's office was.

"This is Helena Davies," I said. "I need to speak to Mr. Ragsdale immediately. This is an emergency."

"One moment, please."

"How long does it take to get a warrant?" I said.

Judy shrugged. "I only know about it from watching *Law and Order* re-runs."

"Ms. Davies," Ragsdale said. "You have an emergency?"

I quickly recounted the episode with the detectives and my concern about them inventorying Abernathy's and voiding the indeterminacy principle.

Ragsdale said, "Leave it to us. Just go on running the store."

"Should I give them the books we still have?"

"Put them aside for our lawyers to handle. Admit to nothing, but don't obstruct the detectives in any way. Don't worry. This isn't the first time Abernathy's has received stolen books."

I didn't like how casual he sounded about the possibility of the store being an accessory to crime, but if Abernathy's had accepted Hallstrom's stolen books in trade, it clearly didn't care about human laws, and there wasn't anything I could do about it. "Thank you," I said, and hung up.

"This doesn't tell us anything about Hallstrom, though," Judy said. "Just that he's a thief and we don't know anyone who knows him."

"I wish I knew what kind of magus he is. If he's a wood magus, and a loner, and a stranger to the community...couldn't he be our serial killer?"

"Why a wood magus?"

"Lucia said they were mostly sure the killer is a wood magus, based on where the attacks happened."

"I don't think Father knows that."

"He's not part of her investigation. I'm not sure she's bound to tell him everything."

"True, but he's trying to catch the killer too. It could only help him to know."

Startled, I exclaimed, "You can't tell him! That might be privileged information!"

"Don't worry, Helena, I'm not going to tell him. But I might lean on Lucia to do it."

I groaned and buried my face in my hands. "Is this day over yet?"

No Ambrosites came in at two o'clock. Around three-thirty, a couple of women in severe business pantsuits with their hair pulled straight back arrived. "The box, Ms. Davies," one of them said to me.

"The—oh, the box." I retrieved the box of Hallstrom's rejects and handed it to her. Both women nodded and left with no other word. It felt like I'd just had a visit from the Mob. If they were representative of the Board of Neutralities' lawyers, I felt suddenly more hopeful.

The store stayed mostly empty for the rest of the afternoon. Derrick and the team didn't appear. The detectives didn't return, with or without a warrant. A few Ambrosites came in toward closing time, moving furtively and checking their surroundings constantly as if they feared being attacked. I asked each of them if they knew Mitch Hallstrom; none of them did. Well, if he was a Nicollien, that made sense.

It occurred to me that I didn't actually know if he was a Nicollien. I'd assumed it because he always came in the morning, but I'd never seen him with a familiar, and if he was a stranger to Portland he might not even know about the curfews. The more I thought about it, the more I was convinced Hallstrom was suspicious. I tried to tell myself I was just desperate to find the killer so Malcolm could be exonerated, but my mind wouldn't let go of the theory.

Judy left early, explaining that she needed to be home for a meeting her father was hosting. "I keep telling him it doesn't look good, me playing hostess at a Nicollien gathering, but he always claims he's not doing anything partisan. I think he just likes having me around, like a security blanket."

"Or a teddy bear."

"Thanks, Helena, I've always wanted to be compared to a stuffed toy." She pretended to snarl at me and left by the front door.

I spent the last hour alternately prowling the shelves, hopelessly trying to identify the stolen books, and sitting behind the counter playing with the antique cash register. My thoughts kept drifting to Malcolm, wondering where he was, whether he'd found the killer yet, if he was thinking of me at all...Every time I drifted too far, I yanked myself back. Now was definitely not the time for daydreaming, not while he was in so much danger.

Once again I thought about the Accords and what they really said. Was it laid out in black and white that a custodian of a Neutrality couldn't be romantically involved with a member of a faction? Were there rules about strong friendships, too? Why shouldn't those be as forbidden as romance? Either way, you ran the risk of being partisan, using your Neutrality's powers on behalf of your lover or your friend. I pounded the glass top of the counter once with my fist. It was just so *unfair*. Hadn't I proved I could be impartial? I was going to find a copy of the Accords and I was going to go over it with a highlighter and a magnifying glass. I was tired of living my life in fear.

The door jangled open. "Ms. Davies," Detective Acosta said. "I'm glad we're not too late."

I checked my phone. "We close in ten minutes."

"We won't keep you long," Detective Green said. He walked a few paces toward the first bookcase and surveyed its contents.

"Did you bring a warrant?"

"Now, there's a funny thing," Acosta said. "There have been...difficulties...in getting a warrant to search this store. Abernathy's has some powerful lawyers, it seems. Don't you think that's odd?"

"I don't know. I just run the store. The owners don't tell me anything."

"I think it's odd." Acosta leaned against the cracked glass of the countertop. "We're glad you were able to find some of the stolen books."

Wow, those lawyers work fast. "They hadn't been shelved yet. I'm afraid I don't know if there are any others."

"We'll find them, if they're here."

Good luck with that. "Did you have any other questions?"

"Just one. Did Mr. Hallstrom give a mailing address when he purchased the books?"

"No, I'm afraid not. I wish I could help you with that." I was totally sincere. If I knew Hallstrom's address, I could get Lucia to send someone to roust him.

"I appreciate that. I believe you do want to help us, Ms. Davies. So anything you know—anything at all—it would be best if you shared that with us voluntarily."

"What else do you think I know?" His words had me genuinely puzzled. I had no idea what he thought I knew, unless he thought I was actually a fence and the frequent recipient of stolen books.

"I know about small businesses like this one. You get to know your customers quite well, don't you?"

Light dawned. "Oh, you think I know something about Mr. Hallstrom I'm not telling you because we're friends! I never met him before last week. Trust me, detective, I want you to catch the guy. Think about it from my perspective. He brought me stolen books, and he's probably taken stolen books to other stores. I paid good money for the ones I gave the police, money I'm not going to get back. Mr. Hallstrom cheated me, and I want him behind bars."

"That's a rousing speech."

"I meant every word. How did you even find out about Mr. Hallstrom to know he'd stolen the books? I wouldn't think book theft was a high priority case."

"It is when the books are as valuable as these. But we found him accidentally. He was camping illegally in the Powell Butte park and someone reported him."

"But—then didn't you capture him?" I wouldn't have thought there was anywhere in Powell Butte Nature Park that someone could secretly camp out.

Acosta smiled grimly. "We found his campsite, along with a box of stolen books and the receipt I showed you. He wasn't there and he hasn't come back. So we owe you thanks for putting a name to our thief."

"Um...you're welcome."

Acosta pushed upright and nodded. "Sure there's nothing you want to tell us?"

"Detective, can I ask you an insulting question?"

He raised one eyebrow. "Ask away."

"Is there something about me that screams 'suspicious character'?"

To my surprise, he laughed. "Good night, Ms. Davies," he said, and beckoned to Green. As the two of them left the store, I stared after them in disbelief. That had been a non-answer for sure. And yet Acosta had told me more than he had to...was it information I could use?

I locked up and turned the sign to CLOSED, then grabbed my car keys and purse and drove to a nearby convenience store. They had a display of maps near the cash register, and I bought one that showed Portland and nearby cities. It was probably too big for what I had in mind, but it was unlikely I'd find a map showing just east Portland.

I returned home and ran up the steps to my office, where I moved my laptop off Silas's desk and spread out the map. Powell Butte Nature Park was off-center and slightly toward the bottom of the map. I got out a red Sharpie and marked the location where Bannister had been killed, close to her house off Foster Road. It was the only address I remembered. I had to go downstairs to look up the other two addresses, then trudge back down a second time to look up the fourth victim, Sydney Eason, in the database for her address. I didn't know the exact locations they'd been killed, but the map was big enough it could handle a discrepancy of no more than a mile.

With my Sharpie I marked the other three deaths on the map and took a step backward to get the big picture. It was possible to draw a circle centered on the park that had all those dots within its circumference, but just as possible to draw a different circle centered somewhere else. I needed more data.

I drew a dot where Tiffany's house was, at roughly Powell and 122nd, and immediately felt heartened: it fit inside the rough circle centered on the park. Still not proof. I fired up my laptop and started doing some White Pages searches on the other victims' names. I only found four of the six, but all four fit within my circle. Either this was a huge coincidence, or I'd found solid evidence that someone based out of Powell Butte park had killed the victims.

I went for my phone, but hesitated to call Lucia. She was likely to blow me off again if this was all I had, as certain as I was of my conclusion. What I needed was to locate Hallstrom so I could have Lucia pick him up for questioning. I just wasn't sure how. If he came into the store...no, it would be too dangerous for me to try to apprehend him myself. And it would be too much to hope that he'd suddenly decide he needed a mail-in augury, complete with mailing address.

I folded the map and logged off. Maybe Judy would have an answer. For now, I was going to eat something and read Silas's diary. When you put it that way, it sounded more like snooping. But I couldn't imagine him not wanting people to read it if he'd left it in the store. Now I'd finally learn the story behind moving the oracle from England to the United States. It was almost enough to make me forget my fears for Malcolm. Almost.

18

July 16, 1938
> *Fifteen auguries today, and all of them received the same book:* Atlas of the Western States, *in varying conditions, but all with broken spines. All, when allowed to fall open freely, revealed the same page, a map of the city of Portland, Oregon. This is not the strangest thing the oracle has ever done, but it qualifies as peculiar as far as I am concerned.*

Events in Germany continue to disturb. Adolf Hitler in control of the German army is the sort of thing one fears happening, but auguries are silent on the question of what he intends to do with those armies. If he and Mussolini make common cause...but my business is that of the oracle, not of prophesying doom. (A little light humor never hurt anyone.)

I set the diary aside and stretched. It was almost ten and Abernathy's would be opening soon, but even though I'd overslept, I still felt weary. I'd stayed up far too late reading Silas's diary, and now that it was getting to the good part, I couldn't bear to leave it behind. I'd just sneak some reading in between auguries.

July 18, 1938
All of today's auguries were for the same Atlas of the Western States *as Saturday's. I wish I dared search the shelves to see how many more of these*

books we have. But that would be against the rules, and I think it might damage the oracle. We do not understand the principles it operates by, only that organization of any kind reduces its effectiveness, and knowing what is on the shelves makes an augury take longer to produce. So long as the auguries continue to be accurate, knowing whether there are a hundred such volumes doesn't matter.

"Are you reading Silas's diary?" Judy said, closing the front door behind her. "Anything interesting?"

"I managed to stop reading last night just at the part where the oracle started giving auguries leading to its moving here. It's fascinating stuff—at least, fascinating to me. How was the meeting?"

"Boring, and frightening, which I realize sounds contradictory. Father is talking about mobilizing his forces to actively defend against Ambrosite aggression. I think it might come to blows again."

"I hope Lucia is on alert to deal with that. I feel sorry for her right now, what with the factions fighting and the serial killer still out there." That reminded me of my map. "Wait a minute. Stay right there."

I raced upstairs and grabbed the map. Judy stood where I'd left her, tapping her toe impatiently. "Look at this."

"It's a big, lopsided red circle. Is it supposed to mean something to me?"

"The detectives came back after you left yesterday. They told me Hallstrom was camping illegally in Powell Butte Nature Park—that's where they found the receipt and some of the stolen books. These dots are all the places where people have been killed, more or less, and if you draw a circle encompassing them, it's about two and a half miles across and Powell Butte is near the middle of it."

Judy chewed a fingernail thoughtfully. "It's kind of a stretch, don't you think? There are a lot of things inside that circle."

"But only one associated with a suspicious character. I think Hallstrom is the killer, and the next person who dies—assuming no one stops him—will be in this circle."

"So tell Lucia."

"Judy, what is Lucia going to say if I call and tell her this?"

Judy cleared her throat. "'Davies, I don't need speculation, I need facts. Stick to selling overpriced books and let me do my job.'"

"That was eerie."

"And accurate." Judy set her purse on the glass-topped counter. "So how do we get facts for her?"

"I was thinking, if we could find Hallstrom and give his location to Lucia, she could take him in for questioning the way she was going to do Mr. Washburn."

"Jeremiah? She can't suspect him!"

"She suspects everyone. And he's a wood magus. That would be another fact, if we could prove what kind of magus Hallstrom is."

"I don't know how to do the latter, but glass magi have magic that can locate a person. The Kellers did it for us back in April when we were trying to figure out why the oracle kept giving wrong auguries, remember?"

"I do now. I should have thought of that."

Judy took her phone out of her purse. "I'll call Harriet and see if they can help us. You—" She jerked her head at the front door—"can deal with the slavering masses."

I looked in that direction. The line wasn't quite as long as it had been on Saturday, but it was more restless, more in motion. Possibly that was the familiars butting up against the plate glass of the window. I shuddered and opened the door.

It should have been a relief that the number of augury requests for hunting Malcolm had dropped significantly. Unfortunately, the auguries that replaced them weren't cheering. They were all questions about how to hurt the Ambrosite cause. Nothing the oracle would reject, nothing criminal, but barely skirting the edges of what was acceptable. Things like *Where will the Ambrosite leader be at 2 p.m. tomorrow?* or *What action will have the greatest negative impact on the Ambrosites?* My temper, which had been soothed by reading Silas's diary, began heating up, until by noon I could barely stay civil with my customers. They, in turn, became nervous, as if waiting for an eruption.

Finally, I slapped the final book into the waiting young man's hands and snapped, "$3000. Make it quick. I want my lunch."

Nodding, the young man fumbled for his wallet. He had thick, messy brown hair and a prominent Adam's apple that bobbed every time he swallowed, which was often. "And I hope you don't have any luck with that," I added, slapping the cover of *Cardenio*. I'd never heard of the play and hoped it wasn't some ultra-rare lost edition of Shakespeare I was giving the guy in answer to the question *Where is Malcolm Campbell?*

"I thought you were supposed to be impartial," he said, swallowing again.

"I'm impartially hoping you don't have any luck with that." I turned away and strode to the break room, where I slammed a container of shepherd's pie into the microwave and stabbed the Quick Cook button. I watched the plastic container rotate and tried to still my thoughts to match the hum of the microwave.

"He's not a bad kid," Judy said from the doorway. "Just easily led."

"Well, if he does get lucky and finds Malcolm, how likely do you think it is he'll survive that meeting? So I was telling the truth. I hope he has no luck for both their sakes."

"I think you're pushing it, but okay. I talked to Harriet, by the way. They won't have time to get here before two o'clock, so she asked if we could stop by and have dinner with them."

I slammed my fist against the top of the microwave, making Judy jump, and swore loudly. "This is *idiotic*. Harry and Harriet are well-known in the community. Everyone likes them, even Ambrosites. They shouldn't have to be afraid to come in here just because it's the wrong time of day!"

"Harry was going to come anyway. Harriet wouldn't let him."

"I never thought she was a coward."

"She isn't. She's just seen fighting in the Middle East, before the area became a no-go zone for foreign magi, and she doesn't want to see any more. I don't want to be responsible for the two of them being attacked by some scared kid or a magus with a vendetta."

The microwave beeped. I took out my pie and sat down heavily at the table. "I wish you didn't make so much sense."

Judy began heating up her own meal. "So do I."

I read more of Silas's diary, not caring that it was a little rude to do so with Judy there. I didn't want any more of my bad mood spilling over onto Judy.

July 21, 1938

Solomon Marchuk's ritual confirmed what the oracle has been trying to communicate. I find the art of the stone magus fascinating, particularly this one. Solomon attuned a stone torus to the stone of northwestern Oregon and used the hole at its center as a magnifier. When he rotated the torus clockwise, the magnification increased. Truly astonishing!

More astonishing, though, was what I perceived through this magnifier as I looked at the map in the atlas. Tiny houses, miniature businesses, all perfect in every way. And then, a spot on the map that glowed with the light of the oracle, and in that spot, an empty store. I think I understand what the oracle wants, but it is too unexpected, too incredible to believe. More magic is required, this time that of the bone magus, as the oracle is alive in some sense.

"I wonder why Silas didn't use a glass magus to figure out what the oracle wanted," I murmured around a mouthful of shepherd's pie.

"There were no glass magi before 1941," Judy said. "And you have truly disgusting eating habits."

"Sorry." I chewed and swallowed. "I forgot. They were invented— do you say 'invented' if it's people?"

"Glass magi were developed. By Hitler."

"Ooh, I remember that." I made a face. "It's so weird to think of something positive coming from the Nazis."

"It was the last time Nicolliens and Ambrosites worked together on anything. Allied and Axis were a more important distinction than factions. But when the war was over, and the war tribunals were in the past, the factions went back to hating each other. It's sad, really."

"Yeah."

July 23, 1938

I can draw no other conclusion from this but that the oracle insists on being moved. I haven't told the Board of Neutralities yet. What can I say that will convince them? I will have to hope my reputation as custodian is enough. To move the oracle not within London, but out of the city and across the ocean, then across a continent to a city that is...rough is probably the kindest word I can use to describe Portland, Oregon. It has a reputation for being violent and dangerous, a hub of criminal activity, and I can't think of any place less likely for a Neutrality to situate itself. But the oracle is clear, and I must obey, even if I haven't the slightest idea how one moves a creature (?) with no physical form outside its thousands and thousands of books.

"Wasn't the Gunther Node here before Abernathy's?"

Judy shook her head. "Yes and no. The magi who settled in the Pacific Northwest as a result of Abernathy's being here discovered it... I think around 1949 or 1950. It shut up the last remaining naysayers who thought moving the oracle was a bad idea—you know, serendipitous finds and all that. The Gunther Node is the richest source of magic in the western United States."

I heard the door bells ring and put the book down. "It's going to be a long afternoon."

Once again, the store stayed mostly empty until two, when the Ambrosites showed up in droves to match their counterparts. Once they were gone, I read from Silas's diary, sometimes aloud. Silas had worked out through trial and error the smallest volume of books the oracle could contain. Then they'd filled hundreds of packing crates, careful to keep them close together. Moving the crates from the store to the ship was the most dangerous part, as they couldn't separate the crates too far apart without depriving the oracle of a "roost," as Silas put it.

"So he thought the books are the oracle's body," I said.

"Which makes sense, if you think about how a human can lose bits and still be alive," Judy said. "And isn't there something about how you replace all of your cells over the course of seven years? We sell books, and we bring books in, but it's still the oracle."

"I wonder if there are any books still in there that came from the Charing Cross store," I said, jabbing my thumb in the direction of the bookcases. "There are so many things I'd like to know that I can't find out without damaging or destroying the oracle."

"Like which of Hallstrom's books do we still have?"

"That would be at the top of my list, yes. I feel uncomfortable knowing we have stolen property on our shelves."

Judy shrugged. "If it was really a bad thing, the oracle would do something about it. Like reject anything stolen."

"The oracle's moral principles aren't like ours. It will accept requests that indirectly would lead to abetting a crime and only rejects the ones that come right out and say they're going to murder someone, for example."

"Because people have free will. There are a lot of auguries you could use to cause harm if you chose, but the oracle gives us the chance to make that decision."

I opened Silas's diary where I'd closed it on my finger, marking my place. "I wish I could say that made me feel better about the ones I know people will use to do evil."

Finally, six o'clock arrived, and Judy and I closed up shop and battled rush hour traffic to the Kellers' home on the west side of the city. Blocky houses that were ultra-modern forty years ago peeked out above the trees that grew heavily on the hills surrounding them. I admired their neighborhood without wanting to live there. It was wealthy enough I felt out of place in my ten-year-old Civic.

Harry and Harriet, however, welcomed us in with no hint that they thought I should have dressed up. Judy, in a vintage dress I could barely identify as being from the '70s, looked chic and well-to-do as usual. "It's so nice to see you both," Harriet said. "Come in, sit down. Dinner will be a few more minutes."

The Kellers' living room looked like something out of a contemporary home décor magazine, with the chairs and couches upholstered in soft gray plush and the cabinets of pale blond wood. Bright paintings made the only spots of color in the room. I heard a howl from deeper within the house, and shuddered.

"Don't worry about Vitriol, dear, it's safely locked away. We've had to keep it inside for the last several days, so it's a little more vocal than usual, but perfectly safe." Harriet patted my hand reassuringly.

"Damned Ambrosites thinking they're entitled to destroy someone's familiar," Harry grumbled. "I hope Will finds this killer soon. Tensions are too high."

"Poor Morena," Harriet said, and I remembered the shooting from yesterday morning. "As if killing Nicolliens will bring back those dead Ambrosite magi."

"Father is working closely with Lucia to solve these crimes," Judy said. She sat on one of the low sofas, and I took a seat next to her.

"And it sounds like the two of you are helping as well," Harry said.

"After dinner, dear," Harriet said. "Let's talk of happier things for now, shall we? How's your boyfriend, Helena?"

I'd forgotten Harriet's mission in life was to marry off all her young, single friends. "Actually, we broke up," I said. "It was a good thing. He turned out not to be who I thought he was."

"I didn't know you broke up with Jason," Judy said, eyeing me suspiciously.

"It was just a couple of days ago."

"Well, that's still too bad, dear," Harriet said. "I'm sure you'll find someone else. How about that nice Gary Stewart over at the Gunther Node?"

"He's gay," said Judy.

"Oh, is he? I'll have to remember that. Or there's Manuel Gutierrez, he's a real rising star at the Board of Neutralities—"

"Actually, I want to be single for a while," I said. "But thanks for caring."

"Helena's got a type," Judy said, smirking. I glared at her.

"And what type—" The oven timer beeped, saving me from having to answer that question. Harry and Harriet both rose. "Why don't you all be seated at the table, and I'll bring in the fried chicken and beans."

Harriet was nearly as good a cook as my mom—at least, that's what I told myself, but the truth was I'd never had a better meal. I ate until I was stuffed and groaning with fried chicken, barbecue baked beans, and green salad. Dessert was homemade ice cream with caramel sauce. By the end of the meal I wasn't sure I could stand, let alone walk to my car, but I managed to waddle back to their living room and drop like a well-fed stone into a chair.

"So, Judy says you need to find someone," Harry said. "A suspect."

"I don't know how safe that is," Harriet said.

"We're not going to confront him, we're going to tell Lucia so she can capture and interrogate him," I said.

Harry and Harriet exchanged glances. "I suppose that's not so bad," Harriet said.

"I'll get the map," Harry said, pushing himself heavily to his feet. He'd eaten even more than I had.

"This works better if you have something that belongs to the person," Harriet said.

"We don't. We had some books he'd stolen, but all I have now is his augury file."

"Stolen books wouldn't work. They'd point to the owner, not the thief. It's all right. It will still work, just not as easily."

Harry returned with a map of Portland he spread out on the glass prism the Kellers used for a coffee table. It was the same map I'd bought, minus the red Sharpie marks. He scattered a handful of glass cubes across the map's surface. They looked like dice, but with blank faces, and their beveled edges glittered in the light. "Did you want to test, or record?" he asked Harriet.

"I'll record." Harriet went to a low cabinet beneath the picture window and removed a thin notebook from it. Harry handed her a ballpoint pen which she clicked rapidly a few times, in and out, then scribbled a line to test the ink. She settled on the couch across from Harry, and I sat next to her. Judy took a seat in an adjacent chair, where she perched on the very edge of the cushion like a bird of prey, her blue eyes intent on the map.

Harry gathered up the cubes and began placing them at what seemed to me like random spots on the map. As each touched the table, it let off a whiff of ozone and a white spark like flint striking steel that vanished without leaving a mark. When he'd laid out eleven cubes, he set the others to one side and dusted off his hands, making more sparks. I glanced at Judy, but she was still watching the map, so maybe this was all normal.

Harry spread his arms wide and placed his hands, palm down and fingers extended, at the west and east sides of the map. "What's his name?"

"Mitch Hallstrom."

"We're looking for Mitch Hallstrom," Harry said, and lines of white lightning speared between the cubes, making an irregular web that crackled over the surface of the map. I sucked in a startled breath and leaned back. Heat rose from the web and played across my face and hands. I released my grip on the arm of the couch and tried to relax.

Harriet wrote something in her notebook. "Are you sure about the name?"

"The oracle was," I said.

"Do you see how it's fighting?" Harriet said to Harry. "If his real name is Mitch Hallstrom, there's another name he identifies with."

"At least one other name. Could be more," Harry said.

"Does that mean you can't find him?" I asked.

"Unfortunately, that's what it means."

Judy flung herself backward in her seat. "Well, it was a nice idea," she said.

"Wait," I said. "What about an object? You could find that, right?"

"If it's something associated with him, sure," Harry said.

I shook my head. "No, no, I mean an object he'll have on him. An augury."

"That's risky. Who knows how many copies of the book there might be in the city," Judy said.

"Then we get locations for all of them and let Lucia do the foot-work," I said. "I remember the title of his last augury. It was *Sinful Cravings*. I remember teasing him about the half-naked man on the cover. He was pretty embarrassed about it."

"Wow, what question did he ask?" Judy said.

"That, I don't remember." I turned to look at Harriet, who had set her pen and notebook in her lap. "Please try. This is really important."

"I suppose we can try," Harriet said. Harry swept the glass cubes, now blackened and cracked, off the map and threw them at the fireplace, where they struck the back of it and shattered. He took out another handful of cubes and began placing them randomly across the map. It looked to me like they were in different places than the first set, but I wasn't sure.

Harry rested his hands on the map again. "A book called *Sinful Cravings*," he said, and lightning once more formed a web between the cubes. This time, it was tinged red and looked like fireworks going off, though it went on and on instead of exhausting itself and vanishing. I heard Harriet scribbling in her notebook, but I couldn't take my eyes off the display. "Do you have it?" Harry asked.

"The first round, yes," Harriet said, and laid down her pen. Harry shifted position, and the lightning vanished. The cubes weren't blackened, but pulsed with red light. The map didn't look any different to me, but Harry examined it closely, tapping his finger against his lips in thought. He shifted some of the cubes, sliding them across the map without lifting them as if playing some fiendish multi-dimensional game of chess. "Let me see that list," he said, and Harriet held it out. "Probably east of here," he muttered, moving a few more cubes around. "All right. Let's do it again."

The web of lightning sprang up, but this time not all the cubes were connected. Four of them pulsed their red light outside the web. Harriet wrote a few more things down. I wanted to ask about the cubes, but was afraid to talk. I knew so little about magic. I never had any idea what was appropriate for me to do or say when it was happening, or whether I'd disturb the magus or ruin the ritual. So I bottled up my impatience, and my questions, and waited.

Finally, Harry picked up the lone cubes with one hand, keeping the other flat on the map, and rearranged them so they were once more part of the web. Harriet made another note. Harry removed his hand and the lightning vanished. "That's better than I expected," Harriet said, showing the notebook to Harry.

"Did you find it?" I asked.

"We found fifty-seven. But eleven of them are at Powell's down-town, and another nine are at Powell's in Beaverton, and there are a lot of smaller groupings, probably other bookstores. There are three individual results, here, here, and here." Harry took the notebook from his wife's hand and referred to it as he pointed at three locations on the map, all of them with glass cubes on them.

"East and south of Powell Butte," Judy said. "Any of those could be Hallstrom."

"How close can you narrow each of those locations?" I said.

"We can give you street addresses," Harriet said. "Harry, do you have a magnifying glass on you?"

Harry drew a brass-rimmed magnifier with an ebony handle from inside his cardigan and handed it over. Harriet huffed on its surface, then examined the little red-tinged cubes. "They should have the addresses written...there." I couldn't see any writing on the cubes, but Harriet confidently read off three addresses, which Harry wrote down on a fresh sheet of notepaper. He tore it off and handed it to Judy.

"Thanks," I said. "We'll give this to Lucia right away."

"You're welcome," Harriet said. "And do be careful, dear. This man, whoever he is, is dangerous."

"Hard to believe he came into Abernathy's all those times, maybe even looking for auguries that would find him victims," Harry said. "He might have killed one of you."

I hadn't thought of it that way, and it chilled me, remembering Mitch Hallstrom's constant twitchiness and the sense of urgency he carried with him. If we were right, we'd been next to the serial killer without knowing it. "We should probably go," I said, feeling a little urgency myself.

"Wait, I'll pack you up some leftovers," Harriet said.

I wasn't going to say no to that.

19

We put the plastic boxes of food in the back seat, filling my car with delicious smells, and I reversed down the Kellers' drive while Judy called Lucia and left a message about what we'd learned. "You really think Hallstrom is our guy?" she said.

"I thought you agreed with me."

"I do. I was just thinking, what if we're wrong, and Lucia harasses an innocent man?"

"Better than ignoring him as a suspect and getting someone killed."

"I guess." Judy's phone rang, a cheerful rendition of the Funeral March that struck me as typically Judy. "Hello? No, I don't think we overstepped our bounds...I'm not telling you that...Because it's irrelevant, that's why." Judy covered the receiver with her hand and whispered, "She's pissed because we didn't let her track Hallstrom herself. Do you want the addresses or not?"

There was a longish pause during which Judy drummed her fingers on the armrest. Then she sat up indignantly. "What do you mean, useless?" she exclaimed. "You don't have one person who can —fine, but I don't think that's ever mattered to you before, so why—"

There was an even longer pause. I could faintly hear Lucia talking loudly on the other end of the call.

Finally, Judy said, "You're making a mistake," and hung up. She was breathing rapidly and her fingers, which had been tapping the armrest, were curled into a fist.

"She's not going to look into it," she said.

"*What?*"

"She says without more evidence, she can't investigate Hallstrom. And she doesn't have anyone to spare to find evidence. We don't even know what type of magus he is—if he's not a wood magus, there's no point, she said."

"But she wasn't certain the killer is a wood magus! And Hallstrom is suspicious."

"It's all circumstantial. Just because he's a thief, that doesn't make him a murderer too. He could have moved here from some other city so we wouldn't have seen him before. And the Powell Butte thing could be coincidence."

"You don't believe that."

"What I believe doesn't matter. Lucia's the one in charge. She's not investigating."

"I can't believe this." Someone honked, and I realized the light I'd been sitting at had turned green. I hit the accelerator and drove on, speeding up until I was going faster than the speed limit by a few miles per hour. "She's making a huge mistake."

"We did what we could. Call her again tomorrow and see if things have changed."

"By tomorrow someone else might be dead, and Malcolm..." I let my voice trail off. Judy didn't care what happened to Malcolm.

"I don't see what else we can do."

I snatched the paper from where it was lying in Judy's lap. "We can find Hallstrom."

"No. We told the Kellers we wouldn't do that."

"That was before it turned out we're the only ones who care about this lead." I glanced over the addresses. "The second one is only a few miles from here."

"You're out of your mind."

"How? Look, it's simple. We'll just scope out the area until we see Hallstrom—or don't see him—and move on. Once we know where he is, I'll ask Derrick and the team to check it out. We don't have to get involved any more than that."

"Do you think they'll care?"

"If it helps prove Malcolm's innocence, I'm sure they will."

Judy sighed. "If we get in trouble, I'm blaming you."

"That's acceptable."

Judy looked at the addresses, holding the paper close to her eyes. The sun had nearly set while we were with the Kellers, and the lights of the street lamps flashed past, illuminating then darkening the car. "I think we ought to go to the first one, though. It's in a more wooded part of town. Wood magi draw strength from the trees and use them in their magic."

"But we're almost at this other place. We'll go to the woods second. Let's just cross this one off the list."

The neighborhood we drove through was overgrown enough to practically be woods itself. Giant oaks sprang up from every front yard; hedges surrounded every house. Dense leaves swallowed up the moonlight and the lights from the street lamps, making pools of shadow along the sidewalk. A few cars were crouched at the curb, a few more parked in driveways. Most of the houses were lit from within, and I saw the bluer glow of televisions blended with the white-gold of light bulbs. It felt strange, looking through those windows and knowing we were there to spy on one of them.

I drove past the address on the page. It was one of the few houses where the lights were out, though there was a slight glow from deep within the house. "Now what?" Judy asked.

"We'll park down the street and walk back this way, then get into the backyard," I said.

"Oh, right, because what this venture needed was trespassing."

"It's just a little trespassing. And no one will know we're there."

Judy sighed, but got out of the car when I parked and walked with me back along the sidewalk. It was a beautiful, warm, clear night, with the full moon shedding its silver light over the street. The moonlight was bright enough to cast knife-edged shadows even where the lamp light fell. Judy and I walked beneath the oaks' branches, obscured from view. "I feel like we should tiptoe or something," I said.

"We'd probably be the worst thieves in history," Judy said. "Besides, it's better if we look like we belong."

"Right. Just two women out for a moonlit stroll. Okay, it's the next house."

All the houses on this street were ramblers, single-story and sprawling. Our target was surrounded by a dark hedge I thought might be arborvitae, cut off flat at the top to end just below the windows in the side wall. We crept quickly from the sidewalk to the house, sticking close to the hedge though the windows were both closed and the blinds drawn. "Around to the back," I whispered, and led the way to the corner.

The arborvitae ended at the back corner, and to my dismay I saw there was no cover from the house across the back lawn to the white-painted wooden fence. There was a broken picnic table that canted to the right, and the aluminum uprights of a clothesline, but aside from that the yard was empty. I beckoned to Judy, and we sidled along the wall toward the sliding glass door. The light coming from inside the house was brighter there and from a window close to it. I stayed close to the wall until I reached the window, then I carefully slid toward it, barely peeking over the sill.

The kitchen beyond was ordinary, with the kind of generic oak cabinets you get when you don't care very much about décor but you want your kitchen to look nice. From my vantage point, I could see the corner of the refrigerator and half a Formica-topped table that ruined the point of the cabinets. I heard, faintly, the sound of streaming water. Then I jerked out of sight just as someone came to the sink beneath the window. My heart pounding, I craned to see who it was, but it was too extreme an angle. If I moved away from the wall, he or she would see me.

I gestured to Judy to move on, pointing at the sliding door. She slithered past me and sneaked up to the door, which was closed, but its drapes were open. The sound of water shut off, and a shadow passed the window. I risked a peek and found the person was gone. Judy was crouched against the wall past the sliding door, waving at me frantically. She tapped her nose, then jerked her thumb in the direction of the house, tapped again. "Hallstrom?" I mouthed a couple of times. She nodded vigorously.

Well, we'd had a one in three chance, and we'd gotten lucky. I sidled along the wall until I got to the sliding door, where I crouched to look inside. It was a typical living room, with overstuffed chairs upholstered in slick, soft brown fabric and a television mounted on the wall above a fireplace. I saw the back of Hallstrom's head and the TV screen. He was watching *Jeopardy!* with the sound turned up loudly enough to be audible as a rising and falling murmur.

Judy motioned to me to join her. I took another look at Hallstrom, who seemed rapt in his show, then took a few steps, still crouched, to cross that vast open space. Hallstrom didn't look around. I reached Judy and took a moment to catch my breath. "Why was he camping if he could live like this?" I whispered.

"Don't know, don't care," Judy whispered back. "Let's just go, and you can call Tinsley."

We made it to the corner, where the arborvitae hedge began again, and crept slowly along it, past the door to the garage. I pressed deep into the hedge, conscious of how my light green shirt stood out at night. "Don't do that," Judy said. She was walking several inches away from the hedge.

"Why not?"

"Wolf spiders love arborvitae."

I squeaked and stepped away from the hedge, which gripped me with a million tiny prickles. "It's hanging onto me."

"Serves you right."

I pulled away again, but came up short. "I mean it's really grabbed me. Like Velcro."

Judy spun around and grabbed my hand, pulling. It made no difference. The hedge held me fast, and every step took more effort.

Tiny green vines came from nowhere to twine about my arms and legs. "Pull harder," I said.

"Wood magus," Judy said, panting with effort.

We both heard a chilling sound: somewhere nearby, a door opened. I let go of Judy's hand. "*Run*," I said.

Judy didn't dither about leaving me. She sprinted for the sidewalk. Vines held me by the waist and throat, choking me, and I thrashed for air.

The door to the garage opened, and distant light spilled out onto the lawn. "What did I catch?" Hallstrom murmured, then, more loudly, "Ms. Davies! What are you doing here?" He was dressed in a worn brown T-shirt and faded jeans, and he was barefoot.

I couldn't speak with the vines throttling me, but I grunted. "Oh, sorry," Hallstrom said, and the vines around my throat loosened. I gasped and sucked in cool, refreshing air. "There, that's better."

Since I was still pinioned by the rest of the growth, I questioned his definition of "better." "Let me go, please," I said, deciding that politeness to a serial killer was probably the safest option.

"You set off my trap. I think I have a right to know why you're prowling around my...it's sort of my home. For now." Hallstrom looked less nervous than usual, though he had a tic in his shoulders that made them jump every few seconds, like a grasshopper's legs twitching.

"You sold me stolen books. I wanted to know why," I said.

"Well, I needed those auguries and I couldn't afford them. It's pretty simple."

"The cops are after you."

"They won't find me. Though I guess, since you did, I should probably move on."

"Let me go."

"Hmmm." Hallstrom stepped back to regard me, and I felt cold inside, because it was the look of a predator deciding which part of his prey to eat first. Eventually, he said, "Why don't you come inside?" The vines and the grasping fingers withdrew, and I brushed myself off and stood more fully upright, away from the bushes. The door swung open without Hallstrom touching it, and he gestured for me to enter.

The garage was unfinished, its two by fours exposed, but there was a workbench in the corner near the door with a fluorescent light dangling above it. My feet came down on loose nails from a spilled box; they rolled uncomfortably underfoot. There was no car, no tools, nothing you'd expect to see in a garage. "Empty," I said.

"It's not my house. I'm just borrowing it without permission. You can stop there."

I stopped about a foot from the inner door and turned to face Hallstrom. "What, we can't go in where it's warm?"

"It's summer—oh, you were joking. We'll just talk here. I'm not inviting you inside until I know what you want."

"I told you. You stole books and sold them to me."

"Something you could have sent the police about. Yet you went to the trouble of tracking me down and then coming here yourself. Who found me?"

"A glass magus."

"Clever of you."

I felt a tug at my sandals and looked down to see a slim vine crawling out of a crack in the floor. I stepped to one side, but it followed me. "So you're a wood magus. I wondered."

"Really? I don't know why you'd care."

The vine grasped my toes, tickling them. I took another step. "Don't move," Hallstrom said, and I froze, because he held a gun in his right hand and had it aimed at me. "The vine is just a precaution. See, I think you're here for another reason."

"What would that be?" The vine had me rooted to the spot and was twining around my calves.

"You think I'm the killer."

"Why would I think that? I don't know anything about it."

"You know my augury questions. And you know my real name. I didn't tell anyone that."

"You can't hide your name from the oracle. I didn't know you were using another one. I don't remember people's questions." Though I did remember his first question, about trusting his business partner, and now I wondered if he'd been asking about Guittard.

"I don't believe you." The tic was growing stronger now, making him look like a chicken jerking its wings back as it strutted through the yard. The gun jerked upward with every movement, making me very nervous.

I shrugged. "Believe what you want." Where was Judy? How long would it take her to call for help? If Lucia was busy, she might not respond immediately. The possibility of my death here in this dirty, empty garage seemed suddenly very real. I had to keep him talking. "So, are you saying you *are* the serial killer?"

"I'm not admitting to anything. I'm not stupid."

"Not like Ms. Guittard."

He jerked his shoulders again. "She deserved what she got, if she was working with the killer. I wonder what she told Campbell."

"Not enough, or he wouldn't be in hiding now."

"Very true. He's not all that bright either, or he would have left her alive."

I was too afraid to be angry at the insult to Malcolm. "So what *were* you after, with all those auguries?"

"Nothing you need to worry about."

That struck me as sinister. "Are you going to let me go?"

Hallstrom tilted his head to one side, regarding me like an inquisitive bird. "I don't know. You *are* the custodian of a Neutrality, and if you just disappear, you'll be missed. On the other hand, I can't let you go running off to tell people what you've learned."

"I haven't learned anything! You're too smart to tell me things, remember?"

"True. But I don't want my affairs pried into by Lucia Pontarelli, and you'll go running to her the second I let you go free. So I have a dilemma."

My mouth was dry. I swallowed painfully and said, "Suppose I promise not to tell Lucia anything."

"I wouldn't believe you. Plus, you're not stupid enough to make that promise."

"Thanks."

"The problem is, I like you," Hallstrom said. "You were always polite to me and you gave me good value for those stolen books. But I don't see any way around the fact that I need to get rid of you."

More fear shot through me. I struggled against my bonds and succeeded only in falling to my knees, my shins painfully bent against the vines like taut wires cutting into them. "You really don't have to."

Hallstrom looked at the gun as if only just realizing he held it. "Are you afraid of this?" he said. "A bullet wound would raise all sorts of questions. No, you'll just be one more victim of the serial killer." He took a step toward me, shoving the gun into his waistband.

I squeaked and threw myself backward, but was still tethered by the vines. I strained, felt some of them give and be replaced by others. Hallstrom kept coming. He walked around behind me and hauled me up, put his left arm around me and hugged me close. It was such a parody of tenderness I wanted to throw up.

He gripped my right shoulder with his left hand and slid his right hand around my waist and under my shirt to lie flat against my stomach. "It doesn't hurt," he said.

I fought him with every ounce of strength I had, clawing his arm and neck, but he just laughed and patted my belly. "Just hold still."

"I am *not* holding still for you, you bastard."

An explosion shattered the stillness of the garage. The outside door, the one we'd entered by, blew in and impacted against the far wall. I flinched away from the sound, closing my eyes briefly. When I opened them, Malcolm stood in the empty doorway, gun in hand, staring Hallstrom down.

20

I felt something cold press against my side. "Put that down," Hallstrom said.

Malcolm's eyes were hard, terrifying. He bent, slowly, and laid his gun on the ground, his left hand brushing the floor as if he were making a bow to a king. "Let her go."

"Ms. Davies and I already agree that I'm not stupid," Hallstrom said, shoving his gun deeper into my side. "Kick it away. Gently."

Malcolm gave the gun a shove with his foot, sending it skittering away and scattering loose nails as it went. "Release her, and I'll let you live." Vines crept in through the empty doorway, twitching like dogs scenting prey. One found Malcolm's leg and wrapped around it. He ignored the thing.

Hallstrom smiled. "How generous of you. Since she's the only thing keeping me alive, I don't think I'll take that offer. No, we'll walk out of here, and you'll stay. I'll release Ms. Davies when I'm safely away. Then I'll leave Portland and never return. How does that sound?"

"You're going to trial for murder, Benedetto or Hallstrom or whatever your real name is," Malcolm said. More vines undulated toward him, creeping around his ankles. "I can't afford to let you walk."

"See? You were lying when you said you'd let me live. How can I trust you?"

Malcolm smiled, a sinister, mirthless expression. "I said I'd let you live. Hurt her, and we'll find out how creative I can be in causing you pain."

"That's so sweet." Hallstrom swiftly raised the gun from my side to my right temple. I stayed as still as I could. "So you've found out the truth."

"I know you came here intending to harvest magic from as many people as possible. I know you and Amber Guittard were instructed to set Nicollien against Ambrosite. What I don't know is who gave you those orders."

"What makes you think it wasn't Guittard?"

Malcolm smiled, but his eyes were still cold and hard. "She confessed her role in the plot to me before I killed her. And you may not be stupid, but you're not a criminal mastermind. You were far too easy to trace. Even Miss Davies, with no experience, was able to do it."

The gun's muzzle was removed from my head briefly. "I was skilled enough to stay ahead of Lucia Pontarelli's investigators. Skilled enough to set all this in motion." Hallstrom pressed the gun to my head again. "Skilled enough to stay hidden all this time."

"Not enough to keep the police—the non-magical police—from finding you. I'm surprised your bosses trusted you enough to send you. What did you do with all the *sanguinis sapiens* you harvested —spill it?"

"It's safe where you won't find it." Hallstrom's tic was making the gun jerk back and forth across the side of my head. The cold metal grew warmer with every jerk. I pictured his finger closing on the trigger and wanted to throw up.

"I wouldn't count on that," Malcolm said. "You've failed, Hallstrom."

"I did everything I was sent to do," Hallstrom said. The gun pressed harder into my temple. I wanted to scream at Malcolm to stop, but I was terrified that Hallstrom would remember I was there and pull the trigger.

Malcolm pressed on relentlessly. "You did it badly. Whoever your bosses are, they've got to be disappointed in you. You weren't supposed to let anyone find you. I hate to think of the kind of punishment they'll unleash on you for your failure."

"*Shut up!*" Hallstrom shrieked, pointing the gun at Malcolm. "I will be rewarded—"

A flash of silver darted from Malcolm's left hand. The gun went off. A streak of fire creased my left shoulder near my neck, making me scream and collapse against Hallstrom's arm. Hallstrom spasmed, then fell, landing atop me and weighing me down. I smacked my forehead against the concrete and black stars spangled my vision. I smelled something bitter and coppery, like tainted blood, and closed my eyes against the pain.

The weight across my body rolled away. "Helena, lie still," Malcolm said. I waited for him to lift me, hold me close, but instead I heard cloth tearing. I opened my eyes and saw only gray, stinking concrete and, farther away, Malcolm kneeling over Hallstrom's body. He was pressing down on Hallstrom's chest with a bloody wad of cloth. Tattered vines still clung to his ankles. "Come on, stay alive," he muttered. "Where the hell are they?"

"Malcolm," I whispered, but he didn't hear me. I rolled onto my side and nearly screamed again at the pain in my shoulder. My legs refused to support me. I reached up with my right hand and felt my shoulder gingerly, sending more pain shooting through me. My hand came away bloody. The flash of silver. The gun. Someone had shot me, but it couldn't have been Hallstrom, not at that angle.

Malcolm. I closed my eyes and tried not to cry. Malcolm had shot me to get at Hallstrom.

I heard footsteps approaching, lots of footsteps, running fast. I opened my eyes just as the first black-garbed figure burst through the door, her gun pointed at Malcolm. I croaked a warning.

Malcolm didn't take his eyes from Hallstrom. "You must save this man's life," he said.

"Hands in the air!" the woman shouted. "Hands up or I shoot, Campbell!"

Malcolm didn't move. More black-clad commandos poured through the doorway, all of them carrying guns. "Malcolm, don't let them shoot you," I said, my voice audible now.

"If he dies, it makes no difference," Malcolm said.

Someone cocked their pistol, an ominous sound that rose above the noises of people moving around to get a better aim on Malcolm. "Don't!" I shouted, though it came out as barely above speaking volume. "That's the serial killer! He has to go to trial!"

"Ms. Davies!" the first woman said. "What are you doing here?"

"Just save his life," I begged. "Malcolm, *please* don't let them kill you."

Malcolm finally looked over his shoulder at me. Slowly, he raised both hands in the air. Three commandos tackled him, and he didn't resist. A short, chubby figure came forward from the middle of the pack and knelt beside Hallstrom's body. "He's almost gone," she said. "Everyone back up."

They'd barely moved when Hallstrom screamed, arching his back as if trying to get away from the worst pain imaginable. I'd been healed once from a severe beating and the healing had hurt worse than the beating. Despite myself, I felt sorry for Hallstrom, having to endure that.

It went on for what felt like forever, and then the short woman sat back on her heels, panting as if she'd run a marathon. She held up a twisted, bloody piece of metal. It looked like three nails twisted together to come to a wicked silver point. "Your work, Campbell?"

"I had to improvise," Malcolm said, sounding unusually calm for someone whose face was being ground into the concrete by three men.

"Malcolm Campbell, you're under arrest for the murder of Amber Guittard and the attempted murder of this man," the first woman said.

"No!" I shouted, and managed to roll one-armed to a sitting position, wincing at the pain. "He's the serial killer! Malcolm had to shoot him to save my life!"

"We'll take that into consideration, Ms. Davies," the woman said. "For now, we have to get out of here before someone calls the cops."

Someone helped me stand, and I discovered I could walk. The pain was fading to a dull ache that only spiked when I moved my arm the wrong way. Malcolm's captors hauled him to his feet, and he didn't fight them. I didn't think much of their chances if he decided to. Two others got Hallstrom, unconscious again, in a fireman's carry, and we all trooped out of the garage and half walked, half ran to the street.

Two vans were parked there, the kind Lucia's people used, and I felt a weight lifted from me. Of course these weren't Nicolliens, because they would just have shot Malcolm. I felt dizzy, and my head ached from hitting the concrete.

"Helena," Judy said.

I opened eyes I hadn't realized I'd closed and saw her trotting along beside me and my support. "Are you all right? You're bleeding!"

"I'm still alive," I said, and winced as the man supporting me jogged my left elbow. "Where are we going?"

"Back to the Gunther Node as fast as possible. The Nicolliens are on the prowl," he said. "You'll need to tell Lucia what happened."

"I'll take your car," Judy said. "Give me your keys. I'll meet you there."

I awkwardly fished my keys out of my pocket as I tried to keep moving. Judy snatched them and ran off down the street toward where we'd parked before I could ask her anything. She must have gotten through to Lucia, but she couldn't have known Malcolm was near, so why did Lucia's people know to expect him?

I climbed into the back of the van and scooted down to make room for Hallstrom and the men carrying him. A few other commandos climbed in after him, and the door shut. "Where's Malcolm?" I said.

"In the other van. We won't let him near you, don't worry."

"I'm not worried! He's not dangerous."

"He shot you, Ms. Davies. I think that's good evidence that he is."

"I already told you, he had to shoot me to stop Hallstrom." I prodded my shoulder again, and pain spiked through it, nearly sending me unconscious. The wound felt deep, like it had torn muscle all the way to the bone, and it was still bleeding. Just as I thought that, someone pressed a thick pad of bandage to the wound and guided my hand to hold it. I hissed in pain.

"Sorry," the woman said, and though it was dark inside the windowless van I recognized the first woman who'd come through the door. "I always knew Campbell was ruthless, but I didn't know he'd shoot an innocent to get at his man." She sounded admiring. I felt sick again. He'd looked so terrifying, like someone ready to commit murder, and he hadn't had one word of reassurance for me. *He had to save Hallstrom's life so he could testify. It doesn't mean anything.* But he'd looked nothing like the man I loved, and a tiny part of me wondered if I'd ever really known him.

The van rumbled across a rough road, jostling all of us. I heard Hallstrom groan and stir beside my feet. "You should keep him unconscious, if you can," I said. "He'll try to escape."

"Don't worry, we've got him under control," the woman said.

Hallstrom lunged for her, getting his hands around her throat to throttle her.

I screamed and scooted backward, out of the way of Lucia's people. It was chaos, people trying to rescue their leader, others trying to subdue Hallstrom. Hallstrom's thrashing feet kicked me in the stomach, and I retched and gagged and made myself as small a target as I could. The van screeched to a halt, rattling us all like dice. Hallstrom let go of his victim and dove for the back door. I threw myself atop him and wrapped my arms around his legs, pinning them. He kicked and thrashed, but I held on tight, bringing my legs up to wrap around his, squeezing my eyes tight shut as if that would give me strength.

"You can let go, Ms. Davies, we've got him," said a man's voice.

"That's what you said before," I said through clenched teeth.

"This time it's true. Sorry we didn't take your warning seriously. This really is the serial killer?"

"Yes." I released Hallstrom and sat back, rubbing the feeling into my wrists where I'd gripped them hard to keep from letting go. "He's a wood magus."

"Where we're going, he'll get no benefit from that," the woman said, her voice raspy. "You ever been to the Gunther Node?"

"No."

The van started up again. I heard someone up front talking into a two-way radio that replied amid bursts of static. "It's hard to describe," the woman said. "Better you see for yourself."

I nodded and retrieved the bloody pad I'd had pressed against my shoulder. Where was their bone magus? I felt a little annoyed that no one had offered to heal my wound. Then again, maybe Lucia would take me more seriously if I were drenched in blood. I felt lightheaded and hoped I wouldn't pass out.

I watched our progress as best I could from the rear of the van, where I could only see glimpses of what was passing through the windshield. I had no idea where we were going, except the road was still rough and there weren't many lights. Occasionally a white corrugated iron warehouse or barn would flash past, but mostly the road was empty. I watched Hallstrom, wary of him erupting into violence again, but he lay on the floor, bound hand and foot with zip ties, his bright eyes glaring at everyone in turn but lingering longest on me. To think I'd once laughed at how awkward and ridiculous he seemed. He would have killed me if Malcolm hadn't arrived. Some self-rescuing princess I'd turned out to be.

The van turned off the road onto an even rougher surface that nearly knocked me off my seat once or twice. Hallstrom's head bounced off the floor of the van, but I couldn't find it in me to feel sorry for him anymore. Then the road was smooth, perfectly free of jolts, and the van came to a halt. The woman opened the door and hopped out. Two of Lucia's people maneuvered Hallstrom's gangly body out of the van, and someone gave me a hand down.

We were inside an airplane hangar, though I only called it that because I'd seen them on TV. There were no planes inside, nothing but empty concrete and the two vans. Malcolm was being guided out of the second van. His hands were secured behind him with zip ties—of course metal handcuffs would be to a steel magus like Malcolm just one more weapon. He looked perfectly composed, but he looked once at me and the emptiness in his eyes chilled me. His guards led him away, and the woman put her hand on my elbow and guided me along after them. Behind us, four of Lucia's people picked up Hallstrom and carried him, thrashing again, in our wake. I heard the ratchet of a gun being cocked, and Hallstrom went still.

The crunch of tires and a spray of gravel brought us all to a halt. Judy leaped from my car and ran toward us. "Don't you dare go without me," she said.

"You're not authorized," said the woman.

"You wouldn't have found them without me. And Lucia will want to speak with me." Judy drew herself up to her full 5'1" height and gave the woman an imperious stare. The woman threw up her hands and waved Judy forward.

"I'm probably going to regret this," she murmured to me.

We headed toward a white circle painted on the floor. As I drew nearer, I saw it wasn't a perfect circle, but was interrupted in places by squiggly lines and curves like giant thorns. It reminded me of a girl's flower circlet, the kind they used to wear dancing around maypoles. I stepped over the white lines, careful not to touch them, though the woman didn't give me any warnings about them and I was sure I saw at least one of Lucia's people scuff the paint with her boot sole. It just felt wrong to do that.

Once we were all inside, the woman pulled an access card on a lanyard around her neck from inside her shirt and knelt at the center of the circle. What I'd thought was a smear was actually a slit she dropped the card into and out of rapidly, like running a credit card. Nothing happened for a moment. The woman continued to kneel. Eventually the concrete rippled, like a pool with water dripping into it, and went glass-bright. "Eleven," the woman said, and between one blink and the next we were elsewhere.

The new place was brightly lit with long fluorescent bulbs hanging from the walls and the ceiling, which was at least three stories up. It was more like a cavern than a room, though one of poured concrete, walls, ceiling, and floor. I could see now why the woman had been sure Hallstrom's being a wood magus wouldn't benefit him here. Even though the faint smell of gardenias hung in the air, I couldn't imagine anything growing in this place.

Seven vast openings outlined in bright colors and a dozen smaller doors pierced the walls of the room. Men and women crossed the vast cavern, some of them pushing carts, others carrying papers or strange equipment I didn't recognize. They noticed us immediately, slowing to look at Malcolm and Hallstrom. Malcolm strode on as if he weren't bound, his head held high. The woman indicated that Judy and I should follow Malcolm and his guards through one of the smaller doors.

We entered a concrete tunnel, again lit by fluorescent tubes, this one empty of people and narrow enough we could only walk two abreast. I ended up right behind Malcolm and kept my gaze focused on the back of his head. Lucia would see reason and release Malcolm. She'd put Hallstrom before a tribunal and the truth would all come out. And Malcolm would stop looking at me like I was an inconvenience.

The tunnel snaked through the...was it under a mountain? It felt like it was deep underground. It curved back and forth for some time before opening on a long, straight hallway lined with metal doors, silver with a dull matte finish. I wondered where the actual Gunther Node was, the part that was a source of magic. This all looked more like an industrial complex than a magical nexus.

The woman pushed past Malcolm and his guards and went to the third door on the right, where she knocked, making a hollow metallic boom. A moment later, the door swung open. "Inside," Lucia said.

The room looked like a bomb shelter, or something out of a *Fallout* computer game I'd watched my ex-boyfriend Chet play. Lucia's desk looked like mine in Abernathy's, black melamine and chrome with spidery legs. A metal bookshelf crammed with papers and a couple of funny-looking purple rocks stood nearby. Plastic milk crates stacked against the back wall were also full of papers. With all of us inside, it was almost too full to move, particularly with Hallstrom still being carried.

"Who's that?" Lucia asked, jabbing a finger at Hallstrom. He glared at her.

"Ms. Davies and Campbell claim he's the serial killer," said the woman.

"*That* long streak of nothing?" Lucia's blue eyes came to rest on me.

"I told you we knew where he was," Judy said.

"I believed you when you said the killer had captured Davies," Lucia said. "I just can't believe that's him. But I've seen criminals come in all shapes, so maybe it's not so strange."

"And Malcolm Campbell came with us voluntarily," the woman said. "He shot Ms. Davies and the suspect and admitted to it in front of all of us."

Lucia's eyebrows raised. "He shot *Davies?*"

"I was standing in the way," I said, successfully keeping my mouth from trembling at the memory.

"Ruthless," Lucia said to Malcolm.

"I made a decision," Malcolm said. His voice was stony, expressionless.

"Did you." Lucia came around her desk to look at Hallstrom. "Got anything to say for yourself?" Hallstrom remained silent. "Davies, what makes you think he's the killer?"

"He more or less confessed it to me and Malcolm," I said. "I don't know if that's enough evidence for you to hold him."

"It's enough. Lock him up, and we'll interrogate him later," Lucia told the woman.

"What about Malcolm?" I said.

"What about him?"

The room swam in my vision, and I leaned on Judy to keep from falling. "Hallstrom admitted Ms. Guittard was his accomplice. That means Malcolm acted in good faith, or something, when he killed her."

"Campbell will stand trial and the evidence will acquit or condemn him. Are you going to give me any trouble?" Lucia said, eyeing Malcolm's tall, well-muscled form.

Malcolm stared her down. "Now that you have the killer in custody, I see no reason to hide. If you can assure me of safety from Nicollien reprisal."

"Cut him loose," Lucia said. "Protective custody for you, as a material witness. Davies, are you still bleeding?" She prodded my shoulder, making me hiss. Malcolm closed his eyes briefly. "Somebody heal her, then return her and Rasmussen to their homes."

"But I—"

"You've done plenty, Davies." Lucia looked unexpectedly compassionate. "Go home and rest. You'll need it after the healing."

I looked at Malcolm again. He wasn't looking at me. I blinked back tears and said, "Thank you."

"I ought to thank the two of you, right after I give you both a couple of good dings round the ear for going into danger like that. Now, out of my office. Campbell, you and I need to talk privately."

The woman guided me out of Lucia's office and down the hall a few more doors. "Sue, how about you do the healing in here," she said. The short, plump woman pulled a chair away from the wall in what looked like a conference room and told me to sit.

"Is this your first healing?" she said.

"No."

"Then you know what to expect. Just grit your teeth and it will be over soon."

I felt Judy slip her hand into mine, but before I could ready myself excruciating pain swept over my shoulder and arm, so painful it burned with an icy cold. I gasped and crushed Judy's hand in mine. Tears leaked from my eyes, and I cried, grateful for the excuse. Malcolm would never look at me the same way again. Either I was an impediment, or I was a reminder of how he'd had to shoot an innocent to get his man, and either way our relationship had changed forever.

As abruptly as it had started, the pain stopped, replaced by a dull, deep muscle ache that hurt, but bearably. I wiped tears from my eyes and thanked Sue, who nodded. "You should go home and have a hot bath. It will ease the lingering pains."

Judy and I walked alone through the serpentine passage back to the cavern. "How do we get out of here?" I asked. I still felt shaky, and my blood-soaked and torn shirt stuck to my shoulder uncomfortably.

"We find a tech to operate the gate."

"Have you been here before?"

"Once or twice, for Father to use the node. And when I was arrested last April."

"Where are we?"

Judy shrugged. "I don't know. Somewhere underground in the Portland area, though I've heard rumors it's actually in Camas, across the river."

I felt bone-weary and heartsore. "I guess I don't much care. I just want to go home."

"Did Campbell really shoot you?"

"He made a...like a dart or something out of some nails. And I was standing in front of Hallstrom and was just tall enough to block his shot at Hallstrom's heart." Saying it aloud made me feel better. Of course Malcolm had shot me. It made sense. "It was only a little cut."

"It was not. It tore most of your muscle away!"

"Well, it's healed now. Can we go home?"

Judy gave me a funny look. "All right." Then she grabbed my arm, making me stop. "Look!"

Crossing the cavern ahead of us was Jeremiah Washburn, his T-shirt rumpled as if he'd been sleeping in it. He caught sight of us and veered around to greet us. "I hope this doesn't mean you've been interrogated too," he said with a smile.

"I'm really sorry," I said. "If I hadn't mentioned your name—"

"No worries. Lucia likely would have hauled me in anyway." Washburn shrugged. "I think she was growing desperate."

"Even so. It wasn't fair."

He shrugged again. "Fairness is a weapon wielded by the underdog, for good or ill, and I choose not to be a victim. I'm going to pick up my familiar from holding and then I'm going home to watch *Cowboy Bebop*."

I had no idea what that was, so I said, "I've heard Lucia won't allow familiars near her."

"And with good reason. They're dangerous tools, and they go crazy around you custodians." He nodded to Judy politely and said, "Be seeing you both."

I watched him walk away and said, "He's unusual."

"He's weird, but I like him," Judy said. "Let's find a tech."

I didn't know how she could tell who the techs were. They all looked the same to me, dressed in black jumpsuits or fatigues. But she found someone who led us to a smaller circle that had the same thorny look, and within seconds we were back in the airplane hangar, several yards from my car. The vans were gone. It was quiet enough to hear crickets chirruping outside, but all I could smell was concrete and the blood drying on my shirt.

I insisted on driving, though my shoulder hurt enough I soon wished I hadn't. But I needed the focus driving provided, needed something to keep my thoughts from circling back around to being a captive, to the deadly expression in Malcolm's eyes, to the pain of being shot by someone I loved.

I dropped Judy at her house, thanking her for her offer to stay the night with me. "You shouldn't be alone after that," she said.

"I'll be fine. Thanks." It meant a lot that Judy, never a particularly caring or compassionate person, was worried about me, but I wanted to be alone for a while.

"All right," Judy said skeptically, but walked to her front door and let herself in.

I drove home slowly, observing every traffic law. What I didn't need was having to explain my gory self to a cop who might insist I go to a hospital. What a waste of time that would be. But no one pulled me over, and I made it home with no trouble other than an increasing ache in my formerly wounded shoulder.

Safely inside, I locked my door and stripped off my clothes in the hallway because going into my bedroom was too much work, and besides, there was no one to see. My pants hit the floor with a thud, and I remembered my phone. I'd turned it off before searching Hallstrom's place, visions of an untimely call dancing in my head, and now I turned it back on and set it on the shelf above the sink. I turned on the taps and watched the tub fill up with steaming water.

My phone buzzed as it came back to life, and I retrieved it. Two texts. The first was from Viv, asking where I was. The second was from my sister. ETHAN THRILLED AM NAMING BABY HELLIE HA HA HA.

I smiled. That was cheering news, almost enough to dislodge the stone in my heart. Cynthia was going to be...well, I couldn't say she was going to be a great mother, because I had no idea whether my sister would be able to cope with a baby. For all I knew, she'd let the nanny raise her. But I was certain Cynthia would do her best, and her best was generally amazing.

I put the phone back on the shelf, well away from the water, and slid into the tub. Tendrils of pink curled through the water. I scrubbed my bloody shoulder and side and the water turned even pinker. I should have washed first so I didn't have to soak in my own blood, but I was too tired to get out and drain the tub. I piled my hair on my head and found a few strands caked with dried blood, so I sank under the water until nothing but the tip of my nose showed. I let myself float, closed my eyes and enjoyed the feeling of weightlessness. When I couldn't hold my breath any longer, I rose up out of the water, making it rush and spill over the edge, soaking the bath rug. I wiped water from my eyes and squeezed it out of my hair. Then I hugged my knees and rested my chin on them. And I cried.

I wasn't sure why I was crying, or rather, which of all the cryworthy incidents of the evening prompted me to sit in pink bathwater and bawl until my eyes hurt. I'd been nearly killed by a serial killer. I'd been shot by someone I loved who I thought loved me. I'd seen him arrested and condemned to stand trial. I'd had to endure healing, which in some ways was worse than the original wound. Any of those things could justify my crying jag. Maybe it was all of them.

I cried until the water was lukewarm, then I drained and refilled the tub. I soaped up and washed myself and my hair and rinsed until I felt clean. I was so tired I didn't even know if I could sleep, which was a ridiculous thought, but one I latched onto as justification for watching a movie instead of going to bed.

I put in *The Magnificent Seven*—hadn't I just talked about that with someone? Not Malcolm, though now I knew where I'd seen that hard, angry look before: Yul Brynner looked the same every time he talked to Horst Buchholz, the young would-be gunslinger. It was a look that said he'd hurt the boy if that would save him. I understood that look so much better now.

I fell asleep just as the Magnificent Seven were defending the village the first time and woke to the sound of the end title. I staggered to my bed without turning on the light and fell deeply asleep, where I dreamed of being engulfed by Hallstrom's arborvitae, swallowed up and trapped in a tiny basement that was filling up with water. No matter what I did, it wouldn't let me drown.

21

The next few days were the busiest Abernathy's had ever been. Most people wanted to gossip about Hallstrom and grill me for details I wouldn't give. A few Nicolliens and Ambrosites still wanted auguries about how to cause trouble for the other side and were undeterred by my glaring at them. A lot of people from both sides wanted to talk about Malcolm. The Nicolliens were furious that he was in protective custody. "As if we'd try to kill a prisoner," one Nicollien woman told me. "I want to face him in the killing fields and prove his guilt on his dead body."

"He'd tear you apart, Emily," Judy said. "You're just making a fool of yourself."

Emily had hmphed and stormed out of the store without getting her augury, which was fine by me.

The Ambrosites, on the other hand, turned Malcolm into some kind of patron saint. "He stopped that serial killer single-handedly," said an Ambrosite man, forgetting I'd been there and knew the story. "He gave himself up rather than be captured. The trial has to exonerate him."

"I hope so," I said.

The man patted my wrist. "You're still new, so you don't know Malcolm like I do. He always gets his man, no matter what it takes."

I smiled and removed his hand from my wrist, wishing I dared slap him. "I'm sure everything will be fine."

When that man had gone, Judy said, "I doubt he's ever met Campbell in his life."

"Probably not."

"But he's right. Campbell has enough evidence to prove he acted in self-defense in killing Amber."

"I thought you hated him for doing that."

"I do, but I have to face the fact that Amber wasn't who we thought she was." Judy let out a long breath. "I just want Hallstrom to tell everything. Why he was working with Amber. How and why she got involved at all. There must be something to explain it."

"I hope there is."

Judy swore, startling me. "Would you stop moping? You'd think your best friend was dead. You're alive. Campbell's going to go free. Hallstrom will testify and everything will work out."

"Since when are you so optimistic?"

"Since you stopped being optimistic. Someone has to."

The door swung open. "Ms. Davies?" said a woman whose face was vaguely familiar. She wore a business suit and pumps and had her hair pulled severely back from her face.

"Yes?"

The woman came toward me, holding out a packet of paper. "You've been summoned to appear before the tribunal."

I took the paper unthinkingly. "What tribunal?" I said, though there really could be only one.

"The tribunal charging Mitch Hallstrom with several counts of murder."

"Oh."

"It's on Sunday. The instructions are in the packet. Miss Rasmussen, I believe there's a summons for you as well."

"Thanks," said Judy.

The woman nodded and let herself out. I opened the packet. The first time I'd been summoned, there had just been a single sheet of paper containing instructions about where to go and what the tribunal was about. This time, there were two other papers in addition to the one headed *People v. Mitch Hallstrom.* One was a lined sheet titled STATEMENT with a few lines instructing me to write up my encounter with Hallstrom and my reasons for suspecting him in my own handwriting. This would be picked up tomorrow and read into the record so I didn't waste the tribunal's time telling my story. *Add pages if necessary,* it said. I thought it probably would be necessary.

"Why can't I type it?" I asked Judy.

"Your handwriting is like a key. It's a way of validating the account as yours."

"Sounds like a pain."

"Depends on how thorough you are. What's this last page?"

The last page was a photocopy of someone else's STATEMENT, and it took just one glance for me to recognize the elegant handwriting as Malcolm's. A Post-It note attached to the top told me to read the statement and initial it at the bottom if I agreed it was factual. I swallowed and began reading. It was excerpted from a longer statement—well, Malcolm's account would naturally be longer than mine—and recounted what had happened in Hallstrom's garage.

It was eerie to see myself referred to as Miss Davies when I was so accustomed to seeing my first name written in that beautiful script. The whole thing read like an abstract to some scholarly journal, dry and lacking the terror I'd felt held hostage by a killer, but it was as accurate as it could be.

I judged Miss Davies not to be in a position where shooting Hallstrom through her would prove fatal to her, I read, and swallowed again. Utterly logical. Would he still have taken the shot if it might have killed me? *A head shot was riskier and would certainly have killed Hallstrom, and I needed him alive to testify.* There was an answer to a question I hadn't thought to ask—why not shoot him somewhere else?

"Are you all right?" Judy asked.

"Just experiencing some good old fashioned PTSD."

"Don't joke about that. PTSD is serious. And it wouldn't be at all surprising if you suffered from it, given all the crises you've weathered here."

"Um...thank you."

"You're my friend."

Judy wouldn't meet my eyes. I hugged her, crushing the papers a little. "You're a great friend," I whispered. "I'm glad I didn't go out to Hallstrom's alone."

Tentatively, she hugged me back. "I don't know how much use I was," she said. "Lucia's people arrived far too quickly to have come because I called."

"I think they were chasing Malcolm. It sounded like he knew they were close." I released her and smoothed out the papers. "I guess I know what I'm doing tonight."

"I hope they don't want one from me," Judy said. "I saw practically nothing."

"So how does it work? Is it the Board of Neutralities that tries him?"

"In this case, it will be the Archmagi, which is probably why it's not until Sunday. It gives them time to get their affairs in order. They're both extremely busy people. They'll read all the statements, then call witnesses to testify."

"What if Hallstrom won't talk?"

"They have ways to make him talk."

That sounded ominous. "You mean...torture?"

"No. Magic to compel honesty, or to make someone feel like talking."

"I thought mind control was impossible."

"It is. This isn't mind control so much as encouragement. Most criminals like other people to know how clever they are in committing crimes. This just gives that natural impulse a little boost."

"Will they let us listen when Hallstrom testifies?"

Judy turned and walked toward the office. "I don't know. I hope so."

"Me too."

SUNDAY WAS A CLEAR, warm day, too beautiful to spend underground like I was about to. At ten o'clock I drove to the location on the paperwork, which was an undistinguished red brick building near the Morrison Bridge. Its many windows caught the sunlight and turned the whole thing mirror-bright. I stopped at the reception desk in the atrium, where a woman handed me a visitor's badge and told me to go to the farthest elevator and push B. This time, I was prepared for the elevator to stop after B3 and move sideways, but instead of S5, where it had gone the first time I'd been here, it stopped at S3 and the door slid open.

The foyer beyond was glittering crystal and mirrored glass like a ballroom, with a white marble floor and lighting that seemed to come from everywhere. It smelled sharp, like fresh lacquer, and I pinched my nose shut against a sneeze. Two halls extended out of sight on each side. I walked forward and heard the elevator door slide shut. I waited. They always sent a guide. I wished Judy had come with me, but she'd been called to testify an hour earlier and I was sure they didn't want me tagging along. We'd promised to tell each other everything when we met afterward.

Eventually I heard shoes tapping across the marble, and a gentleman came into view on my left. Gentleman was the only word for him; even Malcolm never dressed this sprucely, in formal morning attire with a bow tie, black and white saddle shoes, and crisp white gloves. His thinning gray hair was swept back from his forehead, and between that and the clothes he looked just like William Powell in *How to Marry a Millionaire*. "Ms. Davies, welcome," he said, his voice rich as chocolate.

"Thank you," I said, and restrained myself from curtseying.

"If you'll follow me." He swept me a bow, extending his hand back the way he'd come, and I followed, wishing I'd worn a dress instead of slacks and a rose-pink silk shell.

The corridor was mirrored on both sides, making it appear to extend into infinity. My reflections paced me perfectly, though they gradually curved to the right and out of sight. I'd never seen anything like it. Between the mirrors and the length of the hall, I felt like I was in simultaneously the biggest and the smallest space I'd ever seen. I almost wanted to mark my progress with lipstick so I'd be able to find my way back, though it wasn't a maze and the way was straight and clear.

We came to the end abruptly, to a mirrored wall I'd thought was someone else walking toward us. My guide pressed his thumb to a crystal square, and the door opened on darkness. "Walk forward, and don't be afraid," he said.

I did as he said, though the darkness did unnerve me a little. The door closed behind me. I waited in the darkness for a light to come on, letting my senses build up a picture of the room for me. It smelled of caramel and roses, a faint but pervasive smell I could almost taste. The warmth of the room felt like velvet on my face, and my feet trod on something soft and plush. I had no idea how large the room was, but instinct told me it wasn't small enough that I should feel claustrophobic. And my eyes weren't adjusting to the darkness to reveal even the tiniest hint of light.

I stretched out my hand and took a step forward. Immediately a purplish-white line of fire ignited, circling the walls just below the ceiling. The room was round, and probably white when a normal light shone on it. Directly across from me were double doors. I crossed the thick carpet and pushed on both doors at once, and they swung open.

I felt it was a dramatic entrance, but no one in the room beyond paid any attention. It looked just like a courtroom, but without a jury box and with no stand where the judge would sit. Instead, a carpeted dais stood at the far end of the room, and a couple of thrones stood on it. You couldn't call them anything else: they were plated in gold, with padded red velvet armrests and ornate carvings covering the backs and sides. I recognized the woman seated on the right; she was the Ambrosite Archmagus, Yamane Mitsuko. I guessed the man on the left had to be the Nicollien Archmagus, Michael Foster. He was the kind of bald that wasn't sexy, being rather pudgy and jowly and with tiny eyes like sparks of blue flame nearly buried in wrinkles.

But I spared only a glance for them, because in the center of the space between the dais and where the spectator benches began was something I remembered well: a circle of black, irregular stones within which burned a purplish-white fire like the one in the antechamber. The fire wasn't consuming anything, not wood or coal, but it showed no sign of going out. The Blaze, a magical tool for compelling truth from a witness. I'd borne testimony within it before and I was the only one who could see it for what it really was. I wished I'd thought to wear sunglasses.

"Have a seat, Ms. Davies," said a man dressed in the same impeccable formal wear as my guide. I walked forward to the third row from the front and slid down the bench until I could see the Archmagi around the Blaze. They were talking to each other and didn't at all look like mortal enemies, which I'd been told they were.

The two straightened in their seats, facing the Blaze, and another uniformed attendant called out, "Malcolm Campbell."

I startled. I hadn't even noticed Malcolm was there. He was dressed in his usual suit and tie, but looked almost casual next to the attendants. He rose and stepped into the circle of stone. The Blaze rose up higher, but Malcolm didn't react, probably because he couldn't see it. To him, it looked like shifting mist.

"Do you swear the statement you presented this tribunal is true in every particular?" the attendant said.

"I do."

Foster leaned forward slightly. "You admit to killing Amber Guittard." His accent reminded me of the Beatles, but thicker and hard to understand.

"I do."

"You claim you killed her in self-defense," said Yamane.

Malcolm stood straight and didn't flinch. "Yes."

"Why would Ms. Guittard have attacked you to require such a defense?" Yamane continued.

"I accused Ms. Guittard of being complicit in a series of murders and of having committed two of those murders herself."

"What proof do you have of this?" Foster said. "Keep in mind Ms. Guittard's reputation was spotless."

"My proof is recounted in my statement," Malcolm said, "but in short, I found it suspicious that she was present at all but two of the killings, even when being there took her out of her way. From there, I investigated the other two killings and found witnesses who put Ms. Guittard in the area only minutes before the killings took place. I brought this evidence to her, and rather than defend herself, she attempted to kill me."

"Forcing you to defend yourself," Yamane said.

"Yes."

"It's your word against a dead woman's," Foster said.

"Mr. Hallstrom will confirm Ms. Guittard's involvement in the murders."

"I suggest we postpone questioning Mr. Campbell until Mr. Hallstrom's interrogation," Yamane said quickly.

"Agreed," said Foster, just as quickly. I guessed they'd already agreed to this, though I wasn't sure why. I'd have thought Foster would want Guittard's killer crucified.

"Take a seat, Mr. Campbell, and we'll recall you shortly," Yamane said.

Malcolm bowed and returned to his seat. His eyes flicked over me, then moved on, and I felt an ache growing in my heart.

"Helena Davies," the attendant called out, and I shot to my feet like I'd been goosed. Flushing with embarrassment, I walked up the center aisle and stepped into the Blaze, closing my eyes against its brightness.

"Ms. Davies, do you intend to insult us?" Foster said. "Open your eyes."

"Sir, I can see through the illusion placed on the Blaze, and it blinds me," I said.

"Huh," said Foster. "All right. Proceed."

"Do you swear the statement you presented this tribunal is true in every particular?" the attendant said.

"Yes."

"Ms. Davies, what made you suspect Mitch Hallstrom of the murders?" Yamane said.

"It's, um, in my statement, but the short version is there were a lot of little things that added up to him being suspicious. His selling stolen books to Abernathy's, for one, and how no one seemed to know him or have seen him before two weeks ago, when the killings started."

"He might just have been a thief," Foster said.

"True, but I thought it was worth investigating."

"So it was a guess."

"That proved to be true," I retorted.

"And you claim Mr. Hallstrom confessed to the murders, and to being in league with Ms. Guittard."

"He intended to kill me to prevent me going to Lucia with what I'd learned and make it look like I was a victim of the serial killer. That confirmed his guilt as far as I'm concerned."

"Malcolm Campbell shot Mr. Hallstrom."

"I—yes." The sudden change of questions dizzied me.

"Shooting you as well."

Memory seized my heart in an icy grip. "Yes."

"Could Mr. Campbell have intended to kill Mr. Hallstrom to prevent him revealing the truth—that it was Mr. Campbell who was his accomplice?"

"*What?*" I whipped around to look at Malcolm, but couldn't see anything past the fire. "Of course not!"

"Campbell was near all the murder locations. He might have killed Ms. Guittard to ensure her silence."

"That's not what happened!"

"Can you prove it?" Yamane's voice sounded tight, worried.

I breathed in to calm myself. Defensive exclamations would hurt Malcolm's case. "Malcolm tried to save Hallstrom's life. He needed Hallstrom to live to prove his innocence. And I think, sir, even you have to admit if Malcolm Campbell wanted someone dead, he wouldn't be so ham-fisted as to fail at it."

I heard someone chuckle, and wondered if I'd just sealed Malcolm's fate by pointing out what a talented killer he was. And he'd only ever intentionally killed one person. "That is," I began.

"We take your point," said Foster, and I realized he'd been the one who laughed. "Any questions, Mitsuko?"

"I would like the option to recall Ms. Davies later," Yamane said.

"Fair enough. You may take a seat, Ms. Davies."

I turned around and fumbled my way back to the benches, trying not to remember that I'd had help the last time I'd had to leave the Blaze. I sat and opened my eyes in time to see Hallstrom, his hands bound, be led into the stone circle.

"Mitch Hallstrom," Foster said, "you are accused of committing ten murders, including killing four magi. How do you respond?"

"I didn't do it," Hallstrom said. The Blaze went insane, lashing Hallstrom with fire. I couldn't see his face, but he cringed away from the fire.

"Would you like to change your answer?" Yamane said.

"I didn't—ah!—do it," Hallstrom said. The Blaze roared soundlessly higher.

Something occurred to me, and before I could stop myself, I stood and said, "He's trying to get it to kill him before he can tell the truth!"

Two attendants grabbed Hallstrom and pulled him, unresisting, out of the Blaze. "I think she's right," Yamane said. "This is an indirect confirmation of his guilt, but if we want details, we'll have to try something else."

"Siobhan Steele?" Foster said.

"She is acceptable," Yamane said.

I glanced at Malcolm. I wished I dared sit by him, because he would answer all my questions, starting with who the woman with the romance novelist name was. But I didn't want to see him look at me with that cold, indifferent gaze again.

Foster took out a cell phone and began texting. I was impressed. I didn't think I even got service down here. I looked at Malcolm again.

He sat with his arms folded across the bench in front of him, his head bowed as if in prayer. I couldn't stand it any longer. I got up, furtively checking the reactions of the attendants in case this was forbidden, and crossed the aisle to sit beside Malcolm. "Who's Siobhan Steele?"

Malcolm didn't even twitch. "She is a powerful bone magus aligned with neither faction. They will ask her to induce Hallstrom to answer their questions."

"I've heard about that. Is it...I don't know, admissible in court?"

"The laws of the tribunal are not the same as the non-magical court. And a bone magus can't compel a particular answer, merely make the subject relaxed and compliant. Mrs. Steele will make telling the truth feel pleasurable. It is in some ways the reverse of what the Blaze does."

"*Mrs.* Steele? She's married?"

"Magi are allowed to marry, Helena. Where else would little magi come from?"

He sounded just like himself, and it eased my heart even if he was having fun at my expense. "I just wasn't expecting it."

"Mr. Steele is not a Warden. Theirs is an interesting marriage."

"I didn't know that was even possible. Wardens marrying non-Wardens."

"It is rare, and difficult, but they seem happy enough."

The doors opened, and I turned around to see a round-figured woman who looked exactly like Imelda Staunton as Dolores Umbridge, down to the coiffed hair. She walked down the aisle, placing each foot as deliberately as if she were crossing a pond. "Michael, Mitsuko," she said, and the illusion was destroyed, because she had a Southern drawl that sounded cut with honey. "What would you like? Compliance, or compulsion?"

"Lowered inhibitions," Yamane said.

"Easy enough," Steele said.

Hallstrom broke free from his attendants and made a rush for the door. More attendants came out of nowhere and tackled him, picked him up and manhandled him back to the front bench, where they forced him to lie flat. I stood to get a better look. Steele walked away, turning her back on Hallstrom. "Relax," she said to the air, and Hallstrom went limp. "That's better. Now, you're proud of what you've done, aren't you? And you want to tell us everything so we'll know how clever you've been. You don't have to speak, but if you want to, we'll all listen."

I couldn't see more than Hallstrom's arm and leg, but I heard him breathing deeply, not quite panting. "Mr. Hallstrom, can you hear me?" Yamane said.

"Yes." Hallstrom sounded normal, not like someone in a drug haze.

"Tell us about the murders."

"I don't want to."

"Yes, you do. You're proud of what you did."

"You know, not many wood magi are capable of what I did," Hallstrom said in a conversational tone.

"And what is that?"

"I shouldn't say."

"Then let's talk about Ms. Guittard," Foster said. "You knew her, didn't you?"

"She's a bitch," Hallstrom said, still in that conversational way. "Didn't want to admit I knew what I was doing. She shouldn't have tried to take over."

"What happened when she did?"

"People died. Just not the ones who were supposed to. And she lost the *sanguinis sapiens* the first time. So sloppy."

Foster sucked in a breath. Yamane said, "So Ms. Guittard killed someone by harvesting their magic?"

"Yes. She shouldn't have done it."

"I agree. That was your job, wasn't it?"

Hallstrom nodded. "But I'm not supposed to say."

"Why magi?" Foster said. "Wouldn't ordinary humans have been safer?"

"It was ordered by my Nicollien masters," Hallstrom said. "They wanted Ambrosites dead."

Malcolm sat up straight beside me. Yamane took a step back from Foster. Foster said, "That's a lie."

"It's truth," Hallstrom said. "They said, start a war, and I said, how soon?"

"There is *no* conspiracy against Ambrosites," Foster shouted.

"Calm down, Mike, I believe you," Yamane said. "You wouldn't be that stupid."

"But there are those who might be," Malcolm said.

"Shut up," Foster shouted.

"He's right, sir," I said. "There are Nicolliens who were happy for an excuse to hunt Malcolm. Just as there are Ambrosites who would love to be able to destroy Nicolliens. Couldn't there be a faction of Nicolliens within the faction?"

"Impossible," Foster said, but he didn't sound convinced.

"Mr. Hallstrom," Yamane said, "who gave you those orders?"

"My masters."

"Their names?"

Hallstrom shook his head. "I don't know their names. I haven't earned that privilege."

"How do they give you your orders?"

Hallstrom was silent. "Mr. Hallstrom, answer," Foster said angrily.

"I just know," Hallstrom said. "I wake up and it's there in memory."

Yamane drew in a startled breath. "Dream speaking," she said. "A myth."

"Apparently not," said Foster. "You've never met your masters in person?"

"No." Hallstrom's voice was tight, the words forced from his lips.

"He's fighting it. We need those names," Foster said.

"A question for another time," Yamane said. "Under different circumstances. Mr. Hallstrom, how many did you kill?"

"Eight. There were meant to be twenty."

"I'm satisfied," Yamane said.

"I'm not. Malcolm Campbell still committed murder, and he should pay the price," Foster said.

Yamane let out an exasperated breath that told me they'd had this argument already. "Do you really want to tell our people they're not allowed to defend themselves when aggressed on?"

"We have only Campbell's word that he didn't attack first." Foster sounded petulant, like a child denied a treat.

"Amber Guittard was complicit with a group who wanted to start a war," Yamane said. "She was hardly an innocent victim."

"Nevertheless."

"Mr. Foster, I will submit to any punishment you and Ms. Yamane agree on," Malcolm said, standing. "I ask only that you consider what will happen when it becomes known what Ms. Guittard did. I will become a martyr to the cause of those looking for a fight, and then there will be the very war you both wish to avert. That I wish to avert."

Foster glared at Malcolm. "The words of a coward."

"No, sir, the words of someone who wants to see this Long War won by the efforts of two sides working together, not lost by factions tearing each other apart."

Foster and Malcolm stared each other down. Foster looked furious. Malcolm was his usual unflappable self. Finally, Foster spat a blistering curse and turned away, stumping back to throw himself onto his throne. Yamane followed him at a more sedate pace, seating herself like a queen. "Return Mr. Hallstrom to custody," she said. "Mr. Campbell, if you'd take your place within the Blaze?"

Malcolm stood and passed me to stand in the stone circle. "Mr. Campbell, you stand accused of killing Amber Guittard. How do you plead?"

"I killed Ms. Guittard in self-defense."

"Did Ms. Guittard attack you?"

"She did, with a knife."

"Why did she attack you?"

Malcolm shifted and clasped his hands behind his back. "I confronted her with evidence that she had killed two people and had a connection to someone who'd killed several others."

"Why did she use a knife against a steel magus?" Foster said.

"I believe she panicked. She was too intelligent to have chosen that weapon deliberately."

"Could you have subdued her rather than kill her?"

"I tried." Malcolm lowered his head briefly. "I believe she chose death rather than capture and questioning. But that's just a supposition. I have no evidence for it."

"Very well." Yamane turned to look at Foster. "What do you say?"

Foster kept glaring at Malcolm. Finally, he said, "You acted in self-defense. I say you're free to go."

I gasped loudly enough that I drew the Archmagi's attention. "Sorry," I said.

"I have no further questions," Foster said. "Mitsuko?"

"I caution you both not to tell anyone what you have learned here," Yamane said. "Rumor will run wild anyway, and the truth will get out no matter how quiet we try to keep things. Don't let that be an excuse for either of you to spread word of Hallstrom's confession. We *will* find out it was you, and we will make your lives hell. Understood?"

I nodded. Malcolm inclined his head gracefully. "Then go, with our thanks," Yamane said.

I followed Malcolm through the antechamber and into the long, mirrored hall. There was no attendant this time, and we walked side by side in silence. I had a million things I wanted to ask him and couldn't think of a way to begin. Inanely, I said, "I'm glad you're free, but..."

"What?"

"If we can't tell anyone what Hallstrom said, how are you going to explain your freedom?"

Malcolm sighed. "I trust Archmagus Yamane to spin the story in a way that exonerates me while giving the Nicolliens no excuse to fight. Which means throwing Ms. Guittard's name to the wolves in some way. We will have to stay silent, and learn what that story is, and then support it."

"Even so, won't you still be in danger from Nicolliens trying to execute judgment?"

"Probably. I think it's best if I disappear for a while. The idea of fighting a series of endless battles, in the Palaestra or on the streets, wearies me."

"But—" I stopped, and Malcolm stopped with me. "But I don't want—"

"I think what either of us wants is irrelevant," Malcolm said, and walked on. I hurried to catch up to him, biting my lip against tears.

22

I curled into the corner of my couch in my pajamas, cuddling my tub of rocky road ice cream like a baby. On the television, Cary Grant and Irene Dunne faced off. I took another bite of rocky road ice cream, savoring the mix of flavors and textures. I knew *The Awful Truth* well enough not to need the sound, and the distant street noises were calming to my soul.

I'd left Malcolm at the atrium of the tribunal building. We hadn't said anything to each other the rest of the way, and now I was kicking myself for all the things I hadn't said. I had a feeling he was punishing himself for how all of this had gone down, for killing Guittard and hurting me and basically getting away with it. I should have said something. I should have at least told him I forgave him for shooting me. And now he was going to vanish, and I knew he'd said "for a while" but I was certain it was more likely to be "forever."

I'd made quite a dent in the tub of ice cream, but it wasn't soothing my spirits. Mostly it was just making me sick. I slid off the couch and took it to the kitchen, where I dumped it back into my chest freezer to lie with its brothers until I needed it again. I washed my spoon and dried it and put it away, too. I'd come home from the tribunal and cleaned my apartment until it gleamed and you could eat your dinner off any surface you liked. Now I had nothing to do but sit and stare at one of my less-favorite Cary Grant movies until I could justify going to bed. It was Irene Dunne's fault. She always sounded frivolous no matter what role she was playing.

I settled back onto the couch and propped my head on my elbow. There was good old Ralph Bellamy, playing the hapless goody-two-shoes again. I always felt sorry for Bellamy in this movie, where his only crime was falling in love with someone who didn't love him back. That seemed especially poignant now.

Distantly, I heard a knock at my door. Judy. She was the only one with a key to the store, but usually she called before she came over. I checked my phone; no calls or texts. Weird. I got up and padded bare-foot down the hall to the door. "Why didn't you—"

It was Malcolm.

He was dressed casually in jeans and a T-shirt and had a back-pack slung over one shoulder. "I'm sorry I didn't call first, but I still haven't replaced my phone," he said. "May I come in?"

"How do you keep getting in here?"

He smiled. "The back door is attuned to me, in case of emergencies. I should have asked your permission before I did it."

"I don't mind. Come in. You—you're leaving town."

"I am. But I realized I couldn't leave without saying goodbye."

My heart began beating too rapidly. I sat on the couch beside Malcolm and paused the movie.

"*The Awful Truth,*" Malcolm said. "Poor Ralph Bellamy."

"That's how I feel about it. She plays him for a fool."

"Not on purpose. She just doesn't know her own heart."

Silence fell. Malcolm settled his pack at his feet and leaned forward. "I'm sorry I shot you," he said quietly. "Please forgive me."

"I forgive you."

His brow furrowed. "As easy as that?"

I looked at his face and decided if he was going away forever, I had nothing left to lose. "I love you," I said, "and that makes it easy to forgive."

"Helena, no. You have a boyfriend—"

"I broke up with him last week. It was a huge relief. I should never have dated him because my heart has always belonged to you."

Malcolm closed his eyes and drew a huge, shuddering breath. "All I have ever wanted is to protect you. I had no idea I would need to protect you from myself."

"I understand."

He opened his eyes, dark and full of pain. "I don't think you do. There you were, trapped, a gun to your head, and I had to choose— kill Hallstrom and go on the run forever, or take the harder shot, spare Hallstrom's life so I could be exonerated, and injure you, risk having you hate me forever. I can't help feeling I made the selfish decision."

"You made the *smart* decision. And I could never hate you forever."

Malcolm smiled, the smallest quirk of his lips. "Just temporarily?"

"Not even that. If you're looking to me to punish you, look some- where else."

He took my hand and ran his thumb over my knuckles, making me shiver. "You are still the most honorable woman I've ever known."

I closed my fingers over his. "And see what good that's done me," I said bitterly. "Malcolm, I sold hundreds of auguries to people who wanted you dead without refusing once. I *am* impartial and it's got nothing to do with who I do or don't love!"

"Helena—"

"Don't. Just don't say anything reasonable about the Accords, or tribunals, or what Lucia would say if she knew we were together, which she already believes we are, by the way." I dashed away tears with my free hand. "I don't give a damn about the Accords. I'm tired of having my life governed by rules that don't give me even a little credit for—"

"Shhh," Malcolm said, laying a finger across my lips, then stroking my cheek and brushing away a few more tears. "Don't cry."

"I can cry if I want to." It sounded petulant, and I flushed with embarrassment.

Malcolm laughed. "But I don't think you want to," he said,

running his hand along my shoulder to rest on the side of my neck. His fingers brushed the hair at the nape of my neck, and I shivered.

"Oh? What do you think I want?" He was very close now, his breath warm on my cheeks.

"This," he said, and kissed me.

I put my arms around his neck and returned his kiss. His lips were warm and soft and his hands touched me so gently I felt like crying again. I ran my fingers through his hair and gasped as he nipped at my lower lip, making him smile. Touching him, feeling safe in the circle of his arms, I wanted it to go on forever.

His kisses became more intense, moving from my lips to my throat, and his fingers slid from my face down my side to slip under my pajama top and caress my back. I tugged at his shirt until he pulled it off, revealing lean, powerful muscle and silky smooth skin. There was a flat knot of white, ridged scarring the size of a quarter over his heart. "My aegis," he said when I touched it. "I know it's ugly."

I ran my fingers across his chest and the hard ridges of his abs. "Ugly? Malcolm, on your worst day you make Apollo want to turn in his laurel wreath. It's going to take more than a tiny bit of scar tissue to make *you* ugly."

He laughed. "You're making me blush, love."

That one little word set my heart racing again and made a silly smile spread across my face. I trailed my fingers upward, caressing his shoulders and the line of his collarbone. Touching him was almost too wonderful to be real.

He laid me back on the couch until he was propped on one elbow above me and began unbuttoning my top. "That night you fell asleep on me, I sat there stroking your hair until I drifted off, wishing I dared do more. I shouldn't have stayed, but I wanted you so badly, I told myself it was all reasonable and safe."

"You didn't give anything away. I was so sure you cared about me, and you were absolutely indifferent."

He laughed. "Not indifferent, just good at hiding how I felt. It took everything I had not to return your kiss."

"I was so embarrassed. I'd completely forgotten I wasn't free, even without the Accords."

Malcolm stopped with my shirt half-unbuttoned and cradled my cheek in one hand, brushing his thumb over my cheekbone. "I almost convinced myself I didn't care who you were dating. That kiss made me realize I loved you, and I've dreamed of having you in my arms ever since."

I put my arms around his neck and pulled him closer. "It was worth waiting for. Even with all the heartache."

"It was." His lips brushed mine, then moved south as his fingers worked the row of buttons. "Nothing I dreamed came close to this."

I wormed my way out of my pajama top, then put my arms around him again, closing my eyes in pleasure at feeling his smooth skin against mine, almost as soft as the maroon velvet rubbing against my back. "I never dared dream of you," I whispered. "But I've been yours since the first time we kissed, when we thought you were saying goodbye. I love you, Malcolm."

He kissed me softly, a kiss that gradually deepened into a passionate embrace that left me breathless and desperate for more. "I love you, Helena," he whispered back. "Let me show you how much."

WE CUDDLED TOGETHER in my bed, Malcolm idly tracing lines on my skin, me running my fingers over the scar over his heart. The smell of him was everywhere, filling the air, and I closed my eyes and breathed him in.

Malcolm ran his finger over the line of my eyebrow to my cheekbone and kissed my forehead. "I still have to go."

"Way to kill the mood, Malcolm."

"I'm sorry. I just thought you should know I can't stay."

"But you could sleep here just one night—"

"I'd have trouble leaving in the morning. And we still have to worry about the Accords."

My arms tightened around him. "You worry about staying alive. I'll worry about the Accords."

"What do you mean?"

"I mean it's past time I actually read them. I'm going to find a way for us to be together openly. For now—as far as I'm concerned, I'm yours, and you're mine, and if that means we have to be together only in secret, and across long distances, then that's what it means."

He sighed. "I should tell you no and push you away, because the Board of Neutralities won't be gentle with you if they find out about us, but I don't think I can bear being without you one minute longer. I suffered the most terrible jealousy whenever I saw you with your ex-boyfriend."

"You *are* good at hiding your feelings. I was sure you didn't care that I was dating him."

"I indulged in some wild fantasies of making him disappear. I even had him investigated."

"Malcolm! You did not!"

He nodded. "Unfortunately he's a decent enough person who's never even committed any minor crimes, so I had no excuse to dangle him off a building as I did Chet."

"He was very rude to me when we broke up. You could dangle him off a building for that."

"I'll keep it in mind next time I'm in Portland."

That sobered me. "Where will you go?"

"I haven't decided. But I promise to call you when I've replaced my phone. I doubt anyone will think to ask you, personally, my location. I can't guarantee you won't have another rash of augury requests about it, though."

I snuggled into his arms and breathed out pure contentment. "I've never had a long-distance relationship before. I wonder if I'll be good at it."

Malcolm kissed me again, long and tender. "You'll have to be," he said, "because I will think of you constantly, and someday I will show up on your doorstep and throw myself at your feet, and you will have to let me in."

"And I'll kiss you until neither of us remembers our own names," I murmured.

"Mmm. Is this the point where I say 'We'll always have Paris'?"

"We almost didn't. I'm glad you came to say goodbye."

We lay like that for a while, kissing and touching until I knew if I didn't get up, Malcolm would be spending the night, and much as I loved him, he was right: leaving now would be easier. So I sat up and brushed the hair away from his forehead. "I don't want you to go."

"But it's time," Malcolm said, sitting up beside me.

"Do you need anything? Food?"

"No. This time, I'm prepared to go into hiding. The benefits of having a large fortune." He kissed me again, drawing me close until I could feel his heart beating. "I'll stay in touch. I promise."

"Call me soon."

"I will." He kissed me once more. "I love you, Helena."

We dressed, taking our time about it, kissing until it started to feel desperate. Then he held me, the two of us standing beside my door as if defying it to separate us. Malcolm whispered my name, kissed me one last time, and then he was gone. I locked the door and stood leaning against it for a minute. My heart ached, but it was a good, clean feeling, something I could live with.

I walked back down the hall and found my phone where I'd left it on the kitchen table. I pulled out a chair and straddled it while I listened to the phone ring. Finally, someone picked up. "Hi, Judy?" I said. "Where can I get a copy of the Accords?"

ABOUT THE AUTHOR

In addition to The Last Oracle series, Melissa McShane is the author of more than twenty fantasy novels, including the novels of Tremontane, the first of which is *Servant of the Crown;* The Extraordinaries series, beginning with *Burning Bright;* and *Company of Strangers,* first book in the series by the same name. She lives in the shelter of the mountains out West with her husband, four children and a niece, and four very needy cats. She wrote reviews and critical essays for many years before turning to fiction, which is much more fun than anyone ought to be allowed to have.

You can visit her at **www.melissamcshanewrites.com** for more information on other books.

For news on upcoming releases, bonus material, and other fun stuff, sign up for Melissa's newsletter at http://eepurl.com/brannP

ALSO BY MELISSA MCSHANE

THE CROWN OF TREMONTANE

Servant of the Crown

Rider of the Crown

Exile of the Crown

Agent of the Crown

Voyager of the Crown

THE SAGA OF WILLOW NORTH

Pretender to the Crown

Guardian of the Crown

Champion of the Crown

THE EXTRAORDINARIES

Burning Bright

Wondering Sight

Abounding Might

THE LAST ORACLE

The Book of Secrets

The Book of Peril

The Book of Mayhem

COMPANY OF STRANGERS

Company of Strangers

Stone of Inheritance

Mortal Rites (forthcoming)

THE CONVERGENCE TRILOGY

The Summoned Mage

The Wandering Mage

The Unconquered Mage

THE BOOKS OF DALANINE

The Smoke-Scented Girl

The God-Touched Man

Emissary

The View from Castle Always

Warts and All: A Fairy Tale Collection